GITTE TAMAR

MOMMY PRINCESS

To those who favor flesh over love's true hue, wronging those who care, hold this in view: once the bridge is shattered, only you will stay, with no one else around to light your way. That is when the real Hell on Earth, loneliness, will light its flare, being your wrongful guide in your fragile house with broken stares.

Hello to all,

Thank you to every last of you, whether your part was big or small.

Thank you to each of my family and friends; you already know who you are, so I will refrain from listing each of your specific names. Just know I will forever be thankful for each of you who gave me never-ending love and emotional support.

Thank you to all my readers for continuing this journey with me. I am forever indebted to you.

Sincerely,

WARNING: This story includes situations of violence, gore, death, abuse, suicidal thoughts, suicide, implied assault, and swear or curse words.

Contents

Chapter One

HITCHHIKER

The headlights of an old forest-green wood-paneled station wagon cut through the dense gloom of the night. Stopping in the middle of the road, its bright beams pierce the darkness and reveal an unexpected sight—a massive trash bag lying ominously in the middle of the deserted pavement. Its glossy surface pulses softly with an unnatural life, casting an eerie, almost hypnotic glow on the slick, rain-soaked asphalt.

It's as if the bag itself is alive, watching patiently and waiting silently.

Inside the station wagon, a small girl, only five years old, crouches by the open window in the back seat, watching her dad, who has gotten out of the vehicle. The car's chipped green paint reveals patches of dull gray metal beneath, hinting at years of wear and tear. The girl tugs nervously at her cotton floral pants, her tiny fingernails nervously chewed to pink.

Darkness envelops her, with rain whispering secrets as it slips down the windows and streams in gentle rivulets over the car's surface.

The rhythmic tap of water hitting the cracked pavement echoes softly, creating a mysterious, mesmerizing beat. Pooling in tiny fractures, the water seems to echo the unspoken emotions swirling in the silent, tense scene—fear, curiosity, and a hint of something waiting to unfold.

"Oh, where, oh, where has my Mommy gone?" the girl whispers.

The melody echoes like a child's lullaby. Losing sight of her father, she uses her weight to open the door's stiff handle, then turns around and shimmies out of the safety of the car. Shadows stretch and sway ominously behind her as her voice trembles.

"Oh, where, oh, where can she be? With her sea-blue eyes and tall, tall crown—oh, where, oh, where can she be?"

Sheets of rain batter her, icy droplets piercing her skin as her wide eyes nervously scan the dim-lit road while she shields her rosy cheeks. She cups her hands over her eyes, searching for her father, trembling beneath her pink polka dot jacket.

"Daddy!" she screams. Catching sight of his gray coat in the distant glow of the headlights, she runs toward him.

He spins to face her; his facial hair is slick with rain, his lips chapped. "Lillie, get back in the car!" he yells, stopping her in her tracks, his piercing blue eyes filled with urgency as the heavy rain pounds around them. Each droplet serves as a cold reminder of their misery.

A sudden movement from within the sealed black plastic causes a lumpy, oblong object to roll onto its side; it's clear that whatever is inside is still alive.

Lillie squints toward the hazy outline of her father's slender frame and the glistening object and continues singing the childhood melody. "—with her sight nearly gone, and her legs weak and long—oh, where, oh, where can she be?"

Her father shifts his focus back to the bag, softly singing, "—with her sight nearly gone, and her legs weak and long—oh, where, oh, where can she be?" A tear slips down his cheek as he repeats the melody.

A hiss emanates from inside the bag, stirring its contents.

"Is it her?" Lillie murmurs. "Is it Mommy?" She continues to gaze at the faint lumps within the trash bag, then steps closer.

As she moves, the bag shifts toward her, wiggling and then emitting a growl.

In a panic, her father quickly turns to his daughter. "Lillie—" he shouts urgently, voice sharp against the wind.

She jumps, startled by his tone.

"Please, just—" Every word trembles with urgency, breaking under the strain of fear. "—get back in the car."

Her eyes are wide with terror and longing. Her breathing grows uneven as she shields her eyes from the pelting rain, still watching the bag sprawled across the bright yellow median lines.

The rolling has revealed a dark red stain smeared across the newly painted yellow strokes.

Her father fights against the storm's fury, desperation echoing in his voice as he struggles against the howling wind. Every moment that passes, the storm's ferocity roars around him like a living beast, threatening to swallow him whole.

The headlights sporadically slash through the downpour, illuminating the slick pavement and casting strange, flickering shadows. Nearby, the plastic bag's secured top flaps in the wind, and the contents inside are ominously still, no longer shifting. The relentless rain beating the plastic warps its form, giving the impression of movement and causing both to question what they see.

As she peers through the darkness, Lillie winces, her eyes stinging from each drop that slices through the frigid air. Every object touched by the headlights' glow casts a shadow dancing in the darkness, their shifting shapes elusive and unnerving. Each reflection of light creates sparks in her father's thick glasses as he carefully inches closer.

Though it seems impossible, the rain pounds harder, thoroughly soaking the scene. The crimson dilutes as the rain intensifies, creating a gruesome stream that flows swiftly and steadily toward the ditch.

Lillie watches in horror. "Mom—Mommy—" she whispers, voice trembling, when suddenly, an unnatural, stiff movement within the bag stops her breath.

A muffled, agonizing wail emerges from inside the black plastic containment.

A shiver runs down Lillie's spine as she freezes, her eyes fixed on the grotesque mound now writhing and twisting. Her wide eyes bulge as if she's being strangled by fear's icy grip.

John looks anxiously upward, begging for help, before settling back on the heavy, sealed bag. The rough twine is knotted tightly, clutching the opening with oppressive firmness. Over the cord, thick strips of duct tape cling desperately, their shiny surfaces shimmering in the dim light as they resist any attempt to breach their confines.

From inside the bag, another cry erupts—louder, more frantic, almost animalistic in its desperation.

Lillie's lips part suddenly in a gasp. "Daddy!" she cries out, her desperate voice piercing the chaos.

John's face flushes as his thoughts are now consumed with frustration, sweat forming on his forehead as he snaps, "In the car—*now!*" His booming voice carries a sharp urgency, as if the very air around them charges his words with impending danger.

But—" Lillie's voice wavers as she speaks, her brow knit tightly in a line of mounting concern, a fleeting shadow of doubt flickering across her face like a passing storm cloud.

In an instant, a wave of intense anger surges within her father, exploding. Fierce and uncontrollable. His body sways abruptly as he pivots sharply toward her, eyes now filled with an uncontained fury that darkens his expression. "Goddamn it, Lillie!" he shouts, his voice drenched with raw emotion.

His usually steady and composed demeanor is nowhere to be seen, replaced by volatility, instinctively triggering Lillie to recoil. Her gaze flicks nervously toward the trash bag, seeking distraction from the growing tension with her dad.

With every passing second, his movements grow more aggressive and erratic—clenching and unclenching his fists, his stance infected by an irrepressible agitation that contorts his entire body.

Inside the trash bag, the contents squirm wildly, as if fueled by violent energy.

Lillie cautiously steps back, her knees quaking with each tiny clack.

Without hesitation, her father moves toward her, each step forceful and heavy with assertion, closing the distance. Gripping her arm firmly, he leads her to the car and yanks the door open, its metal frame protesting with a groan. "Get inside!" he commands, jaw clenched, eyes blazing with intensity.

She pulls back, and her body stiffens as a sudden forceful motion of his hands grips her waist. In one swift movement, he hoists her upward, lifting her off the ground and leaving her momentarily breathless.

Her eyes widen with alarm, darting past him and fixating intently on the ominous shadowed bag on the road. Its dark silhouette stands stark against the dim lighting.

A fragile gasp escapes her trembling lips. "Daddy … I-I'm scared," she whispers, her voice quivering like a delicate leaf in a gust of wind. The atmosphere thickens with foreboding, each second dragging slowly and painfully as her world shrinks to the threatening presence of the bag, her father's fury, and the terror gripping her core.

He slowly kneels, carefully lowering her to his level. Lillie works to slow her breath. A tangible dread surrounds her, the weight of her fear constricting her throat and making her words feel like they might shatter before reaching her lips.

His gaze remains fixed on hers, steady yet infused with a quiet compassion, as if he is gently trying to erase his reaction and the walls of distress and confusion that cloud her face.

"Everything—" he whispers. Pausing, he takes a moment of silence. For a moment, he tightly closes his eyes, searching for a source of strength buried deep inside. He takes a deep breath, gathering his resolve like drawing water from a hidden inner well.

When he opens his eyes again, a hint of vulnerability flickers beneath his calm exterior. "It's—um—it's going to be okay," he says, the slight tremble in his voice betraying his genuine uncertainty. He tries to force a smile, the corners of his lips quivering as he struggles to keep them steady.

Lillie wrings her hands, her eyes fixed on the water streaking down the folds of the bag. She breathes shallowly, the air thick as the weight of the moment crushes her.

Her father pulls himself to his feet and carefully helps her into the car, gently closing the door behind her. She watches as he slowly retreats into the night.

Taking a deep breath, he clenches his fists and quickly steps deeper into the shadowed center of the road. Meanwhile, she gazes at the cold, fogged window, watching him walk away at a hurried, desperate pace between each swish of the windshield wipers.

"Dear God," he whispers, his voice barely audible over the relentless rain lashing against the pavement. His hands shake as he fumbles with the edges of the bag, feeling the slick material beneath his fingertips. The weight of the situation presses down on him, causing his heart to race faster.

Suddenly, a piercing hiss shatters the oppressive moment, echoing sharply and menacingly. The bag jerks violently, and he scrambles backward.

He freezes in terror. His eyes dilate, reflecting raw fear and confusion as adrenaline floods his veins.

A guttural growl rumbles up from the darkness.

His throat tightens, every muscle tense as he struggles to find a voice. Desperation overtakes him, and he finally forces out a trembling plea: "Please tell me what to do." His voice cracks, reverberating with a frantic need for guidance.

Everything is still in Lillie's world as she continues to peer over the seat and through the blurry windshield between the wiper blades' swoosh ... swoosh ... swoosh.

"Daddy—" Lillie mutters.

The wind howls around the car and rain hammers the roof. Each drop makes a sickening thud, a rhythm that matches the frantic beat of her father's heart.

Sweat beads mix with raindrops on his forehead, cold and clammy to the touch. His palms tremble uncontrollably, and he takes a hesitant, shaky step closer to the bag, anxiety twisting painfully in his stomach.

As he nears, the sound of his footsteps ignites a sinister pulse from within the large sack. Its contents' movement heightens his fear of the darkness and unrest lurking within.

He winces as the biting wind batters him, forcing his weary eyes open wide. He stares into the vast abyss, pummeled by each oncoming drop as it takes a vertiginous plunge that mocks his desperation. "Please, save us from this misery," he pleads, his voice thick with desperation as he looks up at the raging sky. "Lift us, carry us away on angel's wings, and lead us to your warmth and light," he begs, his words heavy with urgency as he scans the stormy sky, searching for any flicker of intercession among the pitch-black. Raindrops batter his eyes, each a sharp reminder of his vulnerability amidst the chaos.

Amid his desperate pleas, a faint hiss interrupts him, a subtle, unsettling sound like escaping steam from a kettle. "Help me—"

John gasps, his breath catching in his throat. Heart pounding fiercely, he inches closer to the bulging trash bag lying haphazardly at his feet, its dark form ominous against the grimy pavement.

Tears well up and spill down his face, emotion overwhelming him. "Delilah?" he says, his voice barely audible. Though he had his suspicions, disbelief claws at his mind as he struggles to grasp what he might find.

"John—pl—please," a muffled voice echoes from within the depths of the bag. "I—I beg you, please help me."

His heart races faster as he strains to hear, frozen for a moment beneath the crushing weight of reality.

Then, with cautious resolve, he steps forward. His fingers close around the cool, reassuring shape of a small silver cross nestled against his jacket fabric. It feels reassuring — a symbol of hope, a talisman against the rising despair.

The hissing intensifies, a jagged, electric sound that rips through the quiet, making him shudder.

His heart pounds fiercely as the noise suddenly halts, plunging everything into an oppressive, ominous silence. He draws a ragged breath, eyes closing briefly to steady his spiraling thoughts. "Delilah—is that really you?" he stammers, voice wavering between terror and hope, struggling to find the right words to bridge the terrifying gap.

"Mo-Mommy?" Lillie's voice quivers, trembling as she stares through the windshield at the sinister stillness. Her heart pounds wildly, and as the silence stretches and thickens, her anxiety boils over.

John, on edge, stares at the bag, his muscles tight, anticipating any motion.

Suddenly, the car door opens. John nearly jumps out of his skin.

"Mommy?" Lillie calls, her voice cracking with desperation. She shifts nervously, trying to get out of the car, panic creeping into her every word. The name erupts inside her, unleashing a whirlwind of fear and longing.

John, sensing her distress, whirls around sharply, his eyes narrowing with frustration. "Not now, Lillie!" With its icy tone, his voice cuts like a knife. Lillie immediately shrinks back into her seat, her small shoulders curling inward as she rocks back and forth, hugging her knees to her chest as she stares at her father.

A sudden rustle erupts at his feet, and the bag rolls toward him. He glances at the wooden rosary dangling from the rearview mirror, and his eyes meet Lillie's as she stares desperately at him through the windshield.

He raises a finger to his lips, signaling silence, then frantically grabs his fingers to steady his trembling hand as the rustling heightens his anxiety.

Nervously, he glances toward the bag, his eyes darting with suspicion and fear. He shuffles closer, every movement careful so as not to provoke anything further. "It's okay—I didn't mean to startle you," he murmurs, desperately fighting to control the rising panic within him.

In the car, Lillie grips the seat, her body rigid with worry. Her eyes are wide and unblinking, fixed on something ahead, as if bracing for the worst.

John takes a hesitant step, his heart hammering and adrenaline surging through him. "Don't worry ... She... um, she's just a little scared of the storm," he stammers, swallowing hard and trying to keep his voice steady. "That's all."

A low, animalistic howl resonates from the bag. The sound pulses with a life of its own, evoking a sense of ravenous urgency as it fluctuates between deep rumbling and piercing screams, creating an unsettling symphony of noise.

Lillie's eyes widen in alarm as the shrieking reaches her tiny ears. Her gaze fixes intently on the bag, which pulses ominously with a strange, otherworldly energy—a silent warning that something profoundly unnatural lurks beneath its surface. Her breath catches as every instinct screams that danger is imminent.

"Jo-John." The voice emerges from the bag, trembling with fear, urgently calling out. "I-I'm afraid! Help me!"

A sharp crack interrupts the tense silence—the crinkling of plastic ripping apart.

Drawn by the familiar voice, John moves closer. His hand rises, fingers trembling, and he blinks rapidly, a flicker of dread flashing across his eyes before he makes the sign of the cross. "It—it's going to be okay," he whispers, voice strained with a mix of faith and fright. "I believe our prayers are answered."

His gaze flicks toward Lillie, then settles on the bag, the crumpled vessel hiding a terrifying secret—maybe salvation, or perhaps doom.

"It's okay, Lillie. You were right. It's just Mommy. God brought Mommy home to us," he shouts, his voice trembling as he tries to hold on to some ounce of faith amid the growing horror.

A sudden violent jolt erupts from the bag, causing both to flinch and John to stumble backward.

His jaw tightens as he approaches. "It's going to be okay," he whispers, his voice thick with a desperate conviction that this time could be different as he tries to reassure himself that this might be divine intervention, a sign of a higher power. "It is okay—"

Suddenly, another brutal thrashing bursts from the bag, like a pack of wild raccoons clawing their way out. The noise is deafening, chaotic, filled with primal ferocity.

John purses his lips, forcing clarity into his speech despite his mounting trepidation. "God came to me in a dream last night," he says. "He told me he's giving us another chance—" His eyes fix on the bag as if expecting it to burst open. "This time is different—I can feel it. He told me so."

A flash of lightning cuts through the darkness, illuminating everything in stark white light.

John flinches at the thunderclap, instinctively leaning closer to the trash bag as if to shield its contents from danger. Though his faith is unwavering, he is still questioning whether what he believes inside may not be.

The bag continues to flail wildly, rolling unpredictably across the ground.

John lunges forward.

Adrenaline surges through his veins, sharpening his senses and focus on the prize. His hand snaps out swiftly, snatching the bag with a quick, relentless motion, feeling its slick, chilling surface cling to his fingertips as he pulls it closer. "Gotcha!" he mumbles, a grim smile tugging at his lips. With a grunt, he heaves the weighty bag, arching his back against the strain, dragging the thick plastic across the rough, unforgiving concrete. The sideways-driven rain stings his face and obscures his vision, smearing his glasses. Squinting against the downpour, he struggles to see clearly in the worsening weather.

Suddenly, a jagged flash of lightning splits the sky, casting a ghastly light over the dark, churning clouds above. They seem alive, swirling with malevolent intent, twisting into grotesque shapes that resemble nightmarish figures that one would expect to find lurking in the shadows.

The wind roars like a furious beast, tearing through the air with relentless force, driving icy rain into John's face, numbing his skin, and stinging his eyes. Yet he remains stock-still, barely flinching despite the fury pounding him. He tightens his grip on the bag, knuckles blanching as he clings to it for stability. His heart pounds wildly, each beat echoing like an alarm's pulsing ring.

He whispers a desperate mantra under his breath, trying to silence the terror-filled thoughts consuming his mind. "Everything will be okay." His voice trembles. "We just have to get you home," he says, fighting to stay calm as the apocalyptic storm delivers another bolt of lightning and boom of thunder.

As he yanks with every ounce of his strength, the bag stubbornly resists, its heaviness a cruel reminder of the challenge ahead. Every muscle in his body screams as he strains, digging his feet hard into the ground, his back straining against the unyielding pull. The weight drags him back, his mind flooded with fear and doubt, but he refuses to let go.

Small tears form in the sack as the weight presses against the cracked, uneven pavement. John's toiling sounds echo in the space between thunder's roar and the silence of the deserted road.

With grim resolve, he presses onward, slowly dragging the bag past the car, each step more exasperated than the last. The station wagon's tailgate opens with an ominous groan. Lillie pivots quickly in her seat, her gaze locking onto her father, who wrestles with the cargo. His struggle is painfully audible. A chill runs down her spine as the air thickens with foreboding, knowing something is terribly wrong.

Each strained breath John takes echoes loudly in the dark, rain-swept night.

"Is that—" Lillie stammers. The rain picks up and pelts down fiercely, smearing the world into a swirling chaos of gray and unsympathetic droplets.

"Mommy," her father huffs, his muscles straining painfully as he heaves the cumbersome load. "She will be just fine," he says, but his voice wavers, laced with a tense tremor that doesn't quite hide his unease.

Lillie's eyes fixate on a jagged tear at the top of the black trash bag—an ugly, bleeding scar from their journey. It reveals a peek of matted dirty blonde hair covered in mud and debris.

A deep, guttural moan bursts from the bag, unsettling in its rawness. Lillie flinches instinctively, ears shutting out the torment she desperately wants to ignore.

Behind her, John forces the last of the bag into the cramped, suffocating space. Still, the brutal struggle he endures feels disturbingly unbalanced, as if an invisible force resists his every move. The moment he releases the weight, a crushing exhaustion overtakes him, and his face blanches as the blood drains from his cheeks.

"She will be just fine," he whispers, almost convincingly, as he seals the tailgate with a thud. His hands tremble briefly, and he quickly brushes them against his jeans to calm them so his daughter won't see.

Lillie quickly faces forward as her father approaches the driver's side.

"Lillie," a voice whispers.

She turns her head slowly, cautiously, to see what's behind her.

But her attention is immediately broken by the sound of the driver's door opening.

John slides into the front seat, his movements stiff and hesitant. His eyes exude a strange mixture of fear and reluctant determination. As he shuts the door behind himself, he takes a shuddering breath, his fingers reaching out to touch the cross hanging from the mirror, as if seeking comfort or protection.

A low hiss emerges from the back, slowly morphing into a deep, menacing growl.

Lillie tries to escape the moment, keeping her eyes fixed ahead, wide with fear. Though the rain pours and drenches everything in a shimmering curtain, she stays focused forward.

Meanwhile, John frantically wipes away the raindrops that cling stubbornly to his glasses, using the edge of his soaked shirt as a makeshift cloth. His movements are hurried and anxious as he takes a deep, steadying breath, attempting to compose himself amidst the storm and his racing thoughts.

Lillie's hands tremble, and she tucks them beneath her coat, clutching her sides to steady her shaking body against the adrenaline surging through her veins.

Her father glances anxiously into the backseat, his brow furrowing as he gathers his thoughts to speak. "Do you want to hear a story?" he asks, his voice strained yet gentle. He shifts slightly in his seat, eyes darting nervously.

Lillie gives a quiet, timid nod.

A rustling sound comes from the bag behind her.

"There once was a princess who lived in a world shrouded in silence." His voice wavers as he speaks.

"A princess?" She asks, her voice laced with cautious curiosity.

He nods, a faint smile curling his lips, eyes flickering with a distant memory. "Yes, a princess," he says, drawing her attention. "She was breathtaking, her long, flowing hair cascading like gold—but behind her beauty lay darkness, an unseen thing that lurked beneath the surface, waiting for night to fall and shadows to rise."

Her dad's words come quickly, hurried and sharp, catching Lillie off guard.

She fidgets, trying to process the sudden rush of information. Her body tenses as she leans forward, inching toward the edge of her seat nervously. The car feels suffocating, the air thick with unspoken tension.

Just then, a menacing sound resonates from the trunk. It's a deep, guttural rumble that cuts through the silence like a hunting predator's growl.

John winces as unease mounts inside him, his voice escalating in pitch and growing more frantic as he desperately attempts to mask his worry. "Her eyes were mesmerizing, as clear as the tranquil waters of the deepest blue sea."

The movement inside the bag intensifies, as if awakening a beast.

"Daddy—" Lillie gasps.

He quickly resumes his story to cover his unease. "They said if you gazed at them too long, you could hear gentle waves crashing against a beach and feel the warmth of sunlight on your face—"

He pauses as a shadow from the dangling rosary crosses his face. "When she met her knight in shining armor's gaze..." he begins again, voice steady and soothing. A grin spreads across his face as he relives the moment in his mind. "All her darkness lifted away—the magic, hope, and inner light were restored, as if a spark reignited."

The growl from the trunk grows louder. "Let me out!" a gritty voice demands.

John looks toward the cross as if seeking reassurance. "And just like that, all the darkness and monsters disappeared. Vanished," he says.

Lillie's voice trembles as she asks, "Monsters?" Her face is pale, reflecting her anxiety.

Her father swiftly turns to look at her, his eyes luminous with concern. "No—there's no reason to worry," he replies, voice steady yet reassuring. "Sometimes, people are born with the ability to see things that others can't see."

Lillie listens intently, her pupils dilating as the idea settles over her.

He stops mid-sentence, his words stumbling over each other. "In their imaginative minds—" He hesitates, then mumbles, "That's where the monsters hide."

He places a hand over his chest, as if trying to shield himself from unseen specters lurking within. A chilling snarl causes him to shudder.

His voice speeds up, becoming agitated and unsteady. Shadows dance behind his eyes, flickering with doubt and dread. "But don't worry, little one, because you've got a knight in shining armor, always ready to defend you," he says. He waves his arms wildly, acting like he's brandishing an invisible sword and fighting off evil forces closing in around them.

Lillie can't help but chuckle, her mind conjuring vivid images of her father fiercely battling mighty dragons in the shadowy realm of nightmares. She imagines him wielding his sword with determination, fighting to keep her safe from unseen dangers.

"Monsters will never come after you," he says confidently, smoothly sliding an imaginary sword into its sheath at his side. "I will always be here to protect you."

She giggles, sharing a smile.

He dismissively shrugs off the possibility of feeling fear. "But your mother..." he says with a darkening tone. "Unfortunately, she wasn't so lucky. When she was a little girl like you, she didn't have a knight to protect her, and by the time I found her, it was too late."

The words hang heavy in the air, weighty with unspoken implications and the unbreakable bond of his promise. He stares at her, trying to decipher what she is thinking.

Immediately, the flicker of happiness fades from Lillie's face. Clearly distraught, she leans forward, trying to suppress her pounding heart and keep her voice steady. Her eyes shimmer with unshed tears as she asks, "Why didn't anyone protect her from them? Didn't anybody care?"

A warm, reassuring tone flashes in the man's eyes as he responds, "What matters most is that we care. Your mother is a strong woman, just like you—" He pauses, attempting to shift the mood to something more hopeful. "She's a warrior ... a survivor," he says, nervously tapping his foot. "That's all that matters."

Lillie yawns, her eyes flicking to the seat in front of her.

"She'll be fine," her father whispers, forcing a hollow smile that doesn't reach his eyes. "She just needs a little rest."

The weight of his daughter's gaze presses down on him, heavy with fears she can't voice.

More rustling from the back of the car echoes through the cramped space. The sound grows louder, heightening the tension as it blends with the relentless rain hitting the metal roof, creating an unsettling symphony. It's as if the eerie noise is woven into the very fabric of the car.

He turns to look at Lillie, his eyes searching hers for reassurance, but there's only fear behind her strained gaze. Both know—deep down—that something is terribly wrong.

"That's all ... Mommy's just a little tired," he says, his voice barely audible over the relentless pounding rain. His eyes flick nervously at the black trash bag, which pulsates like a heartbeat in the dim glow, seeming to have a sinister life of its own.

A guttural moan emerges, making him shudder. He winces, his body stiffening as he tries to block out the sound, but it persists, growing more unsettling.

Lillie gasps sharply, clutching her chest as if struck by a sudden shock. Her breath catches as she slowly looks back toward the sound. Her eyes are wide with terror and confusion.

John opens his mouth to speak again, to reassure her, but the words falter and die in his throat. His pulse pounds in his ears as a shadow shifts in the darkness beyond the car's weak interior light.

The air thickens with dread, each moment stretching longer as the unseen presence waits, watching, in the blackened night.

Lillie holds her breath as she nervously continues to glance behind her.

"You understand—" John says.

"Yes, Daddy," she replies.

He hesitates, staring ahead, trying to keep his concern hidden.

Although he appears outwardly composed, he feels a familiar heaviness pressing down inside him. Handling this scenario feels no different from countless others he has endured.

He forces a strained smile, concealing the ache that lurks behind his eyes. "Good," he says.

Lillie watches him, her eyes fixed on his every movement and her ears on every inflection of his words.

The tension in his voice grows sharper as he desperately tries to mask the rising dread pulsating within him. He attempts to calm himself by saying, "It's just another challenge we'll get through together."

Yet his shaking hands betray his facade.

The whispering symphony from the back of the car fades into the abyss, replaced by the relentless white noise of raindrops pounding against the windows.

Suddenly, a bolt of lightning illuminates the dark sky with a blinding flash, followed by a deafening crack. The thunder rumbles, shaking the car as if it were coming to life. The two of them are trapped in a relentless, storming nightmare.

Lillie tenses in her seat, responding to the thunderous roar. John's demeanor shifts, and an unsettling excitement colors his voice. "Hey," he says softly, leaning forward a bit and gripping the wheel tighter, "do you remember what your mother used to say when she tucked you in at night?"

Lillie offers a tentative smile. "Every princess needs her beauty sleep," she replies, yawning as she stretches her arms above her head, her eyelids heavy with sleep.

"That's my girl," he whispers.

Her smile ignites a sinister gleam in his eyes, a flicker teetering on the edge of madness. Abruptly, a surge of frenetic energy surges through him, and he cranks the volume on the radio, the deafening noise drowning out his dark thoughts.

A lively song bursts forth, its cheerful melody contrasting with the growing unease that permeates the atmosphere. Any faint rustling coming from the back gradually merges with the deep, resonant bass, masking the unsettling soundscape and making it less noticeable.

The familiar melody sparks a flicker of recognition in Lillie's eyes. As the music plays, she struggles to keep her eyes open, and her shoulders sway. Her movements are involuntary, suggesting that the song is awakening long-buried memories and emotions.

For the moment, everything feels unnervingly usual—so eerily calm that it almost seems wrong.

She chuckles softly, but the sound lacks genuineness, echoing hollowly instead.

John sings, voice loud and confident, yet there's a sinister edge lurking beneath the melody, unsettling all who hear it. "That's exactly what I mean!" he exclaims, glancing at the rearview mirror with a flicker of disquiet crossing his features.

A cold, calculating smile spreads across his face as he observes his daughter. "Just like your mother, always unable to resist a good tune," he says.

He pauses, his eyes scanning the interior of the car as he smoothly shifts gears. His voice drops to a whisper, eyes darkening with intent. "Now," he says, "it's time to get my girls back home." He emphasizes each word as if sealing a plan.

He leans over and fastens her seatbelt, then buckles his own. After putting the car in gear, he steps on the gas and starts the long drive home.

Chapter Two

WE'RE HOME

The tension escalates as they arrive at the long, shadowy driveway leading to their home. They pass by a sparse array of slender trees lining the gravel, and as they do, the music gradually diminishes, giving way to an overwhelming silence that weighs heavily on them. The willowy figures appear increasingly gaunt, almost skeletal, intensifying the sense of urgency to get home. It's as though a procession of waving bones is guiding them onward through the darkness.

Lillie is groggy and disoriented, drifting in and out of consciousness. Her senses are dulled, and an unnatural stillness pervades her surroundings, unsettling her deeply.

Even after falling into a deep sleep, she fidgets restlessly, as if she is aware of her house drawing near. It feels alive, as if it were reaching out, trying to grasp and ensnare her. Shadows stretch and pulse around the distant two-story silhouette, whispering secrets she struggles to grasp, their voices unintelligible yet troubling. Even the slightest noise outside seems deafening, making her believe an unseen force is clawing at the glass, watching her through the car windows and waiting for her to get out. Darkness wraps around them like a suffocating shroud, intensifying the sensation that they are not alone—something malevolent lurks just beyond her line of sight.

Amidst the muffled chaos of the car engine and rain, a sinister whisper, sharp and chilling, cuts through the din with deadly precision. It stings Lillie's ears, piercing her consciousness and jolting her awake in her dream state with a surge of terror. Her eyes remain fixed closed, but her ears sharpen, straining to catch any sound.

She listens as the gravel crunches beneath the car's tires with each jolt and shifting movement. Every noise seems amplified, every shadow a potential threat, as she grapples with the encroaching horror lurking just beyond her perception. The faint crackling of the radio generates a strangely calming white noise. The soothing sound clashes with the unsettling tension hanging in the air, creating a sense of unease. She shifts her blurred gaze toward the front seat, heart pounding fiercely as dread grips her.

The hushed voice of her father filters through the silence. His tone is frantic and strained, nearly unrecognizable.

Suddenly, an icy wave of realization hits her—she cannot determine who he is speaking to.

Her eyes dart around the dimly lit car interior, catching an odd flinch from him. Her curiosity compels her; she turns her head cautiously toward the passenger seat. A faint ghostly silhouette sits silently beside him, cloaked in darkness. The figure's hair cascades down its back, moving slightly as if stirred by a sinister wind.

An indescribable chill sweeps over Lillie.

She stares toward the disturbing presence, unable to get a clear view, as her seatbelt keeps it just beyond her line of sight. Its shadowy form sits motionless, whispering of horrors she cannot yet grasp. A foul, musty odor evokes images of decay and mold, twisting her stomach.

She fights a gasp, quickly pressing her hand over her mouth to stifle a scream.

Suddenly, a piercing hiss startles her, like a knife slicing through silence. It spirals into a series of unsettling, fluctuating tones that fill her mind, creating an unbearable soundtrack of dread.

Her father's muscles tense as turmoil erupts between them. "What were you even thinking?" he snaps, his voice strained and cracking. He forces every word past clenched teeth, trembling with fury and fear.

A barely noticeable movement stirs the quiet passenger—an almost ghostly shift that flickers like a mirage in the dark. The ambient light catches the faint shimmer of motion, fleeting and elusive.

Lillie remains frozen, her body rigid, as if turned to stone, sitting rooted in place amid the conflict swirling around her. Her ears are painfully attuned to her father's shouting, each word bouncing off the cramped interior jarring her nerves. She rubs her eyes, desperately trying to dispel the sleepy haze that clouds her mind, but the darkness refuses to lift.

Outside, the gravel beneath the car's tires crunches louder, a sinister, gnawing sound that heralds impending doom; its harsh noise reverberates in the suffocating space, further amplifying the tension.

"Do you understand what might happen if I can't find you?" John yells, his voice raw and strained. Each word hangs in the air, heavy with dread. He slowly shakes his head, his expression grim, resigned. "If something happened to you, your daughter would be devastated—"

A soft, chilling moan escapes the woman's lips, her eyes glassy and unfocused, staring blankly ahead. Disconnected, she remains trapped in her own nightmare, as if her mind has retreated into a shadowy corner, distant and unreachable.

He pauses for a moment, his eyes fixed forward as his grip tightens around the wheel, knuckles turning white. "She'd be devastated," he whispers, his voice trembling with desperation.

Outside, the temperature drops, causing the windows to fog and blur the already dreary view. It is as if the scenery itself is dissolving into shadows.

The car's vents whistle as John cranks up the heat, a soft whooshing symphony that mixes with the warm, stuffy air inside. "She…" he says, his voice breaking. "She needs her mother!" He shrinks back against the seat, trembling, and clutches his hair, squeezing his eyes shut to block out the disturbing image of the woman next to him.

Suddenly, the woman's pupils roll back deeply into her head, leaving only the whites visible. Her mouth gapes open wide, her chin tilting unnaturally.

"Heck…" he says.

The atmosphere feels oppressive as darkness creeps closer, wrapping everything in an unsettling embrace.

He gasps, his voice trembling with despair and frustration. "I … I would be devastated," he says, his chest heaving with a deep exhale. His eyes flutter open, revealing his raw emotion. Slowly, he shifts his gaze toward the passenger seat, eyes widening in alarm.

The static on the radio crackles furiously, drowning out all other sounds as it emits a relentless wave of jarring noise. The screech seems eager to insert its opinion into the conversation, invading every corner of space with its chaotic shriek.

In the passenger seat, the woman's neck hinges and spasms suddenly, her tongue slipping from her mouth in a flickering rush. Distorted Latin-infused words spill from her discolored lips, each syllable curling and hissing like a coiled serpent craving to attack.

He winces, trying to block out the demonic sound. "She needs her mother," he whispers desperately. The words rush from him, tumbling over each other as if trying to outrun the wave of worry rising within. The air thickens, heavy with unspoken dread, as he fights to keep panic at bay.

Amid the unease, a piercing melody emerges—a haunting tune that slices through the moment like a razor-sharp blade, echoing with an unsettling insistence. It's as if a malevolent effort is being made to calm the storm, yet its eeriness only deepens the sense of impending doom.

Lillie flinches at the sound of her father's palms slamming against the steering wheel. "Goddamnit, Delilah," he snarls. The sharp edge of his words splits the tense air.

Lillie is suddenly thrown into a panic when her mother's name is spoken. Her heart pounds in her chest as her father glances at the rearview mirror, peering into the unlit back seat, where she is trying to blend into the shadows.

The scene is bleak: only remnants of a torn-up trash bag lie scattered on the upholstered floor around the little girl's feet, the crumpled, dirty pieces glinting grotesquely in the dim light.

A cold, unnatural chill crawls down Lillie's spine, as if something malevolent lurks just beyond her view. With a gulp, her eyes dart toward the back of the passenger seat, trying to remain unnoticed. "Momma," she whispers apprehensively. Her hands instantly clench over her mouth, as if trying to take back her words. She stares at the dirty, straw-like hair spread across the headrest, taking in every single detail.

Her father's eyes blaze with furious intensity as he glares straight ahead, unseeing and consumed by rage. The veins in his neck bulge, and his voice seethes with a mixture of wrath and torment. "Don't just sit there," he barks, his words trembling with a desperate need for acknowledgment. "Say something!"

Her face shows no emotion, a stitched mask of indifference that slowly shifts its gaze toward him. Her eyes divulge nothing, but still pierce through him, revealing a silent, unnatural calm alive with unspoken secrets.

Lillie remains motionless, trying to escape the moment. Her eyes are fixed intently on her reflection in the backseat window as her fingers trace the contours of her face with meticulous care.

Her mother's gaunt, expressionless face absorbs the dim dashboard light, accentuating her horrific visage. She appears as a shell of the mother Lillie once envisioned, a spectral echo of her former self.

The pallor of her skin and the hollowed look in her eyes evoke hopelessness, creating an aura of dread that engulfs the confined space. Ulcers and raw, torn patches mar her face, with crater-like indentations that deepen her grotesque appearance, as if time and pain have etched her away piece by piece.

From a jagged wound on her cheek, a small maggot wriggles free, slipping over raw flesh that barely conceals her skull beneath. She emits a nauseating stench of rot, amplifying the unsettling horror of her deteriorating form.

As she parts her mouth, her lips—pale and parched—stretch tight, revealing a ghastly, translucent interior that shimmers with an unnatural emptiness.

Her eyes, once vibrant blue, have turned into haunting black pools. The pupils are painfully dilated, swollen, and bloodshot, consuming the whites and leaving only a vast, empty darkness. It is as if her soul has been utterly drained, replaced by an all-consuming abyss. Her strawberry-blonde hair, once beautiful and flowing, is now wet with rain, darkened to a muddy shade. Strands cling damply to her face; the rest hang limp and tangled in despair, creating a nightmarish silhouette.

She slumps to the side, startling her daughter and bringing a clearer view.

Lillie gasps sharply, her eyes widening in terror as they fixate on the grotesque, decomposing creature before her. Every detail of its decayed form oozes malevolence, shadows dancing across its putrid flesh in the dim glow from the dashboard.

Lillie's breath catches painfully in her throat, a shiver crawling down her spine as she clamps her eyes shut, frantically attempting to block out the tormenting vision. Her voice, fragile and cracking, escapes in a desperate, broken cry. "Mommy—" Each syllable is soaked in fear and helplessness. The word trembles on her lips.

She stumbles as she tries to speak, her mind unable to grasp the reality before her, as her trembling hands clutch at the air, desperately seeking something familiar, her heart's pace echoing the horror that grips her in this nightmarish moment.

Suddenly, John yanks the wheel with frantic urgency, slamming on the brakes, causing the car to screech and skid in the gravel as it comes to an abrupt stop.

Lillie jars awake. She groggily begins to speak, but only a frightened whimper escapes her lips, stirring something primal within him. His body stiffens as he sits unmoving, every nerve alert. His eyes dart to the rearview mirror, glancing back cautiously, as if searching for what's unseen. The dashboard's fluorescent glow highlights the beads of sweat forming along his brow, betraying his mounting anxiety.

"Is everything okay back there?" he asks. His voice attempts steadiness, but a tremor of unease slips through. His gaze remains fixed on the mirror, waiting, listening.

"Mommy," she says, her voice quivering as she struggles to steady the chaos of her thoughts. She looks toward the passenger seat, her eyes wide with terror, then suddenly freezes, her gaze locked on the empty seat beside him.

A chilling silence settles over the car, thick with unspoken fears that scrape at the edges of reality.

It's gone.

The figure has disappeared without a trace, leaving behind a foreboding emptiness.

Hellish whispers suddenly materialize, forming a swirling ghostly tornado that spirals ominously in the air around Lillie, weaving in and out of her ears. The scene feels surreal and disorienting, as if the air itself is charged with malevolence.

John, cautious and intensely alert, follows her gaze with a piercing stare, scanning the vacant space where the figure was last visible.

Lillie frantically rubs her eyes, trying to clear the paranoia clouding her senses as she struggles to grasp what is happening. "Where—" she says, but John cuts her off mid-sentence.

"She—" He stumbles over his words, his tongue seeming to tie in knots. No coherent sound emerges. "Uh..." He squints, forcing himself to speak. "Your mother is in the back." His voice sounds strained and unnatural, and she can see the pain it causes him to say those words.

Outside, a thunderclap rips through the sky, its deafening blast illuminating the darkness with a blinding flash of light that streaks across the stormy horizon. The terrible noise reverberates through the car, making Lillie's ears ring painfully.

"Thank God we're almost home," John says, hitting the gas.

Her eyes flit to the window, where the storm rages with ferocious intensity. Through the rain-soaked glass, she sees their house's dark silhouette standing in the distance against the stormy sky, a lone figure trapped in the chaos. The sky churns with a sinister purple hue, casting an eerie, oppressive glow over the home's weathered exterior.

Despite the chaos raging outside, her mind obsessively fixates on her bed just beyond the home's walls.

A sudden, oppressive weight floods her limbs, as if the very night is pushing down with a suffocating force. Her eyes, usually alert and bright, are now dull and heavy like stones, covered in a weariness that makes her feel as if her lids are lead blankets pressing her down into despair. She exhales slowly, releasing a long yawn from her lips.

Every moment pulls her closer to an irresistible sleep, and eventually, she cannot resist it.

Outside, the black clouds churn, swirling in a malevolent dance above, their shadows curling and twisting across the blue-trimmed shutters of what should be a peaceful white two-story farmhouse.

Lillie scans the second-story row of windows, her eyes carefully sweeping across the reflective glass panes. Her gaze finally fixes on her bedroom window, where a strange occurrence draws her attention.

Without warning, the floral curtain inside ripples as if stirred by an invisible, ghostly breeze, its delicate fabric undulating subtly, adding an eerie motion to the otherwise motionless room.

A jolt of alarm shoots through her. She stiffens, her eyes locked on the source of the disturbance. Her breathing quickens, shallow and ragged, as her pulse pounds relentlessly in her ears. A cold, prickling sensation races down her spine, raising the hair on her neck. Every fiber of her being screams to identify what might cause this inexplicable phenomenon.

Silence falls, filling the space with a lurking presence unseen yet profoundly felt.

Something about the house feels different as the rain pounds the roof, creating an unsettling symphony that amplifies its strange presence.

The sharp pounding of heavy raindrops, reminiscent of fingernails tapping the windshield in rapid succession, echoes ominously. *Tap tap tap.*

Lillie's eyes spring open.

John's face drains of color, his eyes peering beyond the streaked window, dimly lit by the glow of the headlights. He sits in the driver's seat, soaked to the bone, with the car parked outside their house. "You were sound asleep," he says gently.

Lillie shifts sluggishly, her focus retreating to the vacant seat ahead. "Mommy?"

His eyes gently turn toward his daughter, her features partly hidden by the low light. A faint yellow glow from the moon seeps through a crack in the darkness, illuminating her dilated pupils. His voice falters, cracking as he struggles to speak. "She didn't want to wake you. It's been a long night, and she thought it best for me to take her to bed and let you sleep. She is already inside."

Her eyes, heavy and dry, flicker with a haunted glow, pupils dilating, revealing worry as she scans the home's windows once more, searching for answers. "Is she—" The words escape her lips in a fractured whisper, but before she can voice her whole question, her father interjects.

"Yes, everything's fine," he replies. A small, uncertain smile appears on his lips, as if trying to hide the concern in his eyes. His voice is soft but flat, tinged with a quiet sadness. "She said she'll see you tomorrow."

He clears his throat, then sighs and says, "I think we've all had a long day."

Lillie looks back to the bedroom window, her eyes tracing the faint, wavering silhouette of the house set against a sky churned by roiling, dark clouds.

A deep rumble of thunder erupts overhead, shaking through the air and vibrating painfully in her chest. Startled, she winces, her eyes quickly finding her father.

In the fleeting flash of lightning, his face illuminates, revealing a reassuring smile. "How about we get you to bed?" he says. His tone is gentle, yet there's an unsettling undercurrent beneath his soothing words. Reaching out with an unsteady hand, he gently touches Lillie's arm, attempting to soothe her.

Even though her father's with her, she's still uneasy. The car feels like it's closing in, with shadows dancing on the walls and creating unsettling shapes. Her stomach tightens as she is consumed by the feeling that unseen eyes pierce through the darkness, watching her every move from some hidden vantage.

Out of the corner of her eye, she notices a figure swaying, its face obscured, features briefly exposed with flashes of lightning, while its sinuous body dissolves in and out of the night beyond her car window.

With each gust of frigid wind, its dark, elongated silhouette sways and contorts, popping into view and then vanishing without warning, creating a haunting spectacle against the ominous sky.

Her father notices she's distracted, and his face shows his concern. An unsettling chill runs through him as he clears his throat, trying to mask his unease. "Lillie?" He peers at her through the darkness, desperately trying to make sense of her silent stare.

But she remains fixed intently on the window as if possessed by an unseen force. Her heart races with a fusion of fear and morbid curiosity.

Her father calls out again, more forcefully. "Lillie."

She refuses to turn her gaze away; her eyes are unwavering on the shadowy figure lurking outside. The silhouette grows increasingly menacing in her mind's eye, its form becoming more distinct and terrifying with every moment.

Then, as suddenly as it appears, it disappears into the inky darkness, as if swallowed whole.

Lillie trembles, a tear tracing a glistening path down her cheek, catching the faint light. She quickly closes her eyes, her body shaking with helplessness.

Her father calls out her name once more, his voice strained. "Lillie!" he says sternly. His lips press into a thin, grim line, revealing his rising anxiety.

She blinks rapidly, trying to clear her distorted vision. Her head turns slowly toward him, as if pulled by an unseen force.

In an instant, the shadowy figure reappears outside her window. Her body stiffens, and a chilling paralysis takes hold, rendering her motionless. It is as if her muscles have relinquished control, trapping her in a silent, immobilized nightmare, staring face to face with her tormentor.

The shadowy figure looms outside the window, its head tilting slightly as it silently observes her every move. Its dark hair blows, covering its face and dripping-wet genderless body. Its pubic bone protrudes, and its hips jut at a sharp angle, stretching its translucent white skin.

She stays silent, her chest rising and falling in a slow, measured rhythm as she watches every movement of the creature before her. Shadows swirl and hiss around her, thick and oppressive.

Then, a sinister voice belonging to the creatures emerges from the darkness. "Lillie..." It calls.

The sound, though barely more than a breath, carries an unsettling weight. The air around her shifts, stirred by unseen entities, their whispers fragmenting and growing more urgent, almost frantic, as the tension in the small space becomes nearly unbearable.

Her eyes lock onto the creature, which defies natural description—twisted flesh, unnerving eyes that gleam with malevolent intelligence. The rhythmic echo of her name drifts through the air like a hypnotic drone, pulling her deeper into a web of dread and fascination.

Yet she remains rooted, unable to look away, caught in the terrible, mesmerizing moment, further sparking her father's worry.

Then he hears what, until this moment, only Lillie's ears have been allowed to hear. "Lillie..." the creature says.

Hearing his daughter's name frightens John, making him jump.

Slowly, the creature leans closer to the glass, revealing a sinister, elongated grin carved cruelly into its toothless face—an expression that radiates evil.

It blows a deep breath onto the window, causing the car's temperature to drop and clusters of frost to form and shimmer on the surfaces of the car's air vents. A sharp, icy wind rushes through the vents into the confined space, penetrating deeply and making the air feel much colder than outside, as if winter's breath has invaded the space. The atmosphere thickens with an oppressive sense of dread, as the creature's malicious grin only further deepens the car's unsettling energy.

Lillie's entire body trembles as she watches the creature remain completely silent, extending a slender, sinewy finger toward the house, beckoning her to go inside.

Every passing second feels unbearably long as the cruel moment of silence stretches to what seems like eternity.

John winces sharply as he catches the gangly arm of the creature in his peripheral vision.

He spins around to face the backseat, eyes wide with alarm. "Oh, geebies," he says, gasping. Taking a deep breath, he tries to compose himself and ignore what he witnessed, hoping to calm both his own nerves and Lilie's. "Are you alright? Did you have another nightmare?" he says as he turns off the car engine.

Startled, Lillie quickly turns to face him, her eyes wide with fear. Breaking the stare, she gasps and abruptly looks back at the figure. It has vanished, along with the shadows, leaving only an oppressive, dark, stormy night behind.

Suddenly, a bolt of lightning splits the sky, illuminating the gnarled branches of a nearby tree in harsh, unsettling light.

She quickly glances back at her father. The beads of sweat on his forehead gleam eerily in the fleeting brightness, almost iridescent, as if reflecting a spectral glow.

She gulps hard, then nervously nods.

"That's what I thought," he says. "Now, let's get you inside." His forced smirk conceals his increasing worry as he pauses briefly, then swiftly opens the door, hurries around the vehicle, pulls her out from the back seat, and carries her to the house.

Chapter Three

THE CURSE

As he rushes inside, Lillie buries her face in her father's shoulder.

The whispering voices resume, rippling through the air, distorted and chilling. Rain lashes against her back, cold and relentless.

John quickly unlocks the front door, ducking inside and carefully shutting it behind them. "Much better," he mutters, out of breath. "Feels good to be out of the rain."

He reaches out and locks the deadbolt, then turns toward the staircase.

Each step creaks as he tightens his grip around his little girl and hurriedly carries her upstairs.

Lillie presses her head deeper into his shirt, worried she might see something lying in wait.

Sweat drips from John's forehead from the exertion as he silently tiptoes through the dimly lit, drafty corridor at the top of the stairs. He reaches the door to his daughter's room, fingers grasping the cool metal of the doorknob. With a deep inhale, he turns it slowly until he hears the soft click.

He steps inside and gently closes the door behind him, the squeak of hinges breaking the stillness. He carefully lays Lillie on the bed and removes her shoes. She slips under the covers, the thin linens feeling ice-cold against her skin.

Glancing over his shoulder, he notices the shadows cast by the dim floodlight outside dancing along the walls.

The girl gazes up with wide, innocent eyes, shivering as her small hands clutch her blanket. A faint crease of worry lines her brow as she whispers, "Is Mommy coming?"

He hurriedly slips behind her, his movements quick and nervous, and carefully pulls out a key and locks the door with a metallic click.

Trying again, her voice full of hope, she asks, "Is Mommy—is she going to tuck me in?" Her eyes search his face desperately.

He looks around quickly, ensuring everything is as it should be, before kneeling slowly, bringing himself to her level. Despite his worry, he says calmly, "Sweetheart, remember that your mother loves you, even if she can't tuck you in tonight." His eyes show concern as he continues, "She's had a long day, and your mother isn't feeling very well. But I'm sure she'll be much better by morning."

The room's light flickers. Lillie's eyes shift nervously toward the shadows it creates on the wall. One stands out: two figures, a towering silhouette beside a smaller one, evoking the image of a mother and child. As she fixates on their distorted outlines, a faint flicker of warmth from memories seeps through.

She whispers to herself, almost as a plea, "I wish that were me." Her voice is filled with longing, her mind drifting to her mother's comforting hugs, now distant echoes in the shadows' unsettling dance.

John takes a deep breath, feeling the sharp, icy air seep into his lungs. His shoulders shudder, and he glances at the window to see if it's open. Noticing a crack at the bottom, he walks over to close it. His hands are clammy as he steadies himself against the cold window frame and pulls it shut. He clears his throat, his voice calm yet resolute despite the turmoil in his thoughts. "Now, don't you worry about a single thing," he says, voice steadier than he feels. "If you hear any funny noises tonight, don't be scared. You need to stay in bed and sleep tight. Don't give it a second thought; with the storm, it's likely just the wind. When we're tired, our brains can mess with us. It's happened to me a bunch of times. Sometimes, you imagine you see or hear things, but it's just your mind playing tricks. Always remember, sweetheart, I will always be here to keep you safe."

He kisses her on the forehead and quickly walks across the wooden-planked floor, his breath quickening as he flips the switch, plunging the room into darkness. "Oh, shoot. Just a sec, Lillie; I'll get your nightlight." He quickly reaches out, feeling along the wall and floor until his fingers find the cold plastic light plugged into the socket. He switches it on.

The device comes to life, instantly casting a turning kaleidoscope of colors shaped like stars that dance and swirl against the walls. As the spinning begins, a faint, childlike lullaby echoes softly, but beneath its innocence lurks an ominous undertone. Each note tugs at a hidden tension, stirring an unsettling presence that seems to animate the projected images with a sinister life of their own.

Lillie pulls the covers tightly to the bottoms of her eyes, her breathing shallow and trembling, as she observes every subtle shift in her father's stance, hoping he won't leave. Darkness grips the corners of the dimly lit room, swallowing what little light remains, except for the faint glow of the swirling stars. An oppressive silence hangs heavy, and an unsettling sensation makes her feel that unseen eyes are watching.

John watches his daughter with an intense, almost predatory focus, eyes scanning rapidly, trying to catch the faintest flicker of movement or sound—anything that might reveal her fear or hint at something hidden and lurking.

The silence is shattered by her racing heart, a rapid drumbeat that sounds like a warning.

His mind races with emotion while the cold grip of fear threatens to unravel him completely, making each second feel like a brittle thread hanging by a ghostly hair. The shadows in the dim light seem to creep closer, twisting into ominous shapes that dance at the edges of the room.

Suddenly, whispers flutter through the air, almost inaudible yet eerily present, weaving through the silence and amplifying her fear. He strains to catch any sound beyond the oppressive silence, but hears nothing. The thick fog of unease clings to the room, choking the air with foreboding.

Lillie gasps, piercing the stillness, her eyes wide with concern. "Daddy ... what is wrong with Mommy?" Her voice trembles, breaking off as she gazes nervously toward the closed door. There's fright in her eyes, as if she fears what might emerge.

John, frozen and unsure, looks desperately at the door, uncertain whether to stay or leave, his nerves tangled in knots of anxiety.

"How sick is she, Daddy?" Lillie stammers, her voice shaking. She glances nervously between him and the door, as though expecting a nightmare to appear at any second, hoping her questions will keep him there a bit longer.

Feeling her anxiety, he reaches out and softly clasps her hand as he says, "I think she just has a little cold. It's nothing serious."

Shadows loom behind him, flickering in the dim light, casting eerie silhouettes on the cracked lath-and-plaster walls. A strange silence hangs in the air, thick with unspoken fears, as an unsettling feeling crawls up their spines.

Lillie's favorite moments are when her Daddy tells stories.

Not the familiar tales from books with worn, yellowed pages that smell faintly of ancient libraries, but the special ones he invents just for her—stories filled with magic and mystery about a castle, the brave knight who guards it fiercely, and the enchanting princess who sometimes transforms into glass when the thunder roars outside.

"Tell me again about Princess Mommy," Lillie pleads, cocooned beneath the heavy blankets, clutching her stuffed bunny tightly as if it's her shield.

John stands silently for a moment. The hallway light flickers, casting a long, sinister shadow underneath the door and across her cluttered bedroom floor. "Are you sure?" he asks. "It's a little late for fairy tales—"

Lillie's eyes lock onto his with an intensity that is unwavering, wide, and bright, as if glowing in the darkness. "Always yes," she replies confidently.

"But aren't you tired? I already told you some of it, and you should probably get some sleep. We can always continue the story tomorrow night—"

Her gaze sharpens, and she cuts him off with a pleading look.

He steps closer, kneeling by her bed, his fingers brushing gently through her hair, trying to soothe her. "Alright," he says. "Long ago, long ago, there was a princess who lived all alone in a towering empty castle, surrounded by darkness that never seemed to end…"

Outside, the wind howls fiercely with a wailing fury, sounding like an angry beast.

Yet in his recounting, an uncanny presence stirs, silently lurking in the darkness, watching them.

Before he can complete his tale, her eyes blur, the weight of exhaustion pressing down on her delicate features. As heavy curtains of sleep fall over her eyes, shielding her from the outside world, her mind drifts into a dream state, racing through the stories she's heard countless times—stories of a woman who gave up everything to become a princess, a title that weighed heavily on her: Princess Mommy.

Chapter Four

MY MOMMY IS A PRINCESS

Unlike other stories, this princess isn't held captive by monstrous dragons or wicked wizards.

Instead, an unseen, suffocating force encases her, a darkness so pervasive it seeps into her very soul, twisting her sense of reality. It creeps into her mind like shadowy tendrils, silent and relentless, stripping away her hope and replacing it with dread.

Before the princess was born, her great-grandmother made a haunting choice. She was consumed by a deep longing to escape her humble beginnings and live within the opulent walls of a castle. Her eyes flickered with obsession as she envisioned herself adorned with glittering necklaces and wearing the most exquisite gowns the land had to offer. She was painfully aware that she had no wealth of her own;

her poverty gnawed at her day and night and even in her dreams.

Driven by desire, she became consumed with the idea that she must find a man of immense fortune to secure her future. Her mind spiraled into darker thoughts as she meticulously planned her pursuit of riches, knowing her survival and happiness depended on it.

The shadows of her ambitions twisted into something more sinister, as she yearned to escape her reality at any cost, even if it meant crossing dangerous moral boundaries, such as selling the souls of her female descendants, into a life of mental anguish and isolation.

This story of her great-granddaughter, Delilah, like many, starts with fairy tales and rainbows and concludes with harsh reality.

In a distant land, hidden among tall trees and dense wilderness, there is a charming little cottage.

It was a place where bees hum softly and birds sing melodious tunes, creating a gentle symphony that plays in your mind, inspiring a desire to dance, sing, and embrace everyone with love and peace.

The cottage itself looks enchanting, resembling a freshly baked gingerbread house. Its creamy white trim, like icing swirls, beautifully contrasts with the warm, red cedar planks on the walls.

Nearby, a small, old stone bridge crosses a bubbling brook, offering a tranquil view. Standing in the middle of the bridge, you can hear the smooth, rhythmic flow of water below, while gentle smoke rises from the chimney, forming billowing clouds that drift lazily across the sky, adding a touch of magic to the peaceful scene.

A young girl—not much older than Lillie—with shimmering, sun-kissed streaks tumbling through her loosely braided hair and skin that glows like polished pearl sweeps the dusty porch with a straw-bristled broom. Her delicate hands flick the broom back and forth, gracefully sending a cloud of dust spiraling into the breeze.

"As I sweep and hum a merry tune, I make a clean, bright space for me and you," the child chirps with glee, her bright eyes sparkling.

She pauses for a moment, reflecting on the cheerful melody she has created, while sunlight bathes her in a golden glow, making her appear as if she's wrapped in a shimmering aura.

The flowers nearby sway gently, entranced by her playful rhythm, and the little yellow butterfly that flutters past seems to dance along with her song.

A herd of adolescent deer gradually moves closer, their curiosity evidently piqued by her presence. They settle near a weathered stone well a little way from the house, their eyes shimmering with alertness as they watch her silently.

She twirls in circles, lifting and fluttering the delicate ruffles of her dress around her ankles, the fabric catching the light with each spin. She giggles softly, her voice light and musical as she says, "There you are..." A warm smile spreads across her face as she calls out affectionately to her quiet companions, "Good day to you, my dearest friends."

Although she appears young for her age, her mannerisms and speech reveal a surprising maturity that feels more aligned with an adult than a child. Her dialect is refined, her movements measured and confident, and her gaze carries a wisdom that doesn't match her youthful face.

Her ears perk, listening intently, alert to any sound as she steps quietly away from the house and onto the uneven cobblestone path that winds between ancient trees. The stones feel cold and rough beneath her bare feet, each step echoing softly with a *pit-a-pat* in the stillness.

She pauses, her eyes scanning the surroundings, then gently calls out, "Have you seen my mother and father today?" Her voice is tentative yet hopeful. She extends her hand gently toward a nearby faun, her fingers trembling slightly.

The doe, sensing her sincerity, lowers its head slowly, nudging its tiny fawn closer before stepping in her direction. The scene feels intimate yet strangely imposed upon, as if they're sharing the space with some silent presence.

A heavy sigh escapes her lips. "It's alright; no one's to blame. I am certain they'll be back soon," she murmurs, trying to mask the unease gripping her chest.

The air thickens with an unsettling quiet.

Carefully, she draws water from the well, the rope creaking as it moves over the pulley, raising the heavy bucket to the surface.

Clutching it tightly, she murmurs, "They've sacrificed so much by taking me in." Her voice shakes with the burden of unspoken truths.

And then, almost as an afterthought, she whispers, "I have a secret I've never told a single soul."

The fawn, eyes fixed on the bucket, inches closer, drawn by the possibility of a drink, its soft breath fogging in the brisk air.

She turns to the creature, her voice gentle, yet tinged with an underlying tension. "I see you every day, and we're like family, aren't we?" she asks, her eyes searching the creature's face, seeking reassurance in the animal's calm gaze.

The mother deer lifts her head slowly, blinking, almost as if in a trance. An ominous silence hangs between them.

The girl leans in, her throat tightening as she clears it nervously. Her voice falters as she speaks, a stammer betraying her, but she presses on with a gulp. "I-I'm—" She hesitates, then finally, with an unsteady breath, says, "A princess." Her words catch, cracking like brittle glass, broken and fragile.

In that moment, her surroundings darken, pulsing with a sinister energy, thick and oppressive. It drapes over everything, concealing the truth behind a cloak of dread. Silence hangs heavy, each breath and heartbeat weighed down by secrets too terrible to utter.

Suddenly, the deer's head snaps up sharply, ears twitching as a series of loud cracks erupt from the forest's edge—sounds like a tree splitting in two under unimaginable pressure. The noise echoes through the silent woods, primal and terrifying.

The girl gasps sharply, dropping the water bucket into the well as her eyes dart towards the worrying noise. An icy terror settles in her chest.

The sky above churns violently, clouds swirling into a monstrous mass of grays and blacks, obliterating the once-bright blue and casting it into an unnatural gloom.

"Silly me," she mutters under her breath, lips trembling as she struggles to keep her rising panic contained. Her eyes dart downward, fixating on her hand as it trembles uncontrollably. "Why, Delilah—why did you do this? That was against the rules. You knew you weren't supposed to say anything—" Her voice grows louder, full of desperation. She narrows her eyes, trying to focus, then presses her fingers to her forehead, as if attempting to clear the chaos in her mind. "Be obedient. Be obedient—*be obedient.*"

Another loud crash sounds from the forest, this time louder than before.

"You ruin everything around you," she says faster. "Mother said you were a nuisance, just like a gnat. Biting and draining the life of everyone who gets near."

The deer freeze momentarily, their sleek bodies tensing as they lift their slender necks with a swift, unnerving grace. From their throats, piercing cries emerge like soulless wails, cutting through the silence of the darkening woods. The sound is desperate, sorrowful, echoing with a primal fear that pierces the surrounding air.

Suddenly, the sky overhead clears without warning, the clouds vanishing without a trace, leaving behind an inky blackness that feels smothering and cold. The wind howls fiercely, whipping through the trees with furious, chilling force, carrying an unsettling cry that makes the hair on the back of the girl's neck stand on end.

A heavy, guttural howl suddenly erupts from the shadows, gradually rising in intensity until it transforms into a shrill, blood-curdling scream that slashes through the darkness with its raw sound.

She glances anxiously toward the dense woods, her face pale and tense. "We have to go now," she whispers desperately, her voice trembling with fear. Her eyes flicker to her friends, voice cracking with urgency. "You can't stay here. You must come with me, or it will get you."

An overwhelming worry hangs in the air as the woods seem to loom closer, shadows twisting and curling like living nightmares, waiting to ensnare anyone who lingers too long near the terrifying darkness.

The deer are paralyzed, frozen in place, their muscles taut and hearts pounding.

Delilah lunges forward, her hands clutching the fawn's fragile neck with fierce determination. She yanks it suddenly, making its eyes bulge in fear and its tongue loll grotesquely from its mouth. A blood-curdling scream rips from her throat. "It's going to eat you!" she screams, pulling even harder as the shadows loom closer. The tiny deer presses her hooves firmly into the damp soil, her delicate legs shaking with fear.

Tears streak down Delilah's face as panic takes hold. She swiftly evaluates her options, then releases her grip on the fawn's fragile neck before darting toward the open door of the cottage. Her breathing becomes ragged and loud as she races away, the distant sound of heavy footsteps pounding closer.

Without looking back, she dashes inside and shuts the door behind her. She spins around slowly, her eyes fixed on the locks.

Four heavy, antiquated locks line the door, their surfaces rough and scarred, evidence of years of stubbornly holding something back. The edges are worn, revealing the many times they've resisted with strength, enduring the relentless pressure to keep whatever is on the other side at bay.

She slides her fingers hurriedly, securing each latch in a frantic pattern. "One, then three, then two, then four," she says, her eyes darting wildly.

As the final bolt clicks into place and the lock secures with a loud clank, she takes a deep breath, a momentary wave of relief washing over her. Outside, the wind roars, tearing through the trees with relentless force.

Suddenly, she hears the cracking of branches—sharp, frantic—getting closer.

Her heart hammers as she eyes the unlatched lock on the sill, thinking that even if latched, it wouldn't be enough. The window is slightly ajar from earlier, allowing a chill breeze to seep into the room, carrying with it the scents of damp earth and decay.

Its shutter groans loudly as the wind gusts, flapping violently back and forth, its metal hinges protesting with each thwack against the siding.

Outside, a distant animal cry breaks through the madness, sounding primal and echoing a warning. Panic grips her as her mind races—they're hunting, or something far worse.

Her breath hitches, shallow and fast, as she pictures the deer, so helpless and vulnerable. "No," she whispers. The word barely escapes her trembling lips before she whimpers louder, a desperate plea for its safety.

Suddenly, overwhelmed by a surge of adrenaline, she lunges toward the window.

The wind howls fiercely, biting at her skin as it lashes her hair into her face. She cringes, reaching out the window and into the cold, gripping the jagged edge of the flapping shutter with trembling hands. With a forceful grunt, she tries to pull it shut, the metal hinges screeching in protest. Her ears catch a deep, visceral growl from the direction of the old well, resonating through the night, adding to the nightmare.

"Come on," she says. Straining every muscle, she pulls harder, the shutter resisting with every ounce of strength.

A powerful gust surges toward her, swirling fiercely around the window frame. Miraculously, it helps push the shutter back in place, closing it with a loud *bang*.

As she fumbles to slide the rusty lock closed, the room's candles suddenly flicker wildly, casting fleeting shadows that dance across the walls and transform the room into an evocative black-and-white picture show.

Every muscle aches with fatigue, yet adrenaline propels her forward in frantic desperation as a flash of lightning splits the dismal sky, illuminating the chaos for a moment. Frightened, she ducks to the ground, desperately trying to escape the deafening roar of the thunder.

Nearby, a deer's chilling cries pierce the air, mixing with the sickening crunch of breaking bones, making her cringe and shudder.

"I tried to warn them," she cries. "I—I tried." She buries her head in her arms. Her heart beats faster. "They didn't listen!" she screams, then concedes, "I didn't listen."

She glances reflectively toward the wall, her eyes catching the subtle dance of glinting light. In the faint, trembling glow of a dying candle, a neatly written list is illuminated just enough to reveal its edges, worn from years of careful handling. Shadows dance across the page as the flame pulses, casting an eerie, unstable light.

Suddenly, she breaks the silence in tears. "I've been a good girl," she cries out, her voice trembling with desperation. "I have followed the list—" Her words falter, now louder, filled with anguish and pleading.

The howling wind slams against the sides of the cottage.

"I have done everything you asked," she wails. Her knees buckle beneath her, and she collapses onto the cold floor, tears tumbling down her face. "I-I swear," she whispers.

Flashes of lightning intermittently illuminate the page, each word barely visible, heightening the feeling of secrecy. Each line, meticulously numbered and inscribed with an ominous rule, outlines the desperate measures she must take to keep the unseen monster at bay, warning of dire consequences should any rule be broken.

Delilah, with unsteady hands and wide, apprehensive eyes, looks at the title of the list: *Official Rules of Being a Princess.*

The words hang heavily in the stale air, each syllable echoing with a discomfort that prickles her skin, as if the shadows themselves are listening, waiting for any slip that could invite the horrors lurking just beyond her sight.

She drills her tongue to sound out the word, but before she finishes, the candlelight draws her focus. Outside the window, a distant howl pierces the night air.

Delilah gasps, her eyes darting to the lock. "It's okay," she begins, but her voice falters. "The monsters can't get you."

A growl rumbles loudly, vibrating through the dark.

Her curiosity wars with her fear as she peers toward the noise, moving quietly, cautious not to make a sound. Every muscle in her body tenses as she steps closer to the window, her heartbeat loud in her ears. She clenches her long skirt in her fists.

Almost at the window, she listens; her senses heighten as her toe nudges a weathered wooden plank.

A slow, groaning creak escapes from the misaligned boards, piercing the silence like the squeal of a dying animal. Delilah freezes instantly, her breath hitching painfully in her throat as a wave of icy dread seizes her.

Her eyes flick to the last bullet point on the list: *Never be saved*. The words pulse ominously in her mind.

A sharp knock reverberates against the door. The candle's flame sputters from the vibration, sending vines of smoke curling upward.

A deep, gravelly voice whispers through the wooden entryway. "Hello?" it snarls, as if the words are dragged from a throat imbued with evil. Another knock ... after knock...after knock thuds relentlessly, each one more demanding than the last. "I've been collecting wood in the nearby forest, and I saw smoke coming from your chimney. I wondered if anyone was home—perhaps a widowed woman or a child waiting for their parents to return. It's stormy outside, and I thought to myself, hmm, you could probably use some firewood to stay warm. However, it's too dangerous for someone as vulnerable as you to go out in this weather to collect it. Going into the woods alone isn't an option with all the dangers lurking, and it would be a pity if you froze to death if the fire goes out," he calls out.

With each passing moment, the knocking's insistence grows, like a ravenous beast clawing to be let in. Delilah trembles, her body stiff with fear as her mind races. The relentless sound batters her ears.

"Can you hear me? I know you are in there. Do you need help with wood for your fire?" the stranger's voice asks again, softer, but still carrying an ominous undertone.

A shiver races down Delilah's spine, her skin prickling with icy unease. She hesitates, then responds with a tentative voice, "No—um, I'm quite alright, thank you." She raises her voice in a fragile attempt to sound certain, even as her hands tremble and sweat beads on her brow.

His fists pound louder, their impact echoing through the small cabin, shaking it and knocking pictures off the walls.

Chapter Five

MONSTERS

A sharp, insistent knocking pierces the silence, each successive bang echoing more urgently than the last.

Lille's eyes snap open as she gasps, torn from the depths of a frightening dream.

The disturbing resonance of the knocks blurs the line between her restless sleep and waking nightmare, each strike reverberating through her mind, filling her with a growing sense of unease.

Although she's alone now, in the dark with only the soft glow of her nightlight and the swirling stars to keep her company, something edges closer in her peripheral vision—dark shapes that look almost alive as the outside world seeps into her fragile consciousness. Every faint sound sharpens into an eerie call that slices through the silence, greater than it should be, more threatening.

A sinister hiss escapes from beyond the door, low and ominous, piercing the stillness. "Lillie…" the voice intones, dripping with menace, a whisper of dread.

"Lillie," it whispers once more, and this time, her nightlight flickers and goes out.

Lillie pulls the covers up to her chin, her body tensing as she scans the darkness surrounding her bed. Her eyes dart frantically, searching for the comforting glow of her night light, but it remains stubbornly off, plunging her into suffocating obscurity. Every shadow appears to breathe, and every sound morphs into a potential threat as fear grips her relentlessly.

The pounding suddenly ceases; the cold, metallic doorknob twists slowly, emitting a piercing screech.

She scrambles back, pressing herself against the headboard, her heart pounding like a war drum. In a trembling voice, she forces out, "Go away." Clinging to a fragile hope of bravery, she adds, "You are not real!"

Her words feel hollow, drenched in desperation.

The doorknob continues its sinister turn; its cringy screech grows louder, more feral, filling her mind.

She screams loudly and forcefully, "You are not real!" But as strong as she tries to be, her voice quivers with terror.

Suddenly, the doorknob's motion halts—frozen mid-action as if paused by an invisible force.

Her breath catches in her throat as a cold, unnatural chill snakes up her spine, causing her entire body to shiver uncontrollably. An overwhelming wave of dread surges through her. Her pulse races and limbs tremble as she sits paralyzed on her bed.

The silence in the room is oppressive, deafening.

"H—hello?" Lillie whispers, sounding unsure if she wants an answer. She then repeats it louder, desperation creeping into her tone. "Hello ... who's there?"

A slow, deliberate clawing sound scrapes from one end of the door to the other, inching closer to the bottom with unsettling persistence.

Her eyes dart to the faint glow beneath the door.

A pair of thin, skeletal fingers appears, hooking under the wood's edge and gripping it with unsettling strength.

She stares at the jagged nails at the tips of the pale fingers, a chilling reminder of the woman outside—an ethereal, sinewy apparition that haunts her nightmares. Her breath catches again, and her trembling lips barely form her whispers. "Momma," she gasps, voice fragile and filled with terror.

"Baby," a woman's voice says softly, tinged with an eerie warmth, "I couldn't wait another moment to see your beautiful face." Her tone is strangely reassuring, yet laced with something unsettling beneath.

"I couldn't sleep another wink without seeing my shining star."

"Mommy, is that really you?" Lillie blurts out, her words stumbling over themselves in shock. She hadn't seen her mother in person for a good while, not since the woman had vanished without a trace at least six months before the night they recovered her.

"I'm finally back, baby," the voice purrs, smooth and hypnotic. "Just open the door."

Lillie slowly peels back the covers, her trembling fingers hesitant as her eyes dart nervously toward the sound of tapping fingernails just beyond the door.

A prickling sensation crawls up her spine as she listens to her mother's voice grow louder, demanding entry. Her mother's nails scrape brutally against the wood, each grating sound punctuating her words and punishing Lillie's ears. "Open the door," her mother urges, her tone sweeter, but laced with an unsettling edge. "I can't wait to hold my little girl in my arms."

Something in her mother's voice sends terror through Lillie's core.

Drawn toward the faint warmth she associates with her mother, she shifts nervously to the edge of the bed, her breath shallow and rapid.

Her mother's ear presses against the door, straining to catch every whisper, every breath. "That's it, my baby," her mother coos softly. "Come closer."

Lillie shivers as she swings her legs off the bed, her bare feet landing on the cold, unforgiving floor. The surface feels gritty and brutal against her skin.

The silence that follows as she crosses the room is deafening, every second stretching painfully as her mind races with fright, unsure of what sight awaits on the other side.

She staggers forward, her sight nearly lost, leaving shadows to flicker across her gaunt face. Her legs are unsteady, yet she persists, her voice fragile as she hums the childhood melody.

A chilling sensation crawls down her spine. She gasps and immediately covers her mouth to stifle a scream. Her eyes dart around anxiously before she takes a cautious step closer. "Oh, where, oh, where can she be?" she murmurs, her voice barely audible and laced with fear.

The sinister hand reaches beneath the doorway, twitches suddenly, fingers curling inward with an unnatural, erratic motion, unmistakably pointing directly at her as if beckoning her into a nightmare. A cold dread pools in her chest.

"Oh, where, oh, where, can she be?" Lillie sings again, her voice quivering as she takes another cautious step closer. Her muscles tense, and she halts abruptly, her eyes drifting to the hand. She strains to hear her own shallow breathing amid the torturous atmosphere.

The hand clenches into a tight fist, the knuckles whitening as if infused with ice. A chilling whisper echoes through the gloom. "Faster now, my child," the voice beckons, smooth and sinister.

Lillie's fingertips sense the sudden drop in temperature; her nose frosts over, raw and numb. "Mommy..." she whispers, voice trembling.

The creature's hand slowly uncurls, revealing even more of the fleshy grasp. "Yes, my child?"

"I'm scared—what if it's not you?" Lillie says, her voice barely audible.

Suddenly, the hand slams against the door with such force that Lillie recoils sharply. The sound echoes, piercing the room's tension. "How dare you question me?!" she screams, shrill with rage and quaking with fury.

Startled, Lillie leaps back, her feet scraping on the cold, worn floor as she loses her balance. She collapses onto the ground, shaking uncontrollably as shadows stretch and slither around her, whispering in her ears.

The creature's hand withdraws abruptly from beneath the door, releasing a flood of sinister hisses that coil into the room like creeping fog. Lillie gasps, clutching her head and covering her ears, desperately trying to block out the malicious voices.

"What's wrong, my child?" Her mother's voice deepens unnaturally, echoing resoundingly among the whispering shadows.

"Are you—" Lillie begins, then stops herself. She clears her throat nervously and whispers, "Are you a princess?"

The room falls silent, as if waiting. Then she nervously continues, "That's what Daddy told me." Her voice wavers, then quickens. "It's okay—I know it's supposed to be a secret, so you don't have to be afraid. I won't tell anyone," she says. "I swear."

The silence stretches, thick and oppressive, as the chilling air around her grows colder, making her shiver uncontrollably.

A muffled cry emerges from behind the door, followed by a heavy thud, as if someone has leaned their weight fully against it.

Lillie pulls her trembling arms tightly around her, exhaling in shallow, ragged bursts. "I promise I won't tell anyone," she whispers, her voice cracking with fear.

She edges closer to the door. "If it's true, knock three times," she says, voice meek and trembling, as if afraid the very act might summon something ungodly. "It'll be our secret."

Scurrying echoes from the hall, tiny claws scratching and skittering like an army of desperate rats clawing their way up the walls.

Without warning, three bashing knocks reverberate against the window behind her, each one louder and more jarring than the last.

"She is a princess!" Lillie says, her eyes wide with a mixture of awe and terror as she whirls around, her heart pounding erratically.

The stories from her father now seem distant and hollow compared to the cold reality staring back at her.

A pale, gaunt face is pressed against the window's glass—a deep, staring void with sunken eyes that pierce right through her.

She hesitates, conflicted, then takes a tentative step forward. "Princess—" Her voice falters, trembling. "Mommy?"

Outside the second-story window, a shadowy figure remains motionless, shrouded in darkness. Her white dress, torn and muddied, billows wildly in the stormy wind, wrapping around her like ghostly vines. The air is thick with the sputter of rain and the shriek of the wind, and the figure's presence feels unnerving, silently tormenting her.

"Is that you?" Her voice cracks, exposing her fear that something darker lurks beneath.

The figure slowly lifts a gangly hand, each finger a skeletal silhouette with peeling, desiccated skin that once stretched over bone, now visible in ghastly detail. Its fingers brush against the rain-soaked window, leaving behind a translucent red smear that runs down the glass.

The window fogs with a mist of icy breath, obscuring the horrifying vision—yet the chilling reality of being watched persists, relentless and terrifying.

A sudden flash of lightning tears across the sky, shattering the pitch-black and causing the floor to tremble beneath her feet. In that brief blaze of light, the ghostly figure emerges in greater detail, its twisted outline shimmering with a sickly glow. Each violent flash reveals patches of rotting flesh, exposing bones beneath—an ever-present reminder of decay and despair.

Lillie's voice trembles with accusation. "You're—" she says, eyes narrowing as she points a trembling finger. "You're—I saw you in the car." Her fists clench at her sides, knuckles whitened, as she takes a cautious step forward, each movement strained with fear.

The shadowless figure's face contorts disturbingly, cheeks twisting as it leans closer, its motion eerily silent save for the faint, rasping sound of breath. Its eyes, if they can be called that, are hollow voids that suck in the dim light around them. It taps softly on the window with elongated, bony fingers, nails clicking against the glass.

A cold, mocking voice hisses from the back of its throat, each word slithering into the air like a serpent. "Your Mommy's not a princess," it whispers, repeating it with deliberate cruelty. The sound reverberates unnaturally, each syllable sharper, menacing.

Desperation seizes Lillie; she lunges toward the window, her intentions frantic and desperate to silence the tormentor. "She is! She is a princess!" she screams, voice trembling—trembling so hard it seems to shake the very walls. The impact of her scream triggers a violent rumble; the walls shudder and groan.

The wraith-like figure tilts its head, observing her with an unsettling stillness as her fingers, like spiders, inch toward the windowsill.

Her limbs weaken as panic tightens in her chest. "Daddy told me so!" she shouts, deafening herself in her desperation.

Suddenly, its fingers stretch outward, transforming into writhing tentacle-like shadows that wedge themselves between the windowsills. They curl and twine, grasping tightly as they burrow through the gaps around the glass pane. Each movement drips with malice, as if the very act is a calculated assault.

A shrill, agonized creak pierces the silence as the window sashes scream in protest. The sound is raw, grating, echoing with wicked intent as the figure slowly forces the window open.

The small child, consumed by fear, spins around wildly, searching for an escape. Her eyes shift back to the source of the harrowing noise battering her ears. "Stop it!" she screams, voice trembling, desperate to scare away the threat. She presses her back against the wall, knees unsteady, as her gaze locks onto the window. Her eyes widen in terror as her breath quickens.

With every passing second, the figure inches deeper into her world, the window giving way to its relentless force, allowing it to climb through the opening and hit the floor with a sickly thud.

The air thickens with dread, e second stretching painfully long.

"Leave me alone!" Lillie cries, her voice cracking, as heavy rain pelts through the open window, smattering against the floor like tiny footsteps in time with her heartbeat.

Slowly, the darkened silhouette crouches like a decaying rag doll, its movements spasmodic and abnormal. Beneath its soaked, tattered dress, its knees bend with a sickening crunch, resembling snapping twigs.

The creature slinks into the room, its body drooping as if disjointed, limbs twitching uncontrollably, as if puppeteered by hidden strings. Shadows cling to its figure, rippling with each subtle movement.

She stands frozen, her body stiff with fright, as the dark silhouette inches closer. Her eyes widen in horror as she observes its matted hair, filthy and tangled, parting from its face to reveal a twisted, oozing visage.

The creature's shoulders lurch back violently, its eyes revealing cavernous, rotten abysses that seem to swallow her whole, igniting a flame of terror within her.

Her throat tightens, and she can barely whisper, "Who—"

The figure extends its neck with a grotesque stretch, raising its head higher above the floor, revealing more of its face, which is riddled with decay. Its voice, raspy, coos, "Yes, my child?" Its fingers curling tightly, dripping a foul sludge into a puddle on the floor.

Lillie swallows hard, her heart pounding. "Who—" she stammers again, trying desperately to force the words out.

The creature's head cocks slowly, a predatory gesture making clear its intent, eyes gleaming with malevolent curiosity, as if relishing her terror. Shadows flicker across its twisted, grotesque features, revealing glimpses of sharp angles and mottled skin that pulse with a life of their own. The air grows heavy with an unsettling silence, shattered only by the creature's faint, raspy breaths.

"Say it," it hisses, its voice rough and grating, like a stick being dragged slowly across gravel.

She gulps, her gaze fixed on the creature's eroded face. She forces herself to speak, her voice barely a whisper. "Who are you?"

The creature's eyes burn with an eerie glow, as if a sinister light has been ignited within. It digs its nails into the floor, its knuckles blanching as it claws at the ground for stability. With a sudden, powerful pull, it arches its back and propels itself to its feet. The creature stands motionless, observing her with a predatory patience.

Lillie inches herself backward, her movements frantic and desperate, trying to escape the menace closing in.

"Your worst nightmare," the creature snarls. From the shadows, whispers emerge, clamoring, creeping, and winding their way toward her.

The small child presses herself against the wall, feeling the carved wood door behind her, as if seeking protection from the unseen horrors lurking beyond. Her trembling hands are crawling up the door's surface, searching for something to hold on to, when a harsh, unyielding grip clamps around her wrists, halting her effort.

Panic floods her as she struggles futilely against the pressure, which tightens with ferocious intent. Her eyes flick toward the faint glow seeping from beneath the door as she frantically searches for salvation or escape.

Horror strikes again as the skeletal hand reemerges from the hall, slipping silently through the gap beneath the door. Its jagged nails dig into her feet, tearing her tender skin and causing blood to stain her toes crimson. She fights against the creature's grip on her wrists, while kicking wildly at the hand that claws and grabs at her feet, desperate to break free.

The creature's mocking snarl echoes sharply in her ears as it loosens its grip and disappears into the darkness.

Whispers swirl chaotically around the dark room, twisting into sinister hisses that slither through the air, dragging her deeper into a relentless nightmare from which escape feels impossible. "Lillie..." they call in eerie unison.

In the far corner of the room, the creature lingers, slowly retreating further into the darkness, its eyes burning with a sadistic glow as it watches her tremble with fear.

Suddenly, a deafening and cruel burst of screams erupts. "Gotcha!"

Lillie's body shudders uncontrollably, desperation pushing her to find an escape.

Without warning, emaciated hands rise from the smothering darkness, their bony fingers grasping her ankles and crawling up her legs, cold and clammy. They tighten around her, immobilizing her as the creature edges closer, its head tilting with a grotesque, fragmented motion.

Strands of hair caked in blood and filth dangle from its putrefying scalp, glistening wetly as they drip onto its dress and onto the floor. The air is consumed with the stench of rot and despair, making each breath a bitter struggle.

Lillie inhales sharply, unleashing a blood-curdling scream, piercing the oppressive gloom.

The door behind her suddenly flies open with a deafening crash as it hits the wall, startling her. Her father bursts into the room, flipping on the light switch with urgency. The harsh fluorescent lights stubbornly refuse to illuminate, leaving them with only a weak glow from the hallway that barely touches Lillie's crumpled form on the floor.

Lillie's eyes remain closed as she reaches out with trembling hands, her fingers grasping desperately at her father's leg in a frantic attempt to escape the terror.

He kneels beside her, gently cradling her in his arms. "Hey, it's okay," he whispers with concern as he cradles her close. "Everything's fine. I've got you."

Lillie sniffles, hiding her face against his chest and clinging to him as if he were the only thing keeping her tethered to reality in this nightmare.

He gently strokes her back, trying to soothe her shivering body. "What's wrong, sweetheart? Did something frighten you?" he asks, voice hushed but filled with genuine worry, trying to calm her fear.

She points across the room with a terror-filled finger. "A-a monster," she stammers, her voice barely audible.

John's eyes dart toward where she is facing, his gaze sweeping across the shadowed corner where Lillie stares at the grotesque, half-decayed form lurking just beyond the pallid glow of the hallway light. Its hollow eye sockets stare at her sightlessly; there is an unmistakable menace in its silent presence as it lurks beneath the darkness.

However, John sees things differently. Though he sees only empty darkness, the sensation of being watched gnaws at him.

He shifts his eyes to the window; the sky is slowly brightening with the rising sun, spilling golden rays into the room. A sense of relief washes over him, but it's fleeting as he sees the wide-open window.

"Huh, I must have left it open last night," he mumbles. Without a second thought, he scoops his daughter up into his arms and carries her, urgency driving him. As he moves across the room, his thoughts race and his words nervously ramble.

"You were out like a light last night—still in your clothes! You looked so peaceful, I didn't want to disturb you, so I just tucked you in. It can get a bit stuffy in here with the windows closed. I thought I'd crack it open a bit to help you sleep, but I must have been tired too, because I completely forgot to close it when I left, and I don't remember opening it that much." He extends a hand, then quickly slams it shut.

The thud of the window frame against the wall echoes sharply through the room.

The sound startles Lillie, who sniffs softly before slowly lifting her head from his chest, her eyes clouded with sleep and unease, as she worries about what she had seen, wondering if it is still lurking in the shadows. "But the monsters—"

"You're just a bit groggy," her father says gently, trying to calm her down. "There aren't any monsters," he reassures her with a warm smile. "Last night was a lot to take in, but your mother is now home, and all is well." He pauses for a moment and sets her down, then continues, pointing around the room with a reassuring gesture. "See? Just look around. There's nothing to be afraid of now."

Lillie carefully scans the room, her eyes flitting over every corner, every object, searching for any sign of trouble. Her gaze finally settles on a faint movement near the window.

"The only little monster I see is a tickle monster," he says with a smirk, "and you know what happens to them."

Suddenly, her breath catches sharply as her eyes fixate on a puddle on the floor near the window. The water's surface shimmers in the scarce light, droplets rippling outward like tiny waves disturbed by an unseen force.

As her eyes remain locked on the water, a chilling sensation grips her as the shadows seem to deepen around it, and an unnatural stillness settles. The air grows heavy, pressing down on her chest as if the entire room is holding its breath.

Suddenly, her father's boisterous laughter erupts, his voice echoing with a mischievous tone as he swoops in to tickle her stomach.

"Tickle, tickle, tickle," he says. She squirms desperately, trying to escape the discomfort.

"Daddy ... stop!" she cries, her voice begging with desperation. She tries to push him away, her small hands gripping at his arms, but he's too strong. "Please ... stop! I'm not a monster!" Her voice breaks as tears well up in her eyes, the sensation of helplessness overwhelming her.

He immediately stops and says, "I was just teasing you."

The room presses in on her, seeming to mirror her fear. Sunlight turns familiar objects into writhing, grotesque shadows that dance with a life of their own. The farthest reaches of the room, untouched by the sun, pulse with a dark energy, suggesting something deeply sinister hidden just out of sight—something patient, waiting in the gloom, ready to claim its victim.

A chilling atmosphere thickens around her, an icy grip that feels almost tangible, wrapping her in a cold, merciless embrace. The surroundings distort into a twisted nightmare where shadows dance menacingly on the walls and the air is heavy with a scent of decay that slowly infiltrates John's nostrils, making him involuntarily cringe.

In a whisper as she tries to silence her shaky breath, Lillie insists, "I'm not a monster." Her voice is barely audible amidst the sinister silence.

John responds gently, pulling her into a tight hug. He remains composed as his nose catches the faint, nauseating odor of rot. He pauses, inhaling deeply, and then offers a reassuring smile. "Of course you're not," he says, attempting to convey calmness. "Just joking, my little honey bun."

Lillie looks up at him, a fleeting wave of relief crossing her face as her shoulders relax slightly. Yet, a flicker of wariness remains in her eyes.

Her gaze shifting and her unease growing, she glances nervously at the room's corners, where shadows seem to creep. "Where's Mommy?"

Caught off-guard, he glances toward the open door, then quickly changes the subject, a forced lightness in his tone. "How about we get you dressed in your favorite overalls for breakfast, and we make pancakes?"

"Will Mommy be there?" Her tiny, anxious voice pipes up.

His lips curl into a vacillating smile, and he forces warmth into his tone. "Of course she'll be there," he says, quick to reassure her.

Her face brightens as her eyes light up with hope.

"We both know she makes the best pancakes," he says with a playful wink, trying to ease her concern.

Lillie giggles softly; her mood is momentarily lifted by the comforting thought of familiarity, even as shadows still linger just beyond her sight.

John gazes at her cheerful smile and continues warmly, "We can't have pancake day without Mommy."

The cheerful sound of her laughter fills the room, echoing vibrantly.

"Isn't that right?" he asks, playfully tickling her to lift her spirits further.

Her laughter grows louder, filling the air with joy.

Smiling affectionately, he declares, "Perfect. Now that's settled, let's get you dressed!" He sets her down gently, and she eagerly runs ahead of him toward the closet, her excitement palpable as she prepares for the day ahead.

He rummages through her clothes and hands her a pair of pink overalls. She notices his shirt sleeve is tightly rolled up, revealing three deep scratches on his skin.

From the corner of his eye, he catches her looking at him. His eyes dart anxiously to the claw marks, and his hands tremble slightly as he frantically pulls the fabric back down, trying to cover the evidence.

Slightly shaken, he casts a quick, worried glance toward Lillie, who has just finished clipping her last overall strap. With a gentle but firm voice, he breaks the silence, saying, "Let's head downstairs."

Chapter Six

CHEWING

At the bottom of the steep, creaking wooden staircase, John carefully lowers Lillie onto the worn floorboards.

A faint aroma of caramelized cakes drifts from the doorless kitchen, seeping into the living room like a whisper from an unseen mouth. Lillie's eyes brighten with innocent excitement. "Pancakes!" she exclaims.

A ball of orange fur brushes softly against John's legs, accompanied by a faint, melodic meow. Lillie's face lights up with a smile as she turns toward her beloved cat, her eyes shimmering with affection. She raises her hands in a familiar gesture, trying to coax him closer. "Huber!" she calls. She leans forward, stretching out her arm, but the cat suddenly leaps away, as if spooked by an invisible presence.

She furrows her brow in confusion, sensing a strange shift in Huber's behavior. There's a coldness in his abrupt retreat, a stark contrast to his usual curiosity. His purring gradually diminishes as he disappears into the shadows, leaving an unsettling silence behind.

"Huber," Lillie murmurs, her voice tinged with longing and uncertainty, her gaze fixed on the space where he vanished. Her eyes search the room, hoping for him to reappear.

John pauses nearby, inhaling deeply as he is drawn to an unusual, tantalizing scent that pulses with a life of its own. He glances toward Lillie, offering reassurance. "I'm sure he'll come back to play later," he says, trying to dispel her worry. He brushes aside his doubts from earlier, shaking off the inexplicable chill that skews the atmosphere.

Lillie sniffs gently, attempting to mask her unease. "Maybe he's just a little tired," she says, her voice wavering with a sliver of hope.

His smile reappears, though it seems strained. "Smells like they're ready," he says, forcing a warmth into his voice.

The room grows warmer as the gas stovetop in the next room robustly glows under the cast iron griddle.

"It's a little too warm in here," he says, voice hesitant. "By the smell of things, your mother must have beaten us to it. Smells like she's cooking up a storm."

A sudden deep growl rumbles from Lillie's stomach. John's eyes glance toward his daughter, a flicker of a smirk crossing his face. "Sounds like someone's hungry," he says. His smile falters slightly as he gazes at her, waiting for her response.

Lillie clutches her stomach, a giggle that feels strained slipping out. "Pancakes are my favorite food," she replies.

John's laughter bubbles up, but this time, there's an edge to it. "I know," he replies, "That's why they're mine too."

She looks towards the kitchen. Something feels off.

As she prepares to step forward, John reaches out, grabbing her hand with an unexpected firm grip. "Shall we?" he begins, his tone eerily calm, but his eyes flashing with something unnatural.

"Can we skip?" Lillie asks, her voice barely a breath, with a subtle nod accompanying the request.

John's expression shows a hint of apprehension lurking beneath the facade. "Is there any other way?" he replies.

Lillie's smile flickers; her eyes remain hollow, devoid of childish energy. Gathering her courage like a fragile shield, she pushes off the ground, leaping into the air with abrupt, frenetic energy. "Wee!" she yells, her voice sharp and urgent as she hurriedly steps ahead.

Her father lurches forward, his movements unsure as he lifts her off the ground, pulling her back with a force that seems to quiver with restraint. "Whoa, there, cowgirl," he says, his tone masking his unease.

He slips past her, moving swiftly, almost nervously, and turns the corner into the kitchen. "Let Daddy go first," he insists.

He stops abruptly, eyes fixed on the kitchen table, a frozen expression on his face.

The room is unusually bright, almost painfully so, its cheerful artificial light starkly contrasting the tension and shadows spilling in from the hallway.

On the table, a steaming stack of pancakes sits untouched, an inviting aroma filling the space—entirely at odds with the atmosphere. On a yellow embroidered tablecloth, spotless plates and carefully arranged utensils suggest a meal prepared for something special, yet there's an unsettling quality to the scene. At the center of the table, a vase displays a handful of freshly picked sunflowers. Their vibrant yellow petals offer a cheerful contrast to the room's heavy atmosphere.

The entire scene appears frozen in a perfect moment, captivatingly beautiful yet frightening, like a wonderful treat poised in a rat trap ready to snap shut.

Unable to remember the last time the kitchen felt warmth, John notices the edges of his lips curling into a gentle, nostalgic smile. Slowly, he releases Lillie's hand.

She immediately rushes inside with excitement. "Yay!" she shouts joyfully. She swiftly pulls out a chair, grunting as she climbs atop it with enthusiasm.

Suddenly, she feels someone pushing her chair from behind. Confused, she turns to find her father standing beside her, seeking answers in his expression.

"There's my little girl," a woman says, her voice gentle and inviting

The comforting sound triggers a deep emotion within Lillie, so profound that it's as if her heart has become whole again, rekindled by the love felt in that moment.

John smiles, a mixture of hopeful anticipation and apprehension in his eyes as he looks past his daughter. "Look who it is," he says with a guarded smile. "I'm surprised to see you up and about so early."

Lillie, hearing the familiar voice, swiftly turns around. Her face lights up as she exclaims, "Mommy!" She immediately extends her arms eagerly, ready to be enveloped in a warm hug.

Delilah receptively leans forward, offering an earnest smile. Her long hair cascades over her shoulders, catching the light with every movement. She wears a white baking apron that hugs her hips, delicately embroidered along the edges, emphasizing a relaxed, homey charm. Imbuing the scene with a sense of innocence, her soft, subtle drawl gently calls out, "Hi, Sugar."

John hesitates, and though he's happy to have her back, each cautious movement reveals unease as he steps forward. His voice wavers, caught mid-sentence, and he clears his throat before attempting to speak again. He pauses, unsure of what to say.

"You—" he stammers. He clears his throat, then makes another attempt. "You—" he says, but the words falter. "Did you sleep all right?"

She locks eyes with him and responds with a forced, brittle smile that barely masks the underlying tension, her lips twitching.

Lillie's eyes gleam with an unsettling brightness, a hint of unpredictability flickering behind their shine, like a glimmer of light in a lightless room. Her voice eagerly cuts through the awkward exchange between her parents as she asks, "Can we play today?" Her tone is laced with nervous anticipation.

John and Delilah continue to stare at one another; their eyes locked in a silent standoff. Neither wants to be the first to break the intense gaze that appears to convey unspoken words. The silence grows thick, stretching between them, as the tension becomes untenable.

"Please?" Lillie begs, her tiny hands clenched into fists at her sides, longing for a response that refuses to come.

"Mommy might need a little more rest," John says, blinking as he struggles to maintain eye contact.

Delilah notices his hesitation and ignores his cue, turning to Lillie and responding, "Of course, my darling." She looks back at John and smiles, her eyes full of affection as she adds, "Anything for my sugar."

John's face instantly drains of color, a wave of unease crossing his features. "But—" he says. "Do ... Do you think that's a good idea? Especially after yesterday?" He tries to protest, struggling to find the right words, his face a look of frustration. "Maybe it would be best..."

She gently places a hand on her daughter's shoulder, her touch light and reassuring. Leaning in slightly, she ignores him and offers a soft, comforting smile and whispers, "Don't listen to your dad." Her eyes linger on her husband for a moment before she adds with a playful smirk, "Now, you have to eat your pancakes first."

Lillie quickly moves to dish up her breakfast. She picks up a fluffy pancake and sets it on her plate. Its golden-brown surface shimmers in the morning light. She cuts a small, bite-sized piece and shoves it into her mouth, her cheeks puffing out slightly as she chews.

John watches her closely, his gaze softening as he notices her concentration. "Delilah..." he says, his voice warm with concern.

"That's my baby," she whispers with a warm smile, gently stroking her daughter's hair, the affection evident in her tender touch. She pauses to enjoy the serene, intimate moment, then reassures her daughter, "No rush now, baby girl. There's plenty of time."

Lillie chews faster as though she fears she will miss something if she takes too long.

"We wouldn't want you to choke," she says, stifling a giggle as she finishes the sentence.

Her father watches her. "Lillie—slow down."

She swallows quickly and stabs a bunch of pancake pieces with her fork, skewering five at a time. She shoves them in her mouth.

"Lillie!" he yells, his voice booming.

Lillie only has one thing on her mind as she homes in on her plate, and before she's even finished her bite, she stabs more pieces.

John lunges forward. "Lillie!" he shouts, slamming his fist against the table.

As the little girl flinches, syrup drips down her chin.

"John!" Delilah shouts. "Look at the fear in the poor girl's eyes!" She glances at her daughter.

Lillie takes a heavy breath, inhaling a soggy piece into the back of her throat. She chokes, hacking and coughing as she struggles to breathe.

Delilah hesitates, taking a step back as she observes the scene unraveling before her. Her face remains eerily blank—an unmoving mask of calm—but a faint glimmer sparks in her eyes like a sudden flicker of realization.

The child's eyes widen in terror as her face begins to pale, her cheeks slowly turning an ominous shade of blue. She gasps desperately, clutching at her throat with trembling hands, her skin cold and clammy.

"Don't just stand there!" John commands urgently, his voice trembling with distress. He swiftly moves around the cluttered table, his hands frantic as he pats the child's back. His eyes stare at his wife, searching her face for reassurance.

There's not a hint of concern, just a look of disconnect. At the corners of her lips, each twitch reveals a tumult of emotions struggling to break free and surface.

As Lillie's condition deteriorates, the tension in the room heightens, with each struggle for breath becoming more desperate.

With a forceful thump on her back, she expels a lodged piece of food, wheezing sharply as her chest heaves for air.

Her father wraps his arms around her; a look of panic etched on his face. "I knew she was eating too fast," he says. He pauses, struggling to find the right words, then blurts, "I knew she was going to choke."

Delilah glares at them, her eyes narrowing as she steps back. Her face contorts in disbelief. "You—you're saying this is my fault?" She snaps, voice cracking, her tone defensive. "You can't blame me for her loving pancakes so much and her ravenous eating habits."

Lillie stares at her plate, her eyes unfocused as she tries to gather her thoughts, the shock still clear in her trembling hands. She takes slow breaths, trying to steady herself, her eyes wide with disbelief at what has just transpired.

Her father takes hold of her, pulling her close. "It's okay," he says, dismissing his wife. "She didn't mean it, Lillie. It's not your fault."

The little girl takes a deep, steady breath and asks, "Mommy ... can we still go out to play?" When she doesn't get a response, she turns around to see. "Where—" she says, voice trembling, but she immediately stops, her eyes darting frantically around the room. "Where did Mommy go?" Her voice is filled with concern.

John quickly shifts his gaze away from his daughter, scanning the room. His eyes linger on various objects, noticing how the vibrant colors he once envisioned now appear muted and dull, as if drained of life. The once-cheerful space feels oppressive, the shadows lurking in every corner giving off a sense of unease.

The sinister quietude is broken by the slow, deliberate *drip.... drip.... drip* of water from the leaky faucet. It punctuates the silence like a heartbeat in the otherwise lifeless room. John's eyes flick toward the kitchen sink, where droplets splash audibly into the battered tin basin, their rhythmic plopping accentuating the silence's weight.

He clears his throat, attempting to exude confidence that masks his nervousness. "Um ... I'm sure she was just a little tired." His words stumble over each other as he momentarily looks away, searching behind him. Then, refocusing on his daughter, he forces a smile, attempting to ease her anxiety. "You know how you need naps sometimes?"

Lillie looks up at him, her wide eyes filled with worry. Her small fingers nervously clutch the legs of her pink overalls tightly as she waits for reassurance.

He pulls her into a gentle hug, fingers softly tracing patterns on her back. "Well, she likes naps sometimes too," he murmurs, speaking more to himself than anyone else as he tries to anchor himself amidst the growing uncertainty of her whereabouts.

"You can't be a princess without a nap," she says, her voice barely above a whisper, carrying a gentle yet firm tone that hints at her youthful but certain sense of self. John gently rests his hands on her shoulders as he assesses her face, searching for a sign of comfort or question.

A flutter of whispers cascades through the air, delicate but almost deafening in their subtlety. They begin practically mute, like the faint rustle of leaves, but grow increasingly persistent. The whispers seem to emanate from the shadowed hallway nearby, their source unseen but their presence deeply felt.

"Follow me..." a ghostly voice bellows, ethereal and hollow, echoing with an unnatural, spectral quality that sends a shiver down her spine.

Lillie's eyes widen as she looks toward the doorway, where shadows flicker and dance just beyond her line of sight.

"What do you say we do something fun today?" John asks, his voice a bit louder now, tightening his grip on her shoulder to garner her attention. His eyes are bright with anticipation, but he tries to mask his concern.

"Something fun?" she asks hesitantly, her gaze drifting toward her father with cautious curiosity. She searches his face for reassurance.

A shadow shifts subtly in the hallway, casting an ominous imprint just outside the doorway.

He glances past her, eyes briefly catching the unsettling movement, and his words quicken. "That is—" he starts to say, but cuts himself off, his attention snagged by a faint, almost inaudible whisper in his ear.

"John."

"John," the voice repeats, more insistent now.

He winces, rubbing his ear as if trying to dispel the ghostly sound, and speaks louder. "That is, if you're done with your breakfast," he says, attempting to sound casual, but with a hint of urgency.

Lillie looks downward at her plate, where a partially chewed piece of pancake still sits. Her stomach knots with a ripple of angst, and she feels the constriction grow tight all the way to her throat. "I'm done," she says and quickly climbs down from her seat.

"So how about we go play outside?" John asks, scooping her up. She giggles, and he attempts to feign enthusiasm. However, despite his best efforts, his concerns get the best of him, and his eyes nervously flick towards the door and the dimly lit hallway, worried and wondering where Delilah could have gone.

Chapter Seven

THE GARDEN

As her father carries her out the front door, he covers her eyes to shield them from the sun.

Unlike the night before, the rain has stopped, and the warm sun is shining on the dewy surroundings.

"Now, I know your mom asked if you wanted to play after breakfast, but hopefully, spending time with Daddy will do for today," he says.

Lillie nods with an enthusiastic smile.

He gently sets her down, and as her bare feet touch the muddy ground, they sink into the soft earth. "Yuckie." She laughs. "My toes look like little worms poking out of the dirt." She wiggles her toes, squishing them deeper into the mud.

"I'd be careful if I were you," he jokes, nudging her arm, a playful glint in his eyes. "I've heard that things live in there." He leans in slightly, voice dropping to a whisper while pressing his finger into the dirt with a mischievous grin.

Lillie widens her eyes, her body stiffening as she freezes in place. "In the mud?" she asks, looking down at her toes with worry.

"No, in there." He gestures toward the woods behind them.

"In the trees?" She asks, her voice rising with a mix of curiosity and worry.

John nods, a mysterious smile on his face.

She curls her toes in panic. "Like what? What lives in there?" she whispers.

A soft breeze rustles the leaves, carrying a gentle whistle that echoes the ominous mood.

John squats down, perching himself on his heels, his eyes locking onto hers. His expression becomes serious. "Did I ever tell you the story about the time the princess tried to run away?" He asks, glancing over his shoulder as if recalling a secret from the past.

Lillie leans in closer as curiosity and concern grow inside her. "She ran away?"

A gentle whisper escapes from her dad's lips, his eyes shimmering with a quiet sadness. "Sometimes ... even princesses need a moment of peace," he murmurs, casting a longing glance back at the house. He takes a slow, deliberate breath, inhaling the scent of the nearby flowers and the crisp air. "When she was not much older than you, living alone in the small cottage at the edge of the woods, she often felt terribly lonely," he begins, his voice tinged with nostalgia.

Lillie's brow furrows. "Was that because she lived all by herself?" she asks, voice sweet with genuine worry.

"Yes," he responds with a nod, his expression pensive. "Not by choice, of course..." His words trail off as he gazes into the distance, lost in memory. He pauses, reflecting before continuing, "Do you remember why?"

Lillie tilts her head, her eyes bright with wonder. "Because she was a princess!" she happily says.

"Exactly," he replies, placing a finger on his lips to shush her. "But remember, it's a secret—something she could never share with anyone."

Lillie stiffens slightly as she pretends to zip her mouth shut in promise.

He asks, "Do you remember the rules? Do you remember why she couldn't leave?" His voice is calm but serious, emphasizing the importance.

Lillie gazes out into the distance, taking a deep, steadying breath, as if trying to grasp the full weight of the story. After a long pause, she whispers, "Because—"

John steps in to fill in the missing words, completing the story with a sense of quiet understanding. "You know what?" he cuts in, his voice brimming with excitement. "How about we continue the story from last night?" His eyes gleam with eagerness as he turns to Lillie.

She hops up and down excitedly, her face lighting up like a summer sun. "Can we go to the castle for the story?" She squeals, clapping her hands in delight and pointing eagerly across the yard.

On the other side of the open space, a weathered slide glints in the sunlight, its surface worn smooth by countless adventures. It's attached to a colorful play structure, sturdy yet showing signs of age.

He turns his head to glance at the structure's roof—an elegant, pointed silhouette that resembles a fairytale spire. Befittingly, a hand-painted sign hangs nearby, vibrant and inviting, reading *Lillie's Castle* in cheerful, looping letters that seem to dance with excitement.

Its jolliness is at odds with the patches of mud and dead grass that surround it.

He gently picks her up, holding her securely in his arms as he walks toward the magical fort they've built together. With a careful lift, he slides her over the edge of the entrance, making sure she's comfortable. "Here you go, my dear," he says.

Lillie giggles, her eyes sparkling with excitement, as she climbs inside the miniature hideaway. She quickly scurries to the back wall, her small hands pushing aside the soft blankets covering the entrance. At the opposite end, there's a bright pink carpet spread out on the floor, accompanied by a charming little white table and two matching child-sized chairs, creating a perfect little play space.

Her father carefully climbs inside after her.

"Hurry, Daddy, shut the door before the monsters see you," Lillie says excitedly, her face pressed to the wall, listening for noise outside.

He crawls on all fours, his knees pressing into the plush rug on the floor. He turns around and draws the fabric doors closed to seal them in their refuge. "I'm hurrying, princess," he replies.

"I don't hear anyone coming," she says confidently, tucking her hair behind her ear to listen intently. Satisfied, she settles into a small, intricately carved chair. Its legs wobble a bit, but it holds steady.

As John finally reaches the small wooden table, he carefully pushes up his slipping glasses from the bridge of his nose with one finger, shaking his head with a bright, mischievous smile. "Are you sure the coast is clear?" he asks, his voice filled with playful curiosity.

She watches him settle into a crouch as she gracefully sits in the seat across from him at the table. He hunches his back, attempting to navigate the cramped space, his body shifting as he seeks a comfortable position on the child-sized furniture.

She dramatically nods, her eyes wide with mock seriousness, eyebrows raised in exaggerated concern. "Yup, I checked everything," she says confidently.

"Good." He leans forward with a smirk. "Now, where were we?" He taps his chin thoughtfully.

Her eyes widen, and she gasps. "The monsters." She looks around nervously, as if searching for hidden beasts lurking in the fort's shadows.

"Yes, yes, that's right—the monsters." He nods slowly, a mischievous glint sparkling in his eyes as he thinks about what to say next. "I think before we get back to the monsters, we should start from the very beginning ... where it all began," he says, leaning back slightly in his chair, gesturing invitingly for her to continue. The room is quiet except for the faint hum of the world outside and a gentle breeze that drifts through the doorway, rustling the fringes of the blankets draped over the entrance.

She leans in, her brow furrowing in curiosity, and whispers, "You mean the rules?" she asks. Her voice is delicate, tinged with nervousness, and she quickly covers her mouth, as if worried she might have been too loud.

A gust of wind suddenly stirs a small cloud of dust, causing the blankets over the doorway to flutter.

John glances over his shoulder, his eyes catching the waning sunlight. "I'm talking about the time before the rules," he begins again, voice low and contemplative, his tone hinting at a deeper story beneath the surface.

Lillie leans forward eagerly, her eyes wide with anticipation. "Before the rules?" She whispers again, her tiny voice barely above a breath, her body tensing with the urge to hear more.

"Being a princess isn't something you choose," he continues. "It's something you receive—something that's given to you at birth, part of who you are from the very moment you open your eyes into this world."

"Daddy ... wait." Her eyes suddenly widen, shimmering with a mixture of wonder and trepidation as she softly gasps. "Since Mommy is a princess, does that mean I'm a princess too?" she asks.

Shadows quietly dance in the corners of the dimly lit room, their whispers like secrets being shared just beyond their ears' reach.

Her father pauses, a darkness dancing across his face as he takes a deliberate breath, his eyes distant, as if recalling something long buried. Carefully, he reaches out, gripping her hand with a cold, steady touch. "Well," he says, "in theory—yes." He replies with a shrug, but there's an unsettling undercurrent to the words.

The whispers grow louder, echoing through the shadows as if the room itself is murmuring warnings. She tightens her fists, knuckles blanching as a shiver runs down her spine.

"You have it in your blood," he continues, voice quickening with an ominous tone, "but it's something you will have to decide for yourself as you grow older." His eyes narrow slightly, darkening with an unspoken warning. "Just like your mother. She made a choice. Being a princess isn't all rainbows and fairytales with happy endings. It's a life shrouded in loneliness, carved from shadows and silence. It's exhausting, relentless, a constant battle against the darkness that lurks beneath the surface."

He watches her expression morph from curiosity to disappointment, but beneath that, something colder, more frightening stirs. He continues, saying, "It can be a tough decision, and sometimes, you must sacrifice things you love to wear the crown. There will come a time when you are asked to choose whether to accept your fate—to be saved or to be lost. The journey is treacherous, and once you step onto it, there's no turning back. The shadows will follow, silent but waiting, and the price may be your very soul."

Her eyes expand, reflecting the faint flicker of the dying candlelight, as the vivid nightmare she just awakened from floods her consciousness once more. The image is so startlingly real, she can almost feel the icy darkness creeping in around her. "Daddy—" she begins, her voice trembling with confusion, but then she hesitates, swallowing her words. The only fairy tales she's ever known are the ones that promise eternal happiness, not those shrouded in shadows and dread.

"Yes, sweetheart?" he replies softly.

"How do you know if you're really a princess?" she asks.

He hesitates, uncertain of how to answer, then attempts to reassure her. "I don't know for sure, but what I can tell you—" Suddenly, he stops mid-sentence, his expression shifting as he senses a presence behind him. His body stiffens, and he quickly pivots around.

The thick blanket covering the entrance to the fort twitches ominously, sliding as if something—or someone—has just entered. It moves silently, intentionally, and then falls still.

John freezes, his eyes narrowing as he adjusts his gaze, trying to pierce the shadows that seem to stretch and writhe around the enclosure.

Lillie turns toward where her father is looking. "Is something wrong, Daddy?" she whispers, sensing that the darkness holding the fort is not just a shadow, but something far more sinister, something waiting in silence, watching them.

"Everything's fine," he says sharply, forcing a smile. His shoulders straighten with a tense rigidity, as if he's bracing himself against an invisible force. He turns slowly, his movement almost mechanical, and his voice drops to a reassuring tone. "Of course it's fine." He takes a slow, deep breath, as if trying to mask the tremor that runs through him. The pallor on his face has deepened, draining away all warmth, leaving only a ghostly, waxen hue that seems almost unnaturally pale in the dim light.

"How will I know when I'm a princess?"

John releases his breath with an audible sigh of resignation—heavy, burdensome. "From what your mother told me, it's like everything in your mind goes dark, as if the lights are flickering and about to go out. First, it's the shadows—slithering, creeping, invading your dreams and twisting them into nightmares. Then, gradually, they seep into your waking life, nestling into your bones and poisoning every thought."

Lillie holds her breath, her eyes wide, pupils dilated. The silence stretches, oppressive and thick, filled only with her ragged breathing.

"She says it's like being haunted by something unexplainable," he whispers, his voice barely audible, laced with a palpable fear. "A constant shade, a malevolent presence that follows you everywhere—a darkness that shields you from the light, but also swallows it whole, leaving nothing behind but empty, suffocating shadows. It's like a waking nightmare, blurring the lines between what's real and what's not, tearing you apart from the inside. Yet, despite everything, she still thinks being a princess is the most important thing. Even when she could have given it all up, she never did."

A faint, unsettling rustle emanates from the far corner, piercing the tense moment and snapping

Lillie's attention sharply. Her eyes dart toward the sound, and she sees a shadow that stretches and contorts in the dim light.

As her father's words continue, the shadow grows, elongating into a sinister skeletal silhouette. Its form distorts, revealing a hunched torso that appears both fragile and grotesquely unnatural. Slowly, thin, spindly limbs emerge, ending in lanky, crooked fingers that seem eager to grasp at the air.

She fixates on the scene around her, the room's shadows twisting and shifting in the faint light. Her father's mouth continues to move, but his words are muffled and distorted as if absorbed by an unseen fog, his voice overlapping with the unnatural silence that surrounds her.

The shadow figure remains, slowly creeping forward with calculated movements. Its form towers over her until the top of its head stretches upward, spreading across the ceiling like a dark stain. The shape parts in the center, revealing a cavernous opening. Inside, jagged teeth gleam with an eerie, glinting menace, their outlines serrated and razor-sharp.

An icy numbness grips her body, leaving her unable to move. Her mouth mirrors the shadow's slow, sinister opening—gaping wide, hunger incarnate. She fights to call out, to summon her father's aid, but her throat feels tight, dry, unable to produce a sound. Her eyes, wide and frozen, deny her the blink she desperately needs; they are dry and shimmering with tears of helplessness.

A suffocating panic wells up as she gasps for air, each breath shallow and ragged. Frustration and fear collide as she watches her father—so near yet so absent—unable to aid her. Her hands hang lifeless at her sides, heavy as if weighed down by despair, while her shoulders ache from the relentless tension, as if the very air around her has compressed, trapping her in this waking nightmare.

Lillie's eyes dart to the shadow's mouth as a serpentine tongue flicks out, slick and frightening, glistening with evil.

From the suffocating darkness, a covert voice hisses, slicing through the silence like a razor, whispering her name. "Lillie..." The voice crawls like icy breath across the back of her neck, unsettling in its softness and filled with loathing.

Beyond her, the world seems to tilt, the familiar twisting into a nightmare; her father's face blurs into a ghostly mask, his words distorted, echoing like distant thunder muffled by thick blankets.

Her chest tightens as she struggles to summon her voice, parched and cracked, craving salvation. "He—help!" she screams inwardly, her voice lost amidst the shadows that stretch and coil around her, suffocating, relentless. Her mind reels, swirling in chaos as darkness and dread intertwine, threatening to consume her completely.

Slowly, the skeleton-thin shadow arms reach toward her, elongated and gnarled like twisted branches in a forsaken forest. The air is thick with silence, broken only by the subtle scrape of bony fingers against the walls.

She is paralyzed, her body refusing to obey, as she watches those ghastly limbs draw near, casting sinister shadows that crawl across the walls like creeping nightmares. Her heart pounds violently in her chest, each thump loud and frantic, as she braces for the moment they will seize her, pull her into a dark abyss. Desperation claws at her mind; she closes her eyes in a futile attempt to block out the dread, to deny the terrible reality.

A voice emerges, faint yet unmistakable, like a ghostly breath: "Garden."

Her eyes snap open in a panic, darting around the dim, bleak room until they settle on the face of her father, staring back at her with unrecognizable eyes.

"That's a splendid idea," he says, voice overly cheerful, a forced brightness. "I know this conversation is heavy, and the garden always lifts my spirits," he adds nervously, the words hanging awkwardly in the humid air. "It always brightens my mood."

Lillie gasps sharply, a sudden, involuntary sound that twists into a cough as she clutches her throat with trembling fingers, trying to suppress the choking sensation that tightens her chest.

"Are you okay?" John leans forward, his face showing deep concern, as his eyes scan her with increasing suspicion.

Feeling momentary relief, she lowers her hand, but her fingers shake as she notices something shiny and wet on her palm. She shakes it away desperately, trying to clear her mind, and quickly nods, forcing a weak smile. She starts to rise, eyes flickering vacantly as her gaze falls on something on the table.

A stunned fly buzzes weakly in a sticky pool of saliva, its wings fluttering against the glistening phlegm. The revolting sight makes her cringe, and it's hard to believe it was once a part of her.

As she continues to look at her father, a brief shiver runs through her, and she brushes her elbow against something, or perhaps someone—she isn't sure anymore. Her movements are mechanical, detached.

"You sure you're okay?" he asks, his voice softer, but with a hint of suspicion. His eyes search hers with growing intensity.

"Mm hmm," she responds, her voice barely audible, her face blanched, as a shadow of something terrifying flickers in her eyes.

"Are you sure?" he asks again, more worried than before. "You haven't noticed anything like what I described, have you?" He probes a bit more.

She nervously glances down, her hands trembling as her head lowers, eyes darting away from the unseen.

Shadows continue to fill the room, clinging to the walls and ceiling while twisting and flickering like candle flames.

She swallows hard, terrified to acknowledge her burden, afraid to share the truth.

A shiver runs down her spine, her breath catching in her throat. Her father gently reaches out, voice comforting but urgent, trying to draw her back from the edge of panic.

"You know, you can talk to me about anything," he says, his tone desperate to cut through her silence.

She lifts her head slowly, eyes shimmering with unshed tears. "I know," she replies.

A faint smile attempts to form on his face, tight and unsure, as he twists the corners of his mouth in an awkward effort to comfort her. "Okay," he says, trying to mask his own unease, "let's go to the garden."

The floorboards creak with age as they make their way to the exit.

As she approaches the final three steps, Lillie glances left and hesitates, then her instinct kicks in, and she sprints past the shadowy corner of the fort to the doorway, heart pounding.

Though she can see nothing in the gloom, a prickling sensation crawls across her skin—she

knows she's being watched, stalked from the darkness.

Chapter Eight

PICKING WEEDS

They dash across the yard, each step hurried and full of purpose, while the distant chirping of the birds persists—singing an eerily distorted symphony. Their calls sound almost identical, but beneath the surface, a subtle, sinister undertone lingers, like a hidden warning.

Overhead, the sky shifts, and the sun struggles to shine through a patch of thick clouds, casting a dull gray overcast that drains the world of its vibrant hues. The colors of the ground and surroundings appear muted, as if soaked in shadow, while an inexplicable static sensation prickles their skin, heightening their sense of unease.

Lillie speeds up, her instincts screaming that she's being watched. She nervously darts her gaze to the side, then over her shoulder, and straight ahead toward the house, searching for the unseen observer.

Her heartbeat thunders in her ears as a dark, oppressive presence seems to cling to her bedroom window, a black void that feels deeper than mere glass, waiting silently in the gloom. As she begins to turn away, the curtain subtly shifts, hinting at a gentle movement behind it.

Suddenly, she hears the distinct creak of the front door's hinges as it slowly swings open, filling the air with a faint squeal.

A burst of sunlight spills inside, casting warm, golden rays across the floor. From the doorway, Delilah's voice resonates loudly and cheerfully, breaking the quiet. "What are y'all up to on this fine sunshiny day?" Her tone is bright and inquisitive.

John quickly glances toward the source of her voice, his eyes meeting hers as she stands in the open doorway. Without missing a beat, he speeds up his steps and calls out, "Just enjoying some time with our daughter!"

"Mind if I join?" she shouts, her voice ringing with enthusiasm as she strides confidently toward them, her steps brisk and purposeful.

The sunlight catches her hair, which is now elegantly curled, contrasting with the casual-yet-polished appearance she maintains. She wears the same apron from earlier, its fabric slightly dusted with dirt, hinting at her recent gardening activities.

From her pocket, she smoothly retracts a small garden shovel, the metal gleaming softly. "You know how much I love to garden," she says with a bright, infectious smile that spreads across her face, her eyes shining with genuine joy.

There's a noticeable spark in her demeanor, a vibrancy that wasn't there before, radiating confidence and contentment, making her appear transformed in this moment.

"Wouldn't you like to get a little more rest?" John asks gently, his voice calm and reassuring. "You still have plenty of days ahead to spend with your daughter—she's not going anywhere."

Suddenly, a chilling sensation seizes Lillie. The icy touch of her mother's fingertips, cold as winter's frost, freezes her in place, a shiver running down her spine as a wave of unease washes over her.

"I am well-rested, but my thoughts are tangled, craving nothing more than to spend quiet moments with my baby girl." Her voice carries a warm, soothing tone, yet it is tinged with an undercurrent of vulnerability.

John pauses, his brow furrowing as he prepares to speak. "But—" he begins, hesitating. "In the kitchen—"

She cuts him off gently, explaining, "I was not myself back there." Her words spill over into his, hurried and evasive. "It's as simple as that." A faint shiver runs through her as she notices shadows lurking at the edge of the yard.

A whisper, sharp and clear, calls to Lillie, drawing her attention. "Come to the garden," it says in a hauntingly soothing tone.

Her eyes scan the surrounding space, searching for the source of the voice beckoning to her, before settling her eyes back on her bedroom window.

Delilah, noticing her daughter's distraction, quickly intervenes, her grip tightening on Lillie's arm, pulling her back to attention with a forced gentleness. "Let's ask her what she wants," Delilah says, laced with a fragile desperation.

She notices Lillie's distant stare and, her tone becoming meek and feeble, asks, "Don't you want to spend time with your poor mother?"

Lillie remains rooted, her face pale, eyes fixed on the darkness in the house's window, from which the whispers seem to emanate.

Delilah's grip tightens like a vise as she pulls Lillie closer, her voice trembling. "What's wrong with you, girl? Do you not love me anymore?" The words are almost staccato—a fractured, trembling sound that barely escapes her lips.

Lillie's head snaps around abruptly, stumbling over her words as she tries to speak. "No—I mean—I—sorry, Mommy—I hear—"

Delilah leans in, her eyes exuding a hint of fear as they reflect shadows that dance in her gaze as she whispers, "That's what I thought..." She spins around, her movement abrupt, and faces her husband. "Alright, so that's settled. We will garden then, as a family." Her tone is tentative yet firm, with a hint of underlying tension.

John glances toward his daughter, observing her stiff posture and the distant look in her eyes. He senses something is wrong, but chooses his words carefully. "Let it be a family affair," he replies.

Delilah giggles, a nervous sound that barely masks her anxiety. She tightens her grip on the small shovel; its wooden handle constricts under her fingers. With a determined nod, she points the blade forward, her eyes fixed on the earth as if trying to convey her intentions beyond words.

John observes her, his eyes sharp with suspicion.

She forces a cheerful expression while her knuckles blanch from tightening her grip on something unseen.

John clenches his jaw, the muscles taut with frustration. "That's right—" he begins, but she cuts him off, her tone colder now, more deliberate.

"Well, this is me trying to be a better mother," she says. Her voice is eerily steady, each word hanging in the tense air.

He tries to respond and argue, but she ignores him, rushing forward with unsettling haste.

Her hand snatches Lillie's, yanking her along as her eyes flash with a disturbing excitement. "Come on, girlfriend, let's go pick some weeds," she says, her voice unnaturally bright and overbearing.

Lillie giggles, skipping along as if entranced.

John, left behind, watches them move ahead, his mind racing. He wipes the sweat from beneath his glasses as a knot tightens in his stomach, sensing that something's wrong simmering just beneath the surface.

"Daddy, aren't you coming?" Lillie shouts eagerly over her shoulder, her voice filled with anticipation. Her face is lit with excitement as she hurriedly strides ahead, her footsteps quick on the gravel path. She turns for a moment, eyes searching, her curly hair bouncing with each step.

"Daddy's being a sourpuss," her mother teases, a playful grin spreading across her face as she tries to coax a smile from her husband. Lillie's cheeks flush with energy, eager for her father's response.

John, feeling a surge of unease clawing at his chest, forces a strained smile, trying to mask his concern. He chuckles softly, attempting to sound unbothered and reassuring. "Of course, I'm right behind you, my dear," he says. His voice carries an undercurrent of tension as he hurriedly catches up to his daughter, determined to appear unbothered despite the storm of thoughts inside.

In the distance, a sprawling field gradually draws nearer, divided into neat, carefully sectioned plots. Rich, dark soil stretches across the expanse, dotted with rows of vibrant green crops that ripple gently as a soft breeze passes through them. Tall stalks of corn sway rhythmically, their golden tasseled tops shimmering in the sunlight, while tendrils of crimson tomatoes twist and intertwine, climbing up trellises.

In front of the abundant crop of tomatoes and corn, a rectangular raised flower bed catches the eye, its edges made from weathered wooden planks, protecting fresh soil and tender, sprouting seeds. Tiny green shoots peek shyly through the dirt, signaling new life.

Nearby, Delilah fixates on this promising greenery, her eyes alight with expectation. She pulls her daughter a little closer, feeling the warmth of her small body. With a spirited skip, she quickens her pace, her hand gripping the little shovel, swinging lazily at her side. Her voice rings out with eager resolve. "Let's go kill some varmints!" A wild, triumphant laugh punctuates her words.

Lillie flinches at her sudden surge of energy, her fingertips flushing with a faint reddish hue as she tugs to free her hand from her mother's grasp. "Mommy—" she says, voice strained, wincing as her small hand trembles.

Delilah, sensing her child's restlessness, gently loosens her hold as they reach the flower bed. "Yes, my darling?" she asks, spinning around to offer a playful distraction.

A gentle breeze stirs the air, carrying soft, elusive sounds that brush against Lillie's delicate ears, distracting her from her worries. "Oh—nothing," she murmurs, her eyes flickering toward the corners of the wooden box, seeking refuge in her own thoughts.

Ignoring her daughter entirely, Delilah's mind drifts elsewhere, preoccupied with darker thoughts. Clutching the dirt-stained handle of the shovel, she lunges forward with sudden ferocity toward a tiny green sprout pushing through the earth. With a sharp, savage motion, she slices it from the ground, a grim satisfaction flickering across her face, as if proud of erasing life itself. The action is disturbingly aggressive, as if driven by a primal urge.

Lillie, still lost in her own world, senses a subtle change in the air—a whisper of movement that's more invasive than the breeze she felt moments ago. It weaves through her hair with an unnerving chill, prickling her skin.

From the distance, a voice, deep and ominous, drips with wicked intent, calling out, "Come hither, my child." The words slither through the field as if pulsing with a life of their own, crawling under her skin.

She gasps as fear grips her, causing her to hold her breath. Her eyes twitch anxiously, darting toward the field of crops.

A sudden rustling disturbs the rows as something shifts. A corn stalk, previously static, quivers violently, the dry leaves whispering secrets in the breeze.

Then, a nearby tree limb snaps—a sickening, sharp crack, echoing like a woodland scream. Shadows dance and stretch across the earth, hinting at unseen horrors lurking just beyond the veil of normalcy.

She looks anxiously at her mother. Her fingers fidget as they stab into the flower bed, yet her expression remains eerily unmoved. Her lips part slightly as she hums a lullaby-like tune, the melody creeping beneath her daughter's skin, unsettling and slow.

A chilling voice joins her, sinister and low, darkly weaving through her tune. "Oh, where, oh, where has my little lamb gone?" The words coil around the melody, each note sinking deeper into the shadowy crevices of her mind. The voice lingers, dragging out the final phrase with a tone that chills the atmosphere. "Oh, where, oh, where, can she be?"

Lillie's eyes flash nervously toward the dense rows of corn, darting as if searching for something unseen. Her fingers, tense and trembling, squeeze the fabric of her overalls, the rough denim a fragile barrier against the growing unease gnawing at her skin.

An abrupt silence rises, oppressive, as if the very ground beneath her is holding its breath, waiting for something dark to surface.

Slowly, a shadowed hand, cold and damp, slips around one of the towering, withered stalks, shifting it aside with a soft rustle. The hand's pallid, near-translucent skin reveals dark bruises and open sores, the flesh marred by neglect; jagged, broken nails dig into its flesh like a raptor's claws. A nauseating smell wafts from it, nearly unnoticeable, yet undeniably sickening.

A voice, raspy and uneven, edges closer, chanting in a low, guttural tone that would make the bravest soul squirm. The sound seems to crawl under the skin, each word darker than the last.

Lillie steps back, her heart pounding like a drum in her chest, every nerve taut and quivering with fright.

The hand continues to pull the stalk back like a curtain, revealing a charred skull and eye, black plastic infused and melted into the clumps of skin left on its elongated face. "Lillie, don't be afraid," it chimes softly.

She takes a hesitant step backwards, her body trembling uncontrollably as if her nerves are fraying with each passing second. Her eyes return to her mother, who, undeterred, presses the blade into the damp earth with greater force, sending a small spray of dirt into the air. She attempts to call out for her mother, to plead for her attention, but no sound escapes her lips, leaving her feelings of helplessness and distress unvoiced.

The creature's lipless mouth slowly stretches open, revealing jagged, rotting teeth grimly exposed in its gaping maw. Its decaying flesh writhes and sags, casting crawling shadows across its deeply contoured features. A damp, foul odor permeates the air, wrapping around her in a suffocating embrace.

John sees Lillie's frantic reaction and races toward her with a surge of panic. "What did you do, Delilah?" he yells as he yanks her little girl into his grasp, hugging her trembling body.

Delilah spins around, clutching a tangled clump of weeds in her hands, her eyes wide with innocent confusion, but tinged with something darker. "Whatever do you mean, John?" She speaks faster. "I've just been minding my own business, picking these ... pests." As she tightens her grip on the unwanted plants, dirt falls between her fingers. "Th ... these little menaces need to be eradicated from our lovely flower beds." Her words falter into a nervous stammer as shadows creep closer, making the garden suddenly seem menacing and alive with hidden danger.

Lillie gasps, air rushing into her lungs after what feels like an eternity of suffocation. A raw, desperate scream erupts from her, echoing through the tense moment. "There—there—there—" she stammers, struggling to form a complete sentence. She raises a trembling finger, pointing toward the dense field of maize. "In there—" she gasps, eyes wide with dread.

The stalks sway in an unsettling, nearly silent wave, as if alive and watching. Their outlines blur at the edges, merging with the darkness that refuses to retreat.

John and Delilah turn their heads toward the ominous swaying of the corn, the heavy silence pressing down on them.

Delilah squints, trying to peer deeper into the shadowy rows, her brow furrowed. Her voice comes out softer, tinged with unease. "I don't see anything," she says, but her eyes betray her certainty, darting back to the threatening gloom within the fields.

John glares at his wife, a look of disgust on his face. "Here, act like a mother!" he snaps, exasperated. He pushes the little girl toward her. "Take care of your daughter."

The sky above darkens, thick clouds rolling in, blotting out the light. An unsettling stillness settles, the air growing heavier with each passing second.

Suddenly, Delilah snaps, her voice sharp and unsteady. "Don't overreact," she says, raising her hands defensively, her eyes darting around nervously. "I can't take care of her; I'm a mess; I have dirt all over me. Why would I want to get her dirty?"

"Just take her," he says firmly, and he nudges his daughter closer. She stumbles, clutching her mother desperately and burying her face in her apron.

John extends his hand toward her, his eyes fixed intently on the small shovel she holds. "Give that to me," he demands, his voice firm, as he slowly reaches out, his fingers brushing the spade's handle.

The air is thick with anticipation as he holds his gaze steady, signaling his quiet urgency. The scene is quietly tense, filled with unspoken words and the subtle motion of his outstretched arm.

Delilah tightens her grip around the implement, her knuckles whitening as she fights to hold on. Her eyes flash with determination. "Why? I still need it!"

Before she has a chance to say more, he quickly pulls the object out of her grasp, his fingers curling around it firmly. "I'm going into the cornfield to see if anything's there," he says, glancing toward the tall, swaying stalks. His gaze lingers on the dirt-smudged blade, which glints faintly in the little bit of sunlight left.

"Don't pay her any attention. She's just a child," Delilah replies with a hint of amusement. She glances down at the little girl tightly coiled around her waist. Lillie's tiny fingers clutch at Delilah's clothing, her face flushed with tiredness and disquiet. Delilah's eyes narrow as she observes her, trying to appear reassuring but with a hint of mockery beneath. "Kids have wild imaginations," she adds with a touch of sarcasm.

Her eyes flick from the girl's face to the cornfield, and then to John, who's standing close by, his hand tight on the handle of the tool.

Delilah's lips curl into a slight smirk. "I don't see anything. She's probably just tired," she says as she gestures towards the fields with a flick of her hand.

John rolls his eyes, his grip tightening around the garden spade-turned weapon. His expression is tense, and he pauses as if weighing his words. "Yeah, she's probably just tired," he says, his voice hardening defensively. "She's definitely not like you! And frankly, I'm glad she's not."

The jarring cacophony of her parents' argument crushes the child. Unfortunately, this type of interaction has become the norm. Overwhelmed by the swelling fear and the relentless bickering, she can no longer hold back her tears, which fall silently down her cheeks.

"Some father you are—" Delilah murmurs, her voice void of emotion as she places her hand gently on the back of her daughter's head, offering a fragile comfort. "Look ... look what you've done. You made our baby cry."

Not wanting to escalate the confrontation any more, John stiffens, shoulders squared, and turns away from the divisive scene. With his jaw tightly clenched, he moves with slow, deliberate steps across the uneven terrain, each footfall cautious yet purposeful. His gaze is fixed on the endless fields of corn, their tall stalks waving gently, casting shifting shadows that dance in the fading sunlight.

Delilah mechanically moves her hand, her fingers trembling slightly as if resisting the urge to pat Lillie's head harder. "Everything is going to be okay, baby," she says. A tiny smirk momentarily lights her otherwise emotionless face as she watches John walk farther away, the ache of her powerlessness lingering in her eyes. "They will take him away soon enough," she murmurs, a hint of resignation in her voice.

Lillie's sniffle catches in the back of her throat, and her petite body quivers with sobs she struggles to hold back. "Daddy—" she whimpers, pulling her head away from her mother's embrace. Her eyes follow him as he disappears farther into the distance, her voice rising in desperation. "Daddy!" she calls out, her voice cracking with a mixture of fear and longing as she steps forward, the sound echoing in the open space.

Her mother grabs her hair, pulling her back. "Know your place, girl," she says through gritted teeth. "He doesn't care; he just wants to control you, just like he controls me," she hisses.

"That's not true! My Daddy loves me!" Lillie cries.

"You think that now, but just you wait," her mother replies, her voice laced with a faint, unsettling resignation. "The second he realizes you're not like him, he'll try to control you. He'll do what he did to me: manipulate and dominate, worming his way into your life and twisting you into something you're not. His eyes will narrow with suspicion, a cruel glint appearing, and his lips will curl into a sneer of disappointment. His words will cut like blades, icy, mocking, and laced with venomous disdain."

The little girl's eyes well with tears, shimmering like fragile glass ready to shatter under the weight of fear and helplessness.

Suddenly, her mother's eyes darken into a sinister shade of black, with veins like spiderwebs creeping across the whites. A shiver crawls down her back as an evil energy twists her mother's features. Her voice dips into a haunting minor key, unrecognizable yet eerily familiar, and her words accelerate into a frantic, almost desperate cadence.

"He wants to control us, to bend us to his relentless will. His insatiable desire to impose his power over us is like a persistent, creeping shadow—an abyss that claws into the edges of our reality and refuses to let go. It darkens every moment of our happiness, like ink spreading through water, tainting everything in its path. He seeks to snuff out our shine, our joy, our spirit—stamp out the light so we're prisoners to his oppressive grip."

Staring at her mother as she rants, Lillie feels like she's looking at a stranger. It's as if the words don't belong to her and are controlled by an evil ventriloquist.

Her mother's tongue wiggles like a snake as her words spill out in a rush, echoing with venom and spite. "It's a shadow that slithers and coils around us, spreading into every corner of our lives, cold and ruthless. It tries to snuff out the fire in our souls, no matter how hard we hold on to hope. We tremble with fear and desperation, yearning for a glimmer of salvation, but the darkness closes in, relentless and consuming. He wants to devour us, seeking to erase our existence and reshape us in his own distorted image, erasing who we are, bit by bit, until there's nothing left but echoes of pain and fear."

Lillie looks up at her mother, tears gathering in her wide, innocent eyes. Her tiny hands clutch tightly onto her mother's clothing, desperately seeking reassurance and safety. "Daddy—" she blurts. "He doesn't do those things. He loves me!" Her gaze shifts quickly toward her father, who is slowly distancing himself, and her face contorts with a mixture of confusion and helplessness.

"Does he?" Delilah sneers, her voice taking on a demonic edge. A look of wicked calculation crosses her face as she continues, "The more I consider it, perhaps we'd be better off without him."

"Please don't hurt him," she stammers, her voice trembling with emotion. "You—you can't!"

Her mother grimaces, a fleeting sparkle flickering in her eye, revealing a complex mix of thoughts and emotions.

Lillie squirms, trying her best to break free from the tight grasp restraining her. "Let me—" she says, her voice trembling and strained, driven by an instinct to escape and find safety.

Her mother tightens her grip, pressing her nails into her skin, holding her firmly.

"Let me go!" Lillie shouts, her voice cracking fiercely, breaking free from the restraint with a burst of raw, unfiltered emotion as her tiny legs flail and kick.

Ahead, John vanishes behind the cornstalks.

Lillie, frantic and breathless, pumps her arms desperately, trying to catch up. The wind cuts through her, carrying the tears and snot from her face, streaking her skin with a mix of salt and moisture. Her body trembles with exertion as her vision blurs with tears.

Meanwhile, her mother stands motionless, eyes wide, watching her daughter retreat. Her gaze is vacant, as if her soul has momentarily left her body. Slowly, as if in a trance, she turns away from the girl. The life behind her eyes is dull, hollow—like a puppet that has lost its strings—as she begins to walk back toward the house. Her steps are unhurried and mechanical, swallowed by the oppressive darkness creeping across the fields.

The child's screams rip through the unsettling quiet, filled with a desperate helplessness. "Daddy!"

she wails, her voice shaking as she stumbles toward the edge of the cornfield.

The towering stalks sway like the pendulum of a clock counting down to her nightmare, their rustling whispering threats in the wind.

She pauses, her breath ragged, eyes searching the sea of green, desperate to find her father. "Daddy, where are you?" she calls.

There is no reply.

She calls again, "Where are you?"

Silence.

Convinced he's gone farther than she'd imagined, she gathers her breath, steeling herself to venture into the shadowy depths of the green labyrinth.

As she weaves into the heart of the towering ten-foot maze, a chilling moan rumbles through the stalks, accompanied by rustling. She freezes, lost and uncertain if it's her father, a figment of her imagination, or something more sinister.

She gasps sharply, her voice trembling as she turns toward the noise. "Hello?" she calls out. "Is—" she stammers, struggling to find words amid the growing fear.

Before she can finish her sentence, a shrill whistle stops her. Her body tenses and her hands clench. Her pulse quickens, adrenaline flooding her veins as her eyes flit anxiously.

She glimpses a long, tattered white cloth—a piece of her nightmare—vanishing into the depths of the tangled cornfield, swallowed by the darkness.

Cold dread coils in her stomach, and an icy shiver runs through her from head to toe. She recognizes the torn fabric. It belongs to the creature that has been haunting her nightmares, a shadowy horror lurking, now clearly close enough to reach out and touch her.

Lillie's words catch in her throat, a ragged gasp choking off her voice as fear constricts her chest. She tries again, voice trembling, to utter the word that feels like a curse lodged in her mouth: "Daddy." Her eyes, wide and unblinking, flicker with terror as she watches the corn husks tremble and rustle.

Shadows dance between the stalks, twisting and merging into dark, unrecognizable figures that loom just beyond her sight.

An icy rush floods her bones, tightening its grip and refusing to let go.

Her body is held captive by fear, squeezing her chest and clouding her thoughts. Her ears catch the crackle of snapping stalks; they are growing closer, each sound sharp, piercing in her solitude.

A whisper drifts toward her, eerily close and clear. "Lillie..." it breathes, stretched and unsettling, as if crawling into her ear like a spider. It cloaks her in chilling anticipation, fueling her terror as the surrounding darkness thickens. The taunting, merciless voice continues, "As you tremble and shake, drowning in fear, I draw closer inch by inch, minute by minute, day by day, year by year."

She tries to tune it out, forcing herself to move forward. Her voice wavers as she calls out, "Daddy?" She takes another step, her words growing louder, desperation creeping into her tone. "Daddy?" She calls out again, her legs trembling and knees knocking together as she searches the shadows.

Whispers drift around her, their voices growing louder and more insistent with each passing moment. Lillie hesitantly takes another tentative step, trying to steady her breath and clear her mind amid the mounting noise. The calls shift and swirl like a brewing storm, echoing in her ears and jostling her nerves.

Suddenly, a piercing screech emerges from the shadows ahead.

Tears well up in her eyes as she fears the worst. "Are—are you there?" she asks, desperately hoping for a sign or response from her father.

With a burst of static-like interference, a hand suddenly shoots out from behind a towering, grotesquely decayed stalk. Its fingers reach out from the soil as if clawing their way from a grave. The hand slaps the dirt harshly, making a dull thud.

She watches intently as each jagged nail digs into the muddy earth, gripping desperately against the wet soil.

The fingers tremble and strain, claws scraping at the muck as the hand slowly retreats, leaving a grisly imprint of mud and decomposing flesh in its wake. It's as if the creature is desperately fighting to free itself from the earth's suffocating grip. Clumps of cold, wet dirt lodge into its rotting skin, matting into its pallid flesh as each spindly finger coils underneath the palm, leaving only a single sinister, elongated finger ominously pointing at her.

She stumbles backward, her eyes wide with horror as she recognizes the ghostly, pearl-white pallor of the creature's skin.

It's the same entity she saw the night before—a nightmare of flesh and bone that has somehow manifested from her subconscious, creeping into her waking world, its presence cold and malign.

Above, the sky roars with thunder, and dark, menacing clouds churn, swallowing the sun in a blanket of oppressive gray. The once-vivid scene transforms into a bleak, suffocating tableau.

Lillie trembles violently, dragging her toes through the dirt as she slowly backs away. A sudden drizzle begins, tiny droplets of chilly rain landing on her cheek, blending with tears of distress.

In a slow, almost predatory motion, the skeletal figure bends its pointing finger, a contorted blend of bone and fetid flesh, as if summoning her with an unholy invitation. Its voice, tinged with a serpent-like hiss, floats through the air. "Come closer, my child—"

Her voice quivers as she desperately retorts, "No … No… No… Please leave me alone. I'm not going anywhere near you." Her voice is barely louder than her pounding heart.

The creature, unyielding, places its palms into the moist earth, pushing into the mud with force.

She observes as its emaciated features emerge—sunken eyes, and cracked, discolored lips that curl into a twisted smile. It contorts into an unnatural backbend, creating a monstrous silhouette against the stormy sky, then remains stock-still, watching her with unblinking, soulless eyes, a predatory presence that exudes impending doom.

"Where do you think you're going?" It sneers, its sharp voice cutting through the chilly, harsh wind. Shadows twist around the creature, elongating its form as it stalks closer, eyes gleaming with malevolent intent.

Lillie squeezes her fists tightly, her knuckles blanching as she fights the flood of terror. "Daddy!" she screams, afraid to look away. Her eyes quickly dart from side to side, searching for safety in the darkness, and she realizes she is lost.

The creature edges closer, its hand extended, moving with a sinister grace, like a venomous spider about to strike its victim, dark and shiny, the wet sheen of rain slicking its skin. Its gaze stays fixed on her as it cocks its head, with an unsettling curiosity shining in its eyes. "He can't save you," it says. Its mouth gapes wide, its jaws splitting open with a loud crack, revealing rows of sharp teeth set in bloodless gums, drenched and dripping with saliva, as though the storm itself has fed them.

Lillie's breath catches as the creature slinks closer, the smell of decay seeping from its mouth. Horror grips her as she watches its shadowed form creep closer, inches away now and smelling of death. "Mommy—" she whimpers, voice breaking, eyes filled with terror.

Above, the sky darkens, thick clouds roiling like a living beast. Lightning flashes and thunder cracks, illuminating the creature's silhouette and the churning storm. The only other sounds are the relentless patter of rain against the crops' broad leaves and the muddied ground, echoing like a funeral dirge.

With trembling lips, she whispers, "Princess Mommy?" Her voice is a fragile plea against the storm's roar.

The creature hisses sharply, its tongue flicking out like a snake's strike. "There are no princesses here," it responds coldly. Its eyes gleam with cruel amusement.

Tears well up in her eyes, shimmering as one slips down her cheek, mingling with the raindrops pelting her. Heavy despair wraps its icy hands around her heart, squeezing tightly.

The creature's voice trickles into the downpour, each syllable dripping like toxic venom, echoing through the storm-lashed air. "It's only a mother who despises little children unless they are cooked and presented like a suckling pig for dinner," it sneers with a wicked grin.

"My Mommy loves me!" she insists fiercely.

The creature's eyes flicker with mockery as it inches closer, shadows casting ominous shapes across its gaunt face.

Falling faster, her tears carve shimmering tracks down her cheeks while she shakes her head, desperately holding onto hope.

The skeletal figure bends forward, its joints creaking and the skin stretching paper-thin, turning transparent and purple, exposing the bones beneath. Suddenly, its neck snaps with a sickening crack, and the head pivots upside-down to stare at her, eyes gleaming.

"She's the one who gave you to me—the woman who sacrificed your soul," it hisses, its voice thick with bitterness.

A strong wind blows through the corn, rustling debris and making the creature sway uncontrollably, creating an opportunity for Lillie to escape.

But as she prepares to run, the skeletal limbs curl and tighten around her like vicious, twisting vines, pressing brutally against her skin. They writhe with a sinister, unnatural strength, coiling around her ankles and wrists with relentless force. She struggles desperately, wrenching her body, trying to break free from their oppressive grip, but they only tighten their hold, constricting her movements with cold, unyielding force.

Without warning, the corn husks twist and ripple in a synchronized wave, almost as if jolted by electricity and brought to life. Then, like gaping mouths, the husks split open, exposing the horrifying visages underneath: horribly disfigured children's faces, their teeth sharp and the color of corn.

Lillie gasps, her eyes wide, staring at the rows of yellow incisors that gleam menacingly with each flash of lightning. Her body melts into a trembling mess; her knees buckle as if giving way to some unseen force kicking them out from behind.

Tiny voices, shrill and filled with malice, chant mercilessly, "Your Mommie's not a princess, she's a *monster*." Their volume intensifies, becoming a chorus of aggressive tormentors.

Lillie, driven by desperation, screams in a voice broken by terror and rage. "Stop! Stop it!" She cries, her voice raw and trembling. "Be quiet! Let me go!"

Her plea is lost in the whine of fiendish voices, high and childish, that loop and escalate into deafening, discordant minor chords, echoing through the rain-soaked field.

Their mouths stretch impossibly wide, the edges ripping open, revealing hidden rows of teeth in the back of their throats that clack insistently, louder now, demanding her submission.

The rain intensifies, pelting her face with relentless force, mixing with the chaos of her panic as she screams, "You're all liars! She loves me!"

Meanwhile, the spectral voices continue their eerie chant, urging and commanding as they sing in unison, "All must struggle to survive, and in the end, you must decide."

Torrential rain lashes the landscape, each drop pounding like a desperate heartbeat, echoing the chaos festering within. Thunder roars menacingly overhead, its deep rumbles resonating with the mounting anxiety in the air.

Lillie fights desperately against the wicked force that claws at her mind and drains her strength. Her ragged breaths are like whispers of her fading vitality, her eyes blazing with terror.

Within the storm's rage and suffocating gloom, thunder crashes overhead as sharp flashes of lightning illuminate the sky. The wind whips through the landscape, carrying with it the scents of rain and decay.

Amidst this chaotic backdrop, desperate voices echo, pleading and commanding simultaneously. "One will live; the other must die."

It's a cruel reminder of the brutal choices forced upon her by her cursed circumstances. She winces painfully, her face twitching with the agony of her predicament, feeling the weight of impossible decisions pressing down on her.

Swiftly, she closes her eyes, shutting out the torment around her. She feels the creature's icy limbs crawling onto her, cold and decayed. She covers her mouth while holding her breath, trying to suppress the nauseating smell of rot that clings to the creature, threatening to overpower her.

Little by little, the creature's added weight pushes her legs deeper into the mud, the dark, sticky substance enveloping her calves like quicksand. It clings to her skin, holding her prisoner, clutching her tighter with each labored movement to escape. Shadows dance over the muck, almost urging it to hold fast as her legs sink deeper into the ruthless grip of the thick, viscous material squeezing around her limbs.

Lillie opens her mouth wide, squealing as loudly as she can into the stormy night. "Daddy!" she cries out, her voice quivering with utter desperation. Her scream pierces the downpour, echoing across a scene of wind-whipped leaves and muddy ground.

Suddenly, the creature lets go and vanishes as a familiar yet panicked voice calls, "Lillie!"

The sound of her father's voice reverberates through her bones, stirring a glimmer of hope. "Daddy," she gasps, her eyes snapping open as she searches the darkness.

Her eyes land on the spot where she imagines she heard him, a row of tall cornstalks directly in front of her, their husks rustling like phantoms in the wind. Cold mud clings to her legs, sending a prickling chill through her. Frantically, her eyes dart from side to side, scanning the shadows for any sign of the creature lurking nearby.

A louder, more ferocious howl rips through the field, shaking the soil beneath her feet.

Driven by fear and urgency, Lillie launches herself forward, freeing her petite legs one by one from the mire. She presses on through the dense, tangled maze of crops, her heart pounding and each breath burning in her chest. "Dad—" Her voice becomes more frantic, and heavy breathing interferes with her words. "Daddy!"

With each step, she brushes aside the rain-soaked foliage, the sharp leaves scraping her skin. Her foot catches, and she tumbles to the ground, lifting her chin from the mud as her eyes lock onto a disturbing sight.

A large, shadowy, indistinct shape is sprawled across the rows. As she sees the cornstalks ahead of her move aside, she trembles, sure that her life is about to end. She closes her eyes, expecting the creature's claws of death to grip her, but instead, she hears her father's voice.

"Lillie, thank God I found you." Her father rushes to her, tense and trembling with concern as he gently lifts her to her feet. "Are you okay?" he asks. She nods in reply.

Suddenly, a noise behind them disrupts their reunion.

John's head snaps around, and the color drains from his face

"Daddy, what's wrong?" Lillie's voice trembles as she takes a hesitant step forward, her eyes trying to see what has captured his attention.

He stammers, trying to find words. His hand raises, pointing straight ahead, voice strained. "Lillie—go back to the house!"

Her gaze drops to the ground, where she notices a patch of matted fur among the stalks. Her stomach heaves, and her eyes flood with tears.

The sky darkens ominously, clouds swirling with a menacing, turbulent energy that mirrors her rising dread. A cold wind whispers past her, carrying a faint, unsettling howl.

"Daddy?" she whispers, her voice cracking as her tears spill over.

His voice cuts sharply through the murmur of the storm, commanding and urgent. "Lillie, there's nothing to see here. Go back to the house now!"

Although soaked and scarred with mud, patches of her cat's bright orange fur remain vivid, creating a striking contrast with the dull browns and grays around it. Amid the tangled fur coat, the tiny paws lie limp and motionless.

Lillie screams for her cat, her legs propelling her forward with frantic desperation toward the small, lifeless body. The muddy ground beneath her feet slings up a splash as she hurriedly presses forward, her toes slipping and skidding in the wet earth.

"No, no, no," she whimpers, reaching for the fragile form, tears flooding her eyes and streaming down her cheeks, blending with the rain that falls more heavily from the stormy sky.

Witnessing his daughter's heartbreaking reaction causes John's knees to weaken and a deep sorrow to consume his entire being. Without thinking, he lunges forward, scrambling to grasp her before she can go any further. His arms wrap around her tightly, preventing her from fleeing.

She wriggles wildly, her small body squirming against his hold. "Let me go!" she shouts, her eyes flickering with desperation as she looks toward her cherished friend nearby.

He tightens his embrace gently but firmly, trying to calm her emotions. "Everything will be alright," he says, his voice steady yet strained as he continues to hold her close.

Her cries grow louder in his arms. He tries to soothe her, his gaze drifting through the last few rows to the house beyond. A flickering light dances in one of the downstairs windows, casting a glow through the darkness. He gently rubs her back, trying to soothe her.

Lillie peers through his arm as her eyes lock onto her dearest companion. Her voice falters as she struggles to find her courage, then clears her throat. "Is—" she stammers, voice trembling, fighting to be heard over her quickening breath. "Is he dead?"

John hesitates for a moment, trying to find the right words. "Yes, my darling," he responds softly, his voice catching as he chokes up. He clears his throat, attempting to compose himself. "He is in a better place now," he says softly.

She sniffles, wiping her nose with the sleeve of her shirt. "With treats?"

He offers a small, tender smile. "Yes, with all the treats he can eat," he replies, a quiet chuckle escaping him despite the sadness. "He's in heaven now," he adds, eyes distant, imagining the peaceful afterlife.

She presses her face deeper into his chest, seeking comfort. "Why did God take him?" She asks as she clings to his shirt.

He gently places a hand on her head, his voice warm and thoughtful. "Sometimes, God takes those who mean the most to us, because they need more soldiers in His army of angels above, watching over us," he replies kindly.

The rain intensifies, droplets pounding onto their skin. The cold makes her shiver.

He glances at her, then carefully pushes her back a little, his eyes searching hers. "Do you feel each raindrop on your cheek?"

She shakes her head slowly, eyes still fixed on her small cat nearby, watching it silently from the corner of her eye.

He kneels, his voice soothing. "That rain is him crying with you, my dear. But he knows he can serve the good Lord better now, watching over you and protecting you from above."

Lillie lifts her gaze to the overcast sky; the droplets of cool rain wash away her tears as she wipes her nose with a palm. John stands, wraps his arms around her tiny frame, and lifts her into his embrace. She wraps her legs around his waist, seeking comfort in his presence.

As he takes a step forward, she tenses, her head snapping up in frantic urgency. "We can't leave him here," she says, her voice trembling, and tears swell anew in her eyes.

Guilt gnaws at John's stomach as he glances back over his shoulder, taking in the small, mangled body of the cat. His voice is soft yet firm. "It will only be for a moment," he quickly reassures her. "You're shivering ... let's get you inside, warm you up, and I promise I'll come right back out to give him a proper burial."

Chapter Nine

MY DARLING

John assists Lillie in getting cleaned up, then selects a floral-print flannel nightgown from her dresser and helps her into it. He gently tucks her into bed with her cherished pink blanket and a light brown stuffed rabbit—both well-loved—and kisses her on the forehead. "Good night, sweetheart," he whispers.

He walks across the room, turns off the light, and switches on her nightlight. Then, he quietly steps out and closes the door.

Then, as promised, he slips out of the house and makes his way to the field of swaying corn.

Lillie quickly rises from her bed. She places her bare feet on the cool hardwood floor, feeling the chill seep into her skin as she tiptoes to the window. Though she's not allowed to accompany her father to the field, her eyes follow his movements through the leaded glass, hopeful to witness her friend's final moments before becoming one with the earth.

As her father walks farther into the darkness, her gaze remains fixed on the lantern he carries, the light flickering like a tiny star. The pale glow from the lantern's flame reflects off the shovel's metal spade, casting a shimmering gleam that makes it easier for her to keep track of his progress.

She squints tightly, watching his figure grow smaller with each passing second until he finally disappears into the abyss.

A soft, meek voice whispers from behind her. "Lillie..." Its tone gives her chills and makes her uneasy. The sound is faint but carries weighty implications. "Lillie..." the ethereal voice repeats, this time louder, more insistent.

She turns around, her eyes adjusting to the darkness, revealing the outline of her door with faint light glowing beneath. Her heart races as she meekly asks, "Who—who's there?"

A tiny meow echoes through the room, piercing the quiet and sending a wave of icy chills through her core.

Though she saw with her own eyes that her beloved cat was dead, something in her still hopes it is not true, and she calls out. "Kitty?"

She cautiously takes a step forward and pauses, eyes fixed on the bottom of the door, her heartbeat quickening. Another meow drifts through the gap, laced with longing and uncertainty.

"Is that you?" she whispers, edging closer while listening intently to the faint scurrying of paws along the hallway outside. The quick movements remind her of her dear friend and the times she would roll a red yarn ball for him to chase in the hall; it's as if he hasn't truly gone.

A shadow of four tiny legs appears, silhouetted by a light outside, their movement flickering under the door like a beacon of hope. She hears a familiar purr.

Her breath catches sharply, and she quickens her pace toward the door. "It is you!" she exclaims, already kneeling, her fingers trembling as they touch the cold wood. A faint scratching noise runs down the surface of the door from the other side, like tiny claws on a wooden scratching post—desperate and relentless.

Leaning forward, she stretches up on her knees and presses her eye against the keyhole, trying to glimpse her four-legged friend. Shadows flicker in the dim glow, casting uncertain shapes that dance across her vision as she attempts to focus.

A whisper seeps into her ear, low and hissed, like the sibilant sound of a snake slithering through dry leaves. "Lillie..."

Suddenly, a sharp snap echoes through the silence, making her jump and her heart pound. Her eyes dart toward the sound, tracking the source with tense anticipation.

At the far end of the hall, obscured by darkness, a shadowy figure crouches silently. Long, tangled hair cascades over its face, obscuring its features, while its joints bend into unnatural, fractured angles, reminiscent of broken bones. Its emaciated hands clutch something tightly—something small and indistinct—guarding it as if it were a secret.

"Hello?" Lillie says, pressing her face more firmly against the keyhole in her frantic attempt to get a clearer view.

The sound of gnawing resonates with a raw, animalistic rhythm.

Suddenly, with a vicious snarl, the creature tilts its head, revealing the stark whites surrounding its glistening black pupils, which gleam menacingly in the dim light. Embedded in its jagged teeth, clumps of orange fur and tiny dangling legs sway as it chews. Its lips curl into a lopsided grin, exposing sharp, bloodied teeth as it continues to masticate.

Lillie struggles for breath as she glimpses her beloved cat's paw swinging back and forth visible through the small spyhole in the door. She quickly pushes herself away, collapsing onto the floor. Using her legs, she backpedals into the shadows, her heart pounding.

The echo of heavy footsteps grows louder down the hall. They halt abruptly in front of her door, and an unsettling silence follows, thick and ominous.

Breathing harder, she covers her mouth and holds her breath, terrified of being discovered. Pressing her cheek to the floor, she stares at the shadows cast by a pair of misshapen, decaying feet looming on the other side of the door. The hall's light highlights the grotesque details of the feet, which seem unnaturally rigid on the ground.

Her eyes dart nervously to the lock, her body tense with apprehension. She quickly crawls toward it.

Slowly, her hand reaches for the brass latch, turning it carefully to the right. It hits a stubborn sticking point, causing a loud snap as it shifts back to the left without her assistance. Her heart pounds fiercely as she watches it click back and forth wildly, faster and faster.

She hears the creature outside, its nails scraping sharply against the wood, leaving ragged gouges as it claws tirelessly for entry. The sound is deafening, an unsettling combination of screeches and thuds that sends tremors through her core. Her heart pounds to the point of destruction, each beat echoing her growing fear.

Her knees weaken, and she collapses onto the floor, unable to support her weight. "Mommy—"

she cries out, desperately searching for reassurance. "Mommy ... please, please help me," she begs.

She presses her back tightly against the door, her fists clenched at her sides. Her eyelids flutter shut as she tries desperately to block out the tormenting noise on the other side of the two-inch-thick wooden barrier. Each aggressive assault against the wood vibrates through her body like a foreboding drumbeat, sending shockwaves down her spine and intensifying her feeling of helplessness.

From the other side, the monster's voice roars, "Your mother is a sinner and a liar!"

Through her small bedroom window, moonlight filters softly, casting a pale glow that dances across the gleaming metal figure of Jesus affixed to the wooden cross hanging above her bed. Its larger-than-life shadow projects eerily across the wall.

Louder and more insistent, the creature's voice chants, "She worships the darkness and denounces the light. She hates your guts with all her might!"

Lillie curls into a tight ball, her trembling body rocking gently as she fixates her gaze on the crucified hands of Christ. Her voice quivers as she whispers, "Daddy said she's a princess—" She pauses. "Daddy said she's a—"

Suddenly, a heavy, thunderous thud crashes against the walls, rattling the floor beneath her. The force makes the cross waver, the nail it hangs from creaking as it slowly and ominously sways back and forth.

Without warning, an invisible force seizes Lillie's hair, lifting it gently yet insistently towards the ceiling, as if gravity itself bends to the will of this unseen power. Her scalp tingles as the tautness builds, every strand rising in a wave of unnatural defiance.

Outside, a voice shifts from a low growl to a snarling roar, resonating through the space with a disturbing clarity; it fractures into a chaotic symphony of octaves, each note piercing the silence like a shard of glass. "I am the demon who dwells inside her—I am the one you call mother—I am the one that haunts your dreams," it says, spitting the syllables with venom, its voice accelerating into a scream.

The creature's gaunt face presses close to the bottom edge of the door, eyes glinting maliciously as it glares to meet her gaze. "You are my child. Your soul belongs to me."

Lillie's body tenses as she fights against the unseen grip on her locks, her hands trembling as she prays, voice shaky but resolute. Her hair continues to lift, shimmering with a crackling static haze that hangs in the air, distorting the dim light. "That's a lie!" she screams, her voice filled with defiance. "You are a liar!"

The creature carefully flattens its translucent hand against the floor, slipping it underneath the door. Its skin darkens to black, and shadows deepen around her as it enters the room. "I see you..." the demonic voice howls. It catches its breath, then finishes in a sinister whisper, "...my child."

Lillie rocks back and forth, overwhelmed by fear, as she whispers frantic pleas. "Princess Mommy, Princess Mommy," she repeats, eyes squeezing shut in hope of her mother's arrival. Her hands clutch her chest as she prays silently, longing for comfort.

Suddenly, a menacing hiss cuts through the silence.

The creature's eye bulges grotesquely as it peeks beneath the door, its unblinking gaze fixed on her. Its voice drips with malice, a raspy, guttural whisper that seems to crawl through the air. "No one will save you," it says with a sneer. "You're mine."

As the creature's menacing words hang heavy, the cross on the wall begins to sway, as if caught in an unseen wind. It flips upside-down, casting an elongated shadow across the cracked plaster.

Lillie's cries pierce the oppressive stillness, her trembling voice filled with despair. "Please, God, protect me," she murmurs through chattering teeth.

Suddenly, she hears a faint scurrying sound behind her, a quick pitter-patter of tiny feet darting across floorboards.

An icy brush against her arm makes her flinch, but she forces herself to stay still, her eyes locked on the inverted cross above her. "God," she whispers again, eyes brimming with tears, "please protect us."

Behind her, the small, rapid shuffling continues, growing nearer and louder. Shadows flicker and stretch across the walls, driven by unseen forces.

As she prays desperately, she glimpses something lurking in the darkness. Its shadowy presence, with what appears to be a tufted outline, is both unsettling and strangely captivating.

"Kitty—" She sniffles as she fights back tears. She hesitates, glancing away briefly to compose herself, then whispers in a fragile voice, "Is that you?" Her eyes shine with a mixture of hope and fear, vulnerability plain to see in her expression.

A cavernous, animalistic call replies—a mew that sounds like a human rendition in its tone and depth. The feline figure stares at her from the dark corner, eyes shimmering with a dangerous honey-red gleam, tracking her every move.

Still refusing to look directly at it, she pushes her palms together harder, speaking louder, begging. "Please protect me," she whimpers, tears pooling at the corners of her eyes, blurring her vision.

Meanwhile, beneath the door, the creature's skeletal fingers inch closer, searching, probing.

The air is thick with anxiety, each moment stretching endlessly.

With a deafening hiss, the demonic figure recoils, claws scraping against the door as it grips the bottom to pull itself in. Its nails gouge into the wood, leaving deep, jagged holes. The creature presses its body flat against the surface, like a piece of cardboard, and its shadowy torso unnaturally lengthens as it drags itself under the door into the room beyond.

Lillie, flooded with adrenaline, spins around abruptly. Her eyes widen as she sees the glowing red orbs of the demon piercing through the darkness and staring up at her.

It slithers and slides across the floor, finally reaching the demonic cat lurking in the corner. Rising from the ground, it stands tall, its true size now apparent. The creature's spindly, rope-like tongue snakes out swiftly, slithering with threatening precision to snatch the furry figure in its grasp. Its mouth opens wide and devours the prey in its cavernous maw, teeth flashing ominously.

It shifts its focus to Lillie.

"I'm going to eat your soul!" it screams. Lillie covers her ears as the shrill sound nearly shatters the window's glass.

Heart pounding, she darts toward the window, her legs weak as she reaches on tiptoe, summoning all her strength to force the window open.

Behind her, she senses the creature's shadow creeping closer. With a desperate burst of energy, she reaches out the window, clutching the gutter's edge, pulling herself out, and scurrying onto the roof.

Lillie spins around, holding on tightly to the cedar shingles as her legs dangle over the edge. She kicks frantically, using her feet to push down on the window with all her strength, forcing it shut and sealing it tightly against the encroaching darkness.

All is silent as if the world is holding its breath as she sits on the roof alone after her escape.

She glances warily toward the cornfield, its tall, rustling stalks swaying gently under the moonlight. The faint glow of her father's lantern swings rhythmically, casting trembling shadows on the landscape beneath the night sky.

She slowly shimmies to the edge of the weathered roof, cautious yet curious, trying to catch a better glimpse. Her eyes track the lantern as it fades into the dark night among the tall stalks. She lifts her gaze to the glowing moon overhead, its cool silver light spilling over her petite features. "He will be back soon," she says. "I know Daddy will be back any minute."

She suddenly feels a shift—a slight movement behind her. The window groans open slowly, revealing a portal to Hell in the night. She stiffens. "It's nothing," she mutters, attempting to summon courage.

But then, an otherworldly voice echoes from the unsealing beneath her, ethereal and haunting, creeping closer and wrapping around her like a cold fog. "Lillie...—" it says.

Panic surges through her veins; she instinctively shimmies further away, feet slipping against the mossy shingles beneath her. Her breath catches as she realizes she's teetering at the very edge of the roof. She has no choice but to leap.

The cool night air brushes against her cheek, transforming her tears into frozen beads on her skin. Desperation surges within her.

"If I have to jump," she whispers, her eyes locked on the dark abyss beneath, "I pray I'm caught in your loving embrace." Her trembling fingers clutch the rough edge of the roofing, searching for strength. "Grant me wings so I can fly," she pleads. Gathering her bravery, she closes her eyes, bracing for what's to come.

Just as she starts to fall, a pair of powerful arms wrap around her waist, pulling her back from the brink.

She swings her arms defensively, eyes wide with fear as she attempts to shield herself from the unseen threat. Gradually, the tension becomes too much to bear; her body trembles, and her vision blurs as overwhelming emotion takes over.

Her father's arms pull her to safety. His voice is soothing yet firm. "Lillie! You're alright. Daddy's got you."

A loud, desperate cry escapes her lips. "Daddy!" she cries, her voice cracking with sobs. "It's you!" She collapses into tears, her tiny frame unsteady as she clutches her father tightly, seeking comfort and safety.

He pulls her in tighter, wrapping his arms around her in a firm, protective embrace. The warmth of his body contrasts with the cool night air, and his voice wavers with fear and relief. "I saw you on the roof when I was coming up from the field," he stammers, trying to process what he just witnessed. "You—you scared the hell out of me." His words tumble out faster. "You know you can't be on the roof. It isn't safe."

Lillie starts to respond, but she hesitates, as if weighing her words carefully.

His body stiffens as he pulls her away, his gaze fixed on her face, illuminated faintly by moonlight. Her pupils dilate, large and round, revealing hints of worry. She glances nervously from side to side, her eyes darting as if searching for an escape. Her breath quickens, and her hands twitch at her sides.

He tries to gather his thoughts, feeling tense and worried. After a moment, he clears his throat and asks, "Why are you out here? Did you—" His voice cracks. "Did you see something in there?" Concern laces his voice as he tightens his grip on her shoulder, holding her firmly so she cannot slip away.

The silent question hangs in the air, thick with worry.

Lillie purses her lips tightly, her brows furrowing as she concentrates hard. Her eyes sweep through the dark toward the window, where faint reflections of trees sway in the night. "No, Daddy," she replies, shaking her head with a determined look.

A gentle breeze stirs the air, carrying with it a chorus of haunting voices that whisper, grazing her ears with spectral murmurs. As she listens intently, the indistinct sounds begin to shift and coalesce into a clear, unsettling clarity. Her name echoes faintly, resonating with an almost sentient presence.

He gently pulls her close, his eyes searching hers. "Nightmare again?" he asks softly, leaning in to study her face, concern etched on his features.

Suddenly, a flash of memory strikes her—a whisper of her mother's advice echoing in her mind, reminding her of the golden rules of becoming a princess: Never allow yourself to be rescued and never reveal that you are a princess.

Her eyes lock onto his, searching for reassurance. "Yes Daddy. That's all," she replies. Exhaling softly and trying to appear strong, she continues, "Just another nightmare." Her voice wavers a little as she gives him a reassuring smile.

Her eyes, unlike before, now possess a deeper, more intense shade of blue, almost shimmering with an unnatural glow. A darkness encircles the iris, resembling a shadowy veil that seems to threaten to seep into her very soul and consume her, lending her gaze an ominous weight.

Her father's lips tremble, caught between pride and concern. "Good, that's my darling," he says. He hesitates for a moment, then finally says, "Let's get you inside."

Chapter Ten

TIMEOUT

Following that night, a quiet, tense routine settles over the house. Although only a short time has passed since John retrieved Delilah, it feels like an eternity in Hell for him.

The late-morning sun filters softly through the curtains as everyone rises.

At breakfast, Lillie emerges from her room; her steps are hesitant.

She finds her father already seated at the table, his face etched with fatigue. Dark circles and puffiness under his eyes reveal sleepless nights and mounting worries, miseries that seem to cling to him as he quietly sips his coffee, lost in thought.

"Daddy?" Lillie says with concern. Unaware of her presence, he quickly wipes beneath his glasses. He slowly lifts his gaze to meet hers with a hint of sadness. A strained smile forces its way onto his face, trying to mask the turmoil inside. "Oh, there is my darling girl! I was wondering when you would get up, it is nearly lunchtime," he exclaims, his voice suddenly becoming overly enthusiastic, almost too loud, as if to hide his true feelings.

Lillie hesitates for a moment, then takes a few tentative steps forward, her small hands clasped together nervously. She peers at the space at the breakfast table, where a plate of toast rests untouched and a glass of orange juice sparkles in the morning light.

There is a noticeable change from the day before; the vibrant flowers have wilted, their fallen petals scattered around the table, leaving behind bare, drooping stems in the vase. The air feels heavy and lifeless, lacking the sweet scent of pancakes and the warm love that once filled it. Instead, a deep sense of emptiness permeates the surroundings, leaving a void that feels almost tangible.

Her gaze drifts to the vacant chair. "No one woke me up this morning," she mumbles, her voice barely above a whisper, glancing around as if expecting someone to appear. Then, her eyes flick to the doorway. "Where is Mommy?" she asks, her eyes searching for her mother's familiar face. John knew the question was coming, just like it had countless times before.

He clears his throat, attempting to steady himself as emotions well up inside him.

Lillie quickly notices the redness in his eyes and the slight swelling around them.

"What's the matter, Daddy?" Lillie asks.

He sniffs, dabbing at his nose with his shirt-sleeve before adjusting his glasses, which have slipped down his nose.

"Oh—everything is fine, sweetheart," he says, his voice thick with suppressed feeling. Sensing her curiosity, he quickly adds, "Daddy just has some allergies, that's all." His words falter, betraying the falsehood as he fights to maintain composure.

She glances back toward the empty seat, her eyes lingering on the space as if expecting someone to appear.

"Here," he says quickly, rising to his feet. He pulls out a chair from the table, the legs scraping against the floor, then gestures invitingly. "Come sit with me."

"Her stomach rumbles, a loud reminder of her hunger that she hopes to ignore.

"Lillie, have a seat," he repeats, his tone warm yet commanding. "I think someone's letting you know they're hungry." He smiles, his hand extended in a gesture of support, waiting patiently for her to take it.

As she moves closer, her gaze drops to his hands, noticing the dark and gritty clumps of dirt lodged beneath his nails, his bruised thumbnail and scraped fingers, like those of a carpenter, a stark contrast to the softened expression on his face.

He nervously shoves his hands into his pockets, fingers curling around the fabric as if seeking comfort. "Late night," he stammers, "I didn't have time to change." His eyes flicker with unease, avoiding direct contact.

"Did you bury Kitty?" Lillie asks hesitantly as she settles onto the worn fabric seat of the wooden chair. Her eyes search his face for any sign of confirmation.

John's gaze drops to the surface of the table; he shifts in his seat, placing one hand on the nape of his neck. He pinches the skin, a silent attempt to suppress a dark memory buried deep inside. His shoulders tense, and a faint tremor runs through him.

Noticing that something is weighing heavily on him, Lillie wrings her hands nervously, her nails tapping against her palms, her fingers trembling as she picks at them. The room feels uncomfortably quiet, with the only constant sounds being John's sighing breaths and the clock ticking on the wall.

John reaches out, grasping a carton of orange juice. He pours some into her glass, the liquid catching the light. "A splash of sunshine to brighten your day," he says with an attempt at a cheerful tone. Then, grabbing a piece of toast from the plate, he swiftly butters it before placing it in front of her.

She watches him lift a spoonful of strawberry jam from the jar. The bright red jam glistens, thick and almost pulsing with fruitiness. The sight makes her flinch; the sticky texture and the squelching sound of the spoon digging inside the jar unsettle her. Her skin crawls at the thought, and she shifts uncomfortably in her seat, the unease lingering in her eyes.

He smiles softly as he sets the toast back on her plate, the warmth of his hand lingering for a moment. "This is a berry good piece of toast," he jokes, trying to break the awkwardness hanging heavy in the room. Glancing at the open chair beside her, he notices Lillie's eyes flick back to it, her expression unreadable.

His hand moves nervously, brushing crumbs from his fingers. "Your mother—" he begins, his voice tinged with concern. He pauses and lets out a heavy sigh that carries the weight of unspoken worry. He purses his lips, choosing his words carefully. "She hasn't been feeling quite herself lately. We decided she should stay in her room for now, get some rest, and recover her strength."

Lillie smiles brightly, her voice light and teasing. "A princess needs her beauty sleep," she says, attempting to hide her worry with a playful tone.

John's gaze shifts from the empty chair back to his daughter, a look of empathy crossing his face. "That's right," he responds. A subtle tension hangs in the air, making it feel heavy and strained. "All she needs is a little rest," he says, motioning toward her plate while the fingers of his other hand tap softly on the table. "Now, eat up—we have a visitor arriving soon to see if they can help your mother recover more quickly."

"Like a doctor?" Lillie asks through a mouthful of food, her eyes wide with curiosity.

"Sure," he replies, a warm smile flickering before fading into a more serious expression. "Something of that sort."

Lillie hurriedly shoves the rest of her toast into her mouth, her stomach rumbling with hunger. John chuckles softly, amusement clear in his eyes. "Someone was hungry," he says, and she giggles, her cheeks bulging as she finishes her last bite.

She rubs her stomach contentedly, then pauses, her brow furrowing in thought. "Wait—" she begins, then takes a moment to gather her thoughts before continuing. "Does that mean Mommy doesn't want to be a princess anymore?"

John turns toward her, his expression gentle but puzzled. "What do you mean?"

She hesitates, then blurts, "If someone saves her, she can't be a princess anymore — that's the rules."

The room falls silent for a moment as John considers her words, the weight of her innocence and imagination filling the space.

"Now, sweetheart," he begins gently, "though it's rare, there are always exceptions, you know—sometimes people just get tired of carrying the weight of their royal duties. They can feel overwhelmed by the constant pressure and endless expectations. Eventually, it just becomes too much to bear, and they reach a point where they can't keep up. In those moments, they decide to give up the burden, their crown, and all that comes with it." He explains it tenderly, trying to reassure her and soothe her worried thoughts.

"Oh," she responds as her unfocused gaze drifts toward the textured wall behind him.

Shadows stretch and ripple along the edges of the room like ominous wallpaper that shifts with a life of its own.

A low, haunting moan echoes from the home's upper floor, serpentine and sinister. "Lillie," a voice whispers, cold and penetrating.

She gasps sharply, jerking her head upward, her heart pounding as if trying to escape from her chest.

The sound continues to emanate from upstairs, growing fainter yet more unsettling.

Finishing his bite, John gently waves a hand in front of her face, breaking her trance. "Lillie," he says softly, his tone calm but tinged with concern. "Lillie—"

She turns toward him, eyes wide and glistening with alarm. "Yes, Daddy?" she replies, blinking rapidly, her mind racing to make sense of what she just heard.

John studies her carefully, sensing her unease. After a pause, he asks, "You haven't seen anything ...

strange...you know, different...have you?" His voice is reassuring, yet laced with genuine concern.

She quickly shakes her head, her throat tightening as images of her mother flood her mind. "No," she stammers. "Nope, not a single thing," She tries to convince herself as much as John.

He smiles, and his shoulders relax, relief washing over him. "Good—that's awesome news," he says, but his eyes quickly dart to the space at the table where her mother would usually sit, and a glint of discomfort crosses his face. He winces as if feeling the absence deeply. Turning his gaze back to her, he suggests, "How about we take your mother a plate?" His tone lightens. "Breakfast in bed—it's the royal treatment, after all. Nothing but the best for our princess."

Lillie looks at him, a gentle smile illuminating her face, her eyes bright with excitement.

"What do you say?" he asks, leaning in, his tone playful yet sincere. "Want to bring her a little treat?" He watches her, anticipation flickering in his eyes.

"Yes!" she responds enthusiastically. With a dramatic nod, she turns her attention to the juice. "Maybe she needs some sunshine in her day, too."

He responds with a smile, a touch of mischief in his expression. "There is never enough sunshine in the world," he replies. Quickly, he pours the vibrant orange juice into a clear empty cup sitting across the table, the liquid catching the light. Then, he reaches for a piece of golden toast. "Do you think she wants butter and jam, or just butter?" he asks, raising an eyebrow as he considers the options.

Her gaze drifts to the jar of bright red strawberry preserves. Her expression tightens slightly, tension apparent in her jaw as she thinks of the sound it creates. She murmurs, "Just butter."

The scrape of the butter knife against the bread's hardened crust reverberates through the quiet room.

"There we are," he says, scooping a generous dollop of butter with the tip of the blade before spreading it over another piece of toast. His eyes are focused, and a hint of a smile plays on his lips. "You can never have too much," he adds.

Lillie shifts uncomfortably, pressing her palms into her thighs to steady herself. The incessant sound grates on her nerves, each scrape etching deeper under her skin, stirring a restless agitation she can't quite escape.

After finishing, John carefully places the butter knife back on the table with a clink.

Lillie loosens her grip on her small, trembling thighs, releasing a breath she didn't realize she was holding. She offers him a hesitant smile, trying to mask her discomfort.

"Ready to go to see your mother?" he asks, reaching for the tall glass of orange juice. His voice remains even, but there's an edge of expectation.

"What can I carry?" Lillie asks, her gaze lowering as she seeks a distraction from her father's tension and her growing nerves. Her fingers twitch, awaiting instructions.

He pushes a simple ceramic plate toward her, on which the freshly buttered toast glistens in the morning light. The warm, fragrant aroma of melted butter and toasted bread fills the air between them, creating a cozy, inviting atmosphere. "You can carry this if you like."

She gently takes the plate, her fingers trembling as she carefully balances the warm toast in the center. With quiet determination, she rises from her seat and follows her dad down the hallway, her bare feet nearly silent on the wooden floor.

From the corner of her eye, she senses something watching her, and a prickling sensation raises the hairs on her arms and the back of her neck. Suddenly, a voice echoes, low and haunting: "Lillie..." The word reverberates, as if it comes from everywhere and nowhere at once.

She continues following her father, frightened and scanning for the source of the voice. They reach the bottom of the stairs to the second floor. After exchanging a foreboding look, they slowly begin to climb.

As they reach the top, the word is spoken again, with greater clarity. "Lillie..."

The sound seems to originate from behind a closed door at the end of the hall.

Her heart pounds faster.

John's posture stiffens as they approach the door, tension lining his shoulders.

Feeling the weight of unseen eyes upon her, she passes by her open bedroom door and catches a fleeting shadow sitting quietly on the edge of her bed—a dark silhouette that seems impossibly still. She nervously quickens her pace, almost bumping into her father, who halts just before reaching the door at the hall's end.

He reaches into his back pocket, his fingers curling as they search for something. The sharp, rhythmic jingling of keys catches her attention instantly, the metallic clatter echoing softly as he fumbles them out of his pocket. She turns her head slowly, her eyes narrowing as she listens closely to the bright, persistent sound that interrupts her attention.

The air thickens as he hesitates, and she quietly asks, "What's wrong, Daddy?" Her eyes are fixed on his hand, waiting.

He grips the jagged edge of the key, fingers curling tightly around it, cold and ridged to the touch. The object feels unnervingly icy, yet it offers a strange sense of comfort. "Sweetheart, can you do Daddy a favor and take this as well?" he asks, passing her the glass of orange juice with an unsteady hand.

Lillie carefully accepts it. She balances a cup and a plate, one in each hand, with her lips pursed in concentration.

He glances at her, notices her nervousness, and asks, "Are you good?" She nods silently. Satisfied, he turns away, refocusing on his task.

"Is Mommy in there?" She asks, watching the door.

"Mhmmm," he replies, trying to focus. As he reaches to unlock the door with one hand, his other hand carefully grips the oddly warm metal knob, feeling it pulse faintly beneath his fingertips. The strange human-like warmth and rhythmic tremor of the object make it seem as though it has a heartbeat of its own.

Lillie's curiosity sparks as she clutches the porcelain and glass more tightly, her eyes wide with questioning. "Why is she in this room and not in her regular room?" She asks, her voice laced with concern. Her small fingers grip the delivery firmly as she looks up at him, searching for answers.

He hesitantly inserts the key into the lock, taking a slow, deliberate moment before turning it. Speaking in a calm, reassuring tone, he says, "I want to make sure I stay healthy so I can keep taking care of you."

Lillie's face reflects her understanding, her brow furrowing slightly as she processes his words. "You don't want to get sick, too?" she asks, her tone tentative.

He chuckles, trying to lift the mood. "Yes, something like that," he teases, a playful glint in his eyes.

She giggles, momentarily caught up in the lightheartedness. Then, with a shy glance downward, she quickly composes herself.

A splash of juice slips from the cup, spilling onto the floor.

"Mom can't fall asleep with Dads snoring," he replies, voice gentle yet determined. "She needs her own big-girl room to rest peacefully and get better." His eyes are steady, reflecting his sincerity.

In that moment, she seems to understand completely, and, her voice small but receptive, she softly replies, "Oh."

Relieved, he turns the key, careful to avoid making any noise. A faint click softly resonates from the lock. He grasps the doorknob and silently gestures for Lillie to stay quiet with a gentle "shush".

He grasps the knob and motions for Lillie to stay quiet with a subtle hand gesture. She leans forward eagerly, ready to slip inside.

He raises a finger to his lips, signaling silence, then swiftly reaches out to take the glass and plate from her hands. He whispers, "We don't want to wake her—she's sleeping."

As he carefully places the tray on a small side table near the door, Lillie's eyes briefly glimpse a shadowy figure under the thick blankets of the sturdy iron bed across the room.

A muffled moan escapes from beneath the coverlet. A faint clang of metal against metal echoes, startling them in the room's darkness.

The room's two double-hung windows are covered with haphazardly taped old newspapers and planks of repurposed splintering wood nailed across them, as if trying to keep something out or in.

"What's that?" Lillie whispers as she notices a metal chain dangling from the head and foot of the bed, disappearing beneath the blankets.

Her father remains focused on his objective, disregarding the question. "We brought you breakfast, honey," he says, gentle but tentative.

The blankets on the bed shift, bunching as someone stirs.

A sudden rush of panic fills his eyes—deep, urgent, flashing like lightning.

Lillie gently tugs on the back of his shirt, her tiny fingers grasping firmly, her voice small but insistent. "Is Mommy awake?"

Grabbing her hand, he pulls her out of the room. He quickly shuts the door, then secures the latch, locking it frantically, hurriedly, and desperately—trying to seal everything shut, to lock the chaos away. "Mommy—she's just a little drowsy," he says, trying to sound calm. But the doubt lingers.

Lillie yawns, her face scrunching as she rubs her sleepy eyes, the exhaustion evident in her every movement. John kneels beside her, his eyes meeting hers with a calm yet strained expression. "What does drowsy mean?" she asks.

He pauses briefly, then answers with strain in his voice. "It just means she's still feeling unwell—you know, tired and icky." Without missing a beat, he straightens up, swiftly putting the key in his pocket. A bead of sweat slips down his forehead, betraying his composed exterior. The atmosphere thickens, heavy with unspoken fears that hover in the silence, each moment feeling like a delicate barrier between what must be concealed and the outside world.

"Oh," she murmurs, her voice uncertain.

A groan resonates from inside the room, the sound distorted through the door's thick wood.

John's gaze shifts anxiously, and then he places a hand on his daughter's back, gently guiding her closer. "That's just your mother stirring around," he says, trying to mask his concern.

Lillie glances over her shoulder, her ears tuned to the faint scraping sound of a metal chain dragging across the floor. "What's that noise?" she asks, eyes narrowing as they lock onto the door.

"That's just Mommy's rumbling tummy," John quickly interjects, pressing a reassuring hand on her shoulder as he gently nudges her forward.

Her eyes widen in alarm, sensing something isn't quite right as she hears a low, deep growl coming from the room. "It sounds like there's a monster in—" she begins, but her words are cut off by a loud pounding knock reverberating through the house, echoing sharply up to the second floor.

John swiftly ushers her toward the staircase, peering down at the front door with a cautious smile. "Would you look at that?" he says, voice steady despite the strain. "It seems our visitor has arrived."

Chapter Eleven
IT BURNS

The door shudders beneath the visitor's hand as John approaches, each knock sounding louder than the last, echoing in the quiet of the old farmhouse. The rhythmic pounding comes in quick succession—three strong knocks that demand attention.

John gradually loosens his grip on Lillie's back, feeling the tension in her body as she moves to stay close. He turns the doorknob, and as the front door creaks open, blinding rays of warm sunlight pour into the dim interior, casting long shadows across the floor.

Lillie raises her hand to shield her eyes while seeking the shadowed safety behind her father's broad, sturdy frame, which offers her a moment of reassurance. The door comes to a sudden stop, and she hesitantly peeks around her father's hip, her gaze darting cautiously toward the visitor.

A man stands motionless in the doorway, clad entirely in black. His figure is rigid and imposing, bathed in a shimmering glow cast by the golden rays spilling through the opening behind him, outlining his silhouette with a luminous halo.

Lille's eyes fixate on the stark contrast—the bright white fabric visible beneath the dark collar of his shirt, peeking out like a secret waiting to be revealed.

"Hello, Father," John says, extending his hand with a mixture of nervousness and anticipation.

The man's hair, short and peppered with gray, is styled with gel that keeps every strand in place, and his skin is clean-shaven, giving him a smooth, composed appearance. He carries a thick burgundy Bible tucked under his arm, its leather cover worn from frequent use.

He grasps John's hand firmly, their connection brief but meaningful. "Sorry, I'm running late," the man says, voice tinged with urgency.

Her father responds with a gentle smile. "It's no problem at all—I feel you are right on time." He turns carefully, shifting his daughter to make more space. "Let's make room for the nice man to come inside," he says, stepping aside.

The priest glances toward her, his expression kind and expectant, as she peers out from behind her father, her wide eyes full of curiosity.

John steps back, his eyes filled with cautious anticipation. "Please, Father, come in." He gestures invitingly.

The priest calmly steps inside. After closing the door, he pauses for a moment and takes a quick glance at the home's modest, dimly lit room, noticing its subtle scent of aging wood and incense, trying to get a sense of the space he's entering.

Lillie tucks herself further behind her father, gripping the belt loops of his jeans for comfort. Her eyes flicker with curiosity and a hint of apprehension as she whispers, "Is he here to help Mommy feel better?" Her voice is barely noticeable, almost swallowed by the room's quiet. John turns toward her, a gentle smile replacing his earlier firmness. "Yes, sweetie," he replies. "This is the man who's going to help her get well and not feel so yucky." Then, with a calm, reassuring gesture, he nods toward the open doorway. "Let's go into the living room and sit down," he says. Without waiting for a response, her father moves toward the seating area, his steps uncertain yet purposeful. He nervously glances back at their guest as he walks, the tension in his shoulders evident.

In the corner, there's a vintage sofa and two oversized armchairs, all upholstered in lush green velvet with detailed floral patterns that show signs of wear. Dark wood wainscoting panels line the bottom half of the walls, their glossy surfaces reflecting the faint glow from the shaded windows.

Lillie rushes behind.

The priest watches him with quiet understanding. Without hesitation, he glides smoothly and calmly behind John, his presence composed and steady. "Of course," the man replies, a reassuring smile on his face. "Whatever makes you comfortable."

As John settles onto the slightly worn plush couch, a tiny cloud of dust rises from the cushion, swirling faintly. He glances at the seat, eyebrows raised in mild surprise, and chuckles nervously. "Oh, would you look at that?" he says with a hint of apology in his voice. "I haven't had much time to clean—you know, with taking care of everything and all."

Lillie observes him, noticing the subtle tremor in his hand as he reaches out to tap the spot beside him. Without hesitation, she hurries over and takes a seat, the fabric creasing softly beneath her weight.

"I know I'm not," John begins, his voice tinged with weariness, "but sometimes, with everything going on with Delilah, I can't help feeling like a single father."

The priest slowly walks toward them, his gaze fixed on an aged crucifix hanging crookedly from the cracked, peeling lath and plaster wall. At the edges, the wooden cross is splintered; the paint is chipped and worn, hinting at years of use. The eyes etched into Jesus's face seem to follow him, eerie and penetrating, as if bearing silent witness to years of suffering.

He pauses, studying the worn sculpture of Christ with tentative reverence. "Where is the mother?"

John's response is quick, but tinged with apathy. "She hasn't been present for some time now."

Suddenly, a loud thud reverberates through the house, piercing the air with sudden tension. The sound echoes sharply, disrupting the conversation.

A brief silence follows, charged with unspoken questions.

The priest turns his gaze toward the staircase, studying the direction of the noise. From his angle, it's obvious the disturbance originated upstairs, the source obscured but unmistakable in its abruptness. "Where is she?"

An unsettling static crackles fill the room with an ominous hum. Each passing second deepens the growing sense of dread as a musty, oppressive smell rises from the floorboards, curling upward like invisible tendrils of stench.

John gulps loudly, a bead of sweat tracing a sluggish path down his face from his clammy forehead, his eyes fixed anxiously on the staircase. "She's in a room upstairs—the one at the end of the hall," he murmurs, glancing nervously toward the shadowy ascent.

Lillie shifts uneasily in her seat, clutching her hands tightly in her lap, her shoulders stiffening as if fighting a surge of emotion. "She's a princess," she says, almost to herself, a faint reassurance. "Princesses need their beauty sleep, so she's taking a nap."

The priest remains still, his gaze fixed intently on the staircase, as if expecting something unseen to emerge from the darkness. "Is that so?" he asks, his voice calm but probing.

Lillie fidgets shyly, her posture rigid and tense. "Mhmmm." She nods, avoiding eye contact, nervously clutching the fabric of her overalls.

He gradually turns his head towards her, a deliberate pause lingering in the tense silence.

"Daddy," she says, turning toward him with a small, tentative voice. She tugs gently on his shirt, her eyes searching his face. "Will Mommy stop being a princess if he helps her?"

John leans down to meet her gaze, his expression gentle yet strained. "Of course not, sweetheart. Your Mommy will always be a princess, no matter what," he replies. After a moment, he nods toward the priest, appearing more assured in his decision to seek help, but still cautious. "He's not going to change her—he's just helping her get better rest so she can be the best and most beautiful princess she can be."

Lillie sinks back into her cushion, still skeptical, curling her slight frame into a tighter ball, her breathing shallow and quick.

John lowers his voice, hoping to soothe her and ease her anxieties. "It's okay," he says. "I spoke with your mom, and she—um—said it doesn't count. Because he's a very special kind of doctor just for princesses. So he is allowed to help, and she can still be a princess."

"Don't worry, my sweet child," the priest says, leaning forward in his chair, his eyes soft yet piercing. He cuts off her father's hurried speech with a calming gesture, his voice smooth and reassuring. "I'm not trying to diminish your mother's status in any way or the divine love that surrounds her. She was crafted by God's own hands, perfect in His eyes."

His gaze drifts to the crucifix hanging on the wall behind them, its faded paint and weathered edges telling stories of longstanding faith. "He has a plan for each of us," he continues, voice steady and reassuring. "And I am here to support His purpose, to ensure that all His children are enveloped in love and compassion."

Lillie shifts in her seat, her fingers twisting nervously in her lap. The muddled light casts shadows across her face, highlighting her concerned expression.

The priest looks deeply into her eyes, his voice both soft and unwavering. "So, what do you think" he asks, his voice laced with curiosity. "Does that sound alright to you ... my dear?"

She purses her lips, a fleeting smile flickering across her face, and then nods.

A high-pitched, piercing whistle, reminiscent of a teapot just beginning to steam, drifts through the space. Hearing this strange sound, Lillie's brow furrows as she nervously fidgets, her pulse quickening.

The priest notices her jittery demeanor and appears contemplative, observing the direction of her gaze with quiet concern as he tries to decipher what has captured her attention.

She flinches sharply, her body tense, as if trying to push back a cacophony of noise that assaults her senses. Her eyes are wide, darting around anxiously, desperately seeking an escape.

He leans closer, his movements slow and deliberate, placing a reassuring hand gently on her trembling knee. "Child," he says, lowering his voice to soothe rather than startle her further, the warmth of his palm a tiny anchor amid her chaos.

She jumps at his words, her breath catching in her throat. "Yes?" she manages, her voice trembling and barely audible.

"Can you lead me to her?" he begins again, voice gentle yet urgent. "Can you take me to your mother?" His eyes scan her face, looking for any sign of understanding or willingness.

Lillie glances nervously toward her father, searching for reassurance, her lips trembling as she waits for his nod of approval.

"It's okay, sweetie," he says, his tone tender and reassuring, encouraging her to speak. "You can show him where she is."

She hesitates, eyes flickering between the priest and her father, her pallid complexion betraying her fear. Finally, she swallows hard and nods, extending a tiny hand with a fragile resolve. "I can show you where Princess Mommy is," she says, her voice just barely strong enough to carry.

He takes her hand in his, his fingers warm and steady against her skin, ready to follow her lead through the dimly lit space. "Be my guide," he says with a smile as he rises to his feet. She tugs on his hand with a determined grip, pulling him toward the staircase with quiet urgency.

The floorboards beneath them creak loudly, each step echoing through the house as if the very wood is trying to warn her mother of their impending arrival. The uneven planks seem to bend under their weight.

"I got to tell you, Father—" John stammers, stumbling over his words as he struggles to find clarity. His face is tense, eyes darting as he attempts to explain. "I've never seen her this bad. It got out of control so fast; I was completely lost on how to handle it or what to do."

The priest looks at him with a serious expression, his forehead creased in concern. Without slowing his pace, he continues forward, eyes fixed on the path ahead as they ascend the staircase, passing family portraits hanging on the wall. The images are fuzzy in the faint light, but he notices the subtle, almost spectral quality of the faces, hinting at memories long past.

"Does she frequently experience episodes like the one you mentioned during our phone call?" the priest asks.

"Yes, but it's usually manageable," John replies. "It's been several years since she's had an episode even close to this one. This is definitely the worst I've ever seen."

Lillie squeezes his hand; her eyes fixed on the far end of the dimly lit hallway. "This way."

The corridor grows colder; the warmth is long gone. An unexplainable gust of wind sweeps through, casting a thin layer of icy mist over the short, plush carpet runner lining the floor. Shadows stretch in the flickering overhead light, amplifying the feeling that something unseen lurks around them.

"Lillie..." a woman's voice calls, its tone playful yet taunting, echoing down the dim hallway and beckoning the child with a hypnotic allure. She flinches at the sound of her name, her petite frame tensing. The voice grows louder, and she perceives it as coming from the door of her mother's room at the end of the corridor, where shadows dance across its surface.

Keeping a wary distance, the priest begins to question the situation, his eyes fixed on the faint glow emanating from beneath the door. He asks, "How long has she been in the room?" His voice is tinged with concern as he studies the subtle flickering of light, unsure of what might lie behind the closed barrier.

"Um..." John begins as he nervously wrings his hands. He averts his gaze and stammers, "Only since yesterday." His fingers fumble as he quickly reaches into his back pocket, rummaging through the contents in a hurry.

Hearing the jingling of keys, the priest glances over at him, his eyebrows raising in curiosity. He studies John carefully before speaking again, his tone calm but probing. "Is she locked inside?"

John's fingers close around the cold metal bundle of keys. Beads of sweat form on his palms, making the metal slick and nearly slip from his grasp as he pulls them out. He momentarily holds the keys before him, making sure he chooses the right one before putting it into the lock.

"Did something happen to result in such harsh treatment?" the priest asks.

"She—um—" John hesitates as if weighing his words with great care, the muscles in his jaw tightening.

Lillie hurries forward, stopping just before the door. She scans her father's face, seeking reassurance, or perhaps a reason to stay.

They stand in painful silence, the only sound the soft rustle of their breath as he clutches the keys, their ridges biting into his white-knuckled hand, and finally murmurs, "Lillie." He tries to steady his voice, his lips quivering slightly as he continues. "Sweetheart," he says, trying to infuse warmth into his tone, though it sounds strained and fragile, "why don't you wait in your room?"

Lillie hesitates, her brow furrowing as a shadow of doubt plays across her features. A quiet tension hangs thick in the air.

As each moment passes, the priest maintains focus on John, his gaze steady and expectant. Every second feels stretched thin as he patiently awaits John's response, eyes filled with quiet anticipation.

He tightens his grip, voice hardening with resolve. "Now." The single word is unwavering.

A whisper emerges from beyond the door, audible only to Lillie's ears. It is carried by a gentle breeze that stirs the surrounding air, sending a faint chill across her skin. Her mind perceives an unfamiliar comfort in the voice, a subtle warmth amid her fear.

She closes her eyes, listening intently to the ethereal sounds around her. Then she tilts her head as if trying to catch a hidden message in the noise. The words from before seem to dissolve into a gentle melody that she recognizes—one she has heard many times before.

She tries to make sense of it, humming softly, the sound slipping between her teeth like a fragile secret.

The priest's complexion pales as he looks at the child, his eyes widening in surprise and suspicion. His brow furrows, sweat beading on his forehead, dripping into his graying bushy eyebrows. A flicker of unsettling recognition crosses his face.

"Lillie." John's voice cuts through the sound with a sharp, commanding tone, causing her to startle.

She snaps open her eyes and faces the open doorway of her room, instinctively lowering her gaze to the floor. "Yes, Daddy," she replies, her voice barely more than a whisper.

"Can you tell me what that melody was that you were humming?" the priest asks, his voice quivering with curiosity and a subtle note of nervousness.

Lillie shrugs loosely.

Something about the tune stirs a memory deep within him. More sweat beads form on his forehead as his stress increases, and he struggles to identify it.

"Is something wrong, Father?" John asks.

Quickly burying his feelings, the priest inhales deeply and stammers, "No—a memory ... it just came to me...nothing more." He speaks in a rush, already turning for the door.

Suddenly, a strange change overtakes Lillie. Her usual mechanical demeanor shifts, replaced by an animated expression. A crooked smile tugs at her lips, glinting mischievously. Her eyes light up with curiosity and a hint of challenge as she gazes at the priest's back.

"Did your mother sing that song to you when you were young?" She asks, but with a deep, almost knowing tone.

Noticing the unusual weight in her voice, the priest pauses, refusing to turn around. "Send her to her room," he commands, his jaw clenched. "No distractions now—I can't have any interference."

Lillie clenches her fists so tightly that her short nails stab into the tender skin of her palms. Her knuckles blanch, tension radiating from her grip as her fingers curl, holding back a rush of emotion.

"Of course," John replies, reaching out to grasp Lillie's shoulder gently but firmly, guiding her to move.

She glares at him with lingering suspicion, her eyes narrowing. "I'd be careful if I were you—" she begins, voice low and gravely.

But John cuts her off, his tone firm. "That's enough, Lillie."

She scoffs, her voice cold and harsh as she lowers her head dismissively. Her eyes flash with disdain as she resumes humming the melody in a minor key, each note tinged with hostility. Her fingers tap impatiently against her leg, betraying her controlled exterior, while the dim light shadows her features, emphasizing the icy resolve in her expression.

John grips her shoulder firmly, his face tense. "Enough!" he repeats sharply. He guides her into her room and, with a commanding push, shoves her inside, slamming the door shut behind her with a decisive bang. He quickly searches his pocket, fingers fumbling as he juggles the set of keys before retrieving the right one from the ring. Without hesitation, he slips the key into the keyhole, turns it swiftly, and locks her inside.

The priest stands motionless, muscles tensing as he hears the click of the lock. A surge of protectiveness and an unshakable sense of foreboding cloud his face. He winces at the sound of John's footsteps approaching from behind, each step deliberate and heavy on the wooden floor.

Taking a guarded breath, he carefully slides past the key used to lock Lillie's door and finds the one for the door in front of him. His lips part slightly as he steadies himself, and with a deep breath, he says, "Now"—he pauses, inhaling deeply— "where were we?"

"I'm sure it's hard on her, given the circumstances," the priest says. His eyes hold a quiet understanding as he continues, "These are pivotal years, and missing that traditional love from your mother leaves a difficult void."

John's grip tightens around the key in his hand. His voice wavers as he struggles to maintain composure. "She has my love—she feels it, I'm sure. She has the love of a father—" His words falter, a flush of heat rising to his face as a hot flash overtakes him.

The priest's eyes fixate on John's face, observing the emotional reaction and vulnerability evident in his expression, hinting at the burden of unspoken worry weighing heavily on him.

After a brief pause, John uses his sleeve to wipe the sweat off his forehead. "I'm sorry, Father," he says. Slowing his words, he continues with difficulty, "It's just ... it's just that it hasn't been easy. I'm trying to do what's best for our family, but it's so hard to know what that really is." His eyes flicker with a mix of hope and doubt. "Lillie needs her mother, but when do things get better?" he asks softly, voice nearly cracking. Nervously clearing his throat, he quickens his speech, desperation evident in every word. "I pray every night, pray and pray, hoping that God will give me an answer—begging Him for a sign, for any sign that things can improve—"

Suddenly, a warm hand rests gently on his shoulder, offering silent reassurance. The simple act of compassion moves him to tears as he fights to steady himself.

The priest looks him directly in the eyes, his gaze steady and reassuring. A gentle smile tugs at the corners of his mouth as he speaks, his voice thick with compassion. "I know this isn't an easy time for you," he says softly, "but remember that all these small turbulences in our lives are only meant to test us and strengthen us."

John sniffles, his shoulders trembling as he tries to hold back the tears, his grip tightening on his hands.

The priest pauses, his gaze unwavering as he slowly leans in just a little closer. "There will be brighter times ahead for you, my son," he says gently, his eyes filled with warmth and hope. "The Lord never gives us more than we can handle."

John feels a wave of relief wash over him as he gently stretches his neck, muscles easing of tension. The priest lifts his hand, and it feels as if a weight has been lifted from his chest. A breath escapes him, steady and firm, imbued with newfound strength.

With a calm but resolute tone, his voice resonating with conviction and purpose, the priest says, "Let us go in. It is critical that we remain strong."

"Yes, Father." Nodding confidently, John takes the key, fingers wrapped around it securely. As he slots it into the lock, he takes a deep breath, preparing himself for what they shall endure.

Chapter Twelve

DON'T COME IN

A creak emanates from the hinges as he slowly turns the lock and pushes the door open, his trembling hand exposing his anxiety.

The air shifts silently, thickening into a stagnant, heavy quiet that settles over the room. All previous sounds fade away; there is no humming or chatter, no whirring, no distant noises—only the deep stillness of silence.

The priest inhales deeply, feeling the cool air fill his lungs. Suddenly, he catches the faint laughter of a child echoing softly behind them. Recognizing its origin, he turns towards the doorway of Lillie's room, his senses heightened by the eerie, lingering sound.

John takes a step back, his eyes darting into the impenetrable darkness beyond the room's threshold. "She is straight inside," he whispers, his voice unsteady as he gestures toward the inside of the dark room with a hesitant hand.

A piercing cry echoes from the far corner, shattering the tense silence like a breaking glass.

"Everything is going to be okay, dearest," John stammers, attempting to soothe her.

The woman's pleas take on a noticeably different tone, with her voice rising, creating a sense of separation. At points, her speech almost sounds bi-tonal, with contrasting pitches that emphasize her emotional intensity and the complexity of her feelings.

As the crying intensifies, growing louder and more desperate, John raises his voice, trying to assert calm amidst chaos. "I brought a man here to help us get through this trying time." He shifts his weight, stepping aside to clear the path for the priest's entrance.

Suddenly, a woman's voice erupts from the shadows, filled with pain and anger. "Why are you doing this to me, John?!"

He hears the torment in his wife's voice, a raw, trembling edge that cuts like a serrated knife. Each word she speaks is tinged with despair, her voice quivering as if carried by a fragile breath. A deep discomfort wells up within him, unfamiliar and overwhelming, as he struggles to find the right words to soothe her suffering.

Her voice cracking as her chains jangle with the agitation of her movement, Delilah bellows, "Why did you chain me here?" Her words hang heavy in the air, accusatory and desperate.

The priest, standing nearby, lifts an eyebrow, his gaze steady and contemplative as he listens to the exchange. He observes the scene in measured silence, absorbing every word and every emotion.

The clank of metal lashes against the bed's metal frame. Delilah screams, her voice trembling with pain as she strains against the restraints. Tears well up in her eyes, and her body thrashes, desperate to break free from the iron's grasp.

"Miss?" The priest's voice is gentle yet firm, his tone trying to soothe her as he works to calm her trembling form. "I am here to help you. Just stay calm." He slowly shifts his foot forward, feeling the uneven floor beneath him in the darkness, his senses sharpened. "Just stay put," he repeats softly, trying to keep his voice steady.

As the last word leaves his lips, a faint, unsettling creak echoes from the wooden plank beneath his foot, shattering the heavy silence. The door slams shut and locks behind them.

Delilah shrieks, her body writhing on the bed, flailing wildly as panic overtakes her. Her eyes are wide with terror, darting around the obscured room.

The priest shifts nervously, unsure whether to move closer or step farther away. In his indecision, his foot bumps the small side table, which holds the breakfast. The table tips over, sending the plate and glass of orange juice flying. They crash to the floor, shattering and scattering broken glass, porcelain, toast, and juice everywhere.

He gasps for a breath, and John nearly jumps out of his skin, clutching his chest to steady his breathing.

Delilah remains unfazed by the commotion, continuing her pleas. "Why did you bring him here ... John? He's hurting me?"

Her voice suddenly shifts, escalating into a demonic shriek. "Can't you see he's hurting me!" Delilah screams, her voice cracking with rage as she fights the restraints.

John clenches his fists tightly, his knuckles turning white. Despite his inner turmoil, he forces himself to speak with conviction. "He's here to help," he asserts, his voice resonating with determination. "He's here to help us—get our family back to normal—"

But Delilah's response pierces the air, her voice rising in a venomous crescendo. "Liar! You don't want to help me; you want to change me, fix me. Be honest, John, you'd rather I was dead than be who I am!" The words slice through the air, each one laced with fury and despair.

"No—no, that's not true," John says, panic in his voice as he adjusts his glasses, sweat glistening on his brow. His eyes dart nervously around the dimly lit room, desperately trying to find the reassurance that isn't there. "I just want to help—I want to help you get better—"

The priest steps forward with caution, carefully placing each foot with barely any weight on the toes to avoid creaking the old floorboards beneath him. He keeps his gaze fixed downward and ears alert for any telltale creak that will reveal his approach.

"I can't keep doing this—I can't help you like I could before." John's voice quivers, wavering between a desperate plea and profound regret. He sniffles loudly, swiping at his wet eyes. "Our daughter ... she's getting older, she's starting to ask questions..." He pauses, then takes a shaky breath. "She needs her mother."

A sudden icy chill washes over the room, cold as a winter wind, rising from the cracked floor and curling around them like a ghostly breath. It defies gravity, climbing higher, illuminating the shadows with a spectral glow.

"I don't want to be saved," she says viciously, her voice guttural yet sharp, slicing the air with tangible malice. An acrid stench, thick and foul, invades the space, like gas seeping from a broken chamber—putrid and choking.

Suddenly, a deep, rasping groan reverberates from beneath the bed, causing the wooden posts to rattle and shudder. The priest braces himself firmly against the floor, his body tensing. Whispering shadows swirl and spiral across the room, darting from corner to corner in eerie, wavering shapes and flickering patterns.

The priest glances slowly from left to right, his eyes narrowing as he focuses. He deliberately avoids blinking, maintaining his concentration, tracking every subtle shift in movement with keen attention. The room itself seems to whisper; the voices are indistinct, like the hissing of a hundred snakes.

Suddenly, the whispers merge into a single woman's voice, screaming in unison, "Get out!" The pitch is so sharp it feels like a poisonous sting against the back of his neck.

Her words dissolve into an ominous silence, heavy and unnerving.

The priest carefully slides his hand into his pocket, avoiding any abrupt movements that might betray his plan. His eyes dart around the dimly lit room, searching for any signs of threat as he nervously grips the wooden beads of his rosary. "Are you alone?" he asks, his voice steady, but tinged with underlying concern.

As he waits for a response, an unusual warmth radiates from the smooth spheres of the rosary between his fingers. "Answer me!" he shouts, tightening his grip.

"I want to stay a princess," she replies, a fragile wisp of sound that barely penetrates the heavy atmosphere.

A multitude of hellish voices emanate from her, whispering and twisting through the shadowed air, their unsettling murmurs playing tricks on his mind. They weave through the darkness like elusive specters, tormenting him with every breath. A cold, unseen force grips the back of his neck, causing him to recoil.

His fingers grip the rosary in his pocket, and he pulls it out, clutching it tightly in front of him, with the large crucifix hanging from it like a talisman. With a trembling voice, he demands, "Reveal yourself—*now*." His eyes dart around the obscured surroundings, searching for any physical sign of threat.

A deep, foreboding laugh resounds from the dark corner of the room, echoing like a sinister melody.

"In the name of God, I command you!" he shouts, his voice trembling with fear and authority.

John nervously shifts his gaze, his eyes darting around frantically for a light source. He reaches out, his trembling fingers searching for the switch. Finally, he grasps the smooth surface embedded in the wall.

With a desperate, hurried flick upward, he expects the room to flood with light—but nothing happens. The shadowy figures draw nearer, their darkness growing and creeping like living creatures.

"John," the priest calls out sharply, voice strained but commanding, clutching the worn cross tightly in his fist. "Come here quickly. I need your assistance."

John rushes toward him, urgency etched across his face. "Yes, Father. Anything—whatever you need."

The priest's grip tightens on the weathered cross dangling from the rosary as he commands in a stern voice, "Remove the boards from the windows." He insists, "We must let in the light to fight the darkness."

Delilah shifts, her form wavering in the abyss as the clinking of chains that restrain her to the bed grows louder. She wails, her back arching wildly as she thrashes, the springs of the old mattress protesting with a loud, grating metallic screech. "The light won't save you," she snarls.

Her eyes burn with a wild intensity, dark and fierce, reflecting a primal rage as she declares, "The shadows are my sanctuary." Her voice, laced with threat, deepens the room's growing sense of dread. "I thrive in the darkness," she continues, her voice rising. "This is my domain. Darkness ... my haven," she says, her words now sharp and demanding.

A chilling wind swirls through the room, carrying a sickening stench of rotting meat that seeps into the air, thick and nauseating. Shadows dance across the walls, deepening the darkness, flickering as the breeze stirs tattered curtains and loose debris.

"Faster, John!" the priest yells, his voice strained amid the churning chaos.

John pushes forward through the suffocating darkness, his hands grasping for the rough-cut planks covering the windows. He grabs the boards and pulls with all his might, but the nails stubbornly resist. His muscles tense, veins bulging as he throws his weight into the effort, finally forcing the boards loose.

Splinters lodge painfully beneath his skin, sharp and unforgiving, digging into his fingers and palms. The pain scorches through his nerves, a relentless, excruciating gnawing that sharpens his focus and drives him to work faster.

"Hurry!" The priest shouts, his voice echoing through the dimly lit chamber. He whips around, his eyes blazing with a mix of anxiety and determination, searching for any possible escape route, just in case things go bad.

Delilah screams at the top of her lungs, her voice consuming every square inch of the room. Her tone is markedly different from before—filled with torment. It sounds as if she is being burned alive, her flesh melting from the bone. Her body trembles as she pushes her vocal cords to their limit. The cold shackles dig into her ankles and wrists, her muscles straining as she thrashes against their hold. Sparks of frustration flit across her face as she jerks her limbs, trying to free herself.

John strains, pulling with all his might. His muscles tense as he rips the boards off the windows, one by one.

Delilah's voice quivers, shifting from a desperate cry to a pleading whisper. "John," she says, eyes wide with fear. "Please—help me—the man you have brought here is going to hurt me—"

The tension in the air thickens as adrenaline surges through John's body, torn between questioning his decisions and his urgency to save her.

"I don't want to die," she whimpers, her voice trembling with fear and desperation. Tears shimmer in her eyes in the shadowy light.

John summons all his strength, gritting his teeth as he heaves a battered plank towards the window, using it as a lever to pry other boards free. Finally, a second board gives way, then a third, a fourth, and so on.

A burst of sunlight floods the room, slicing through the thick shadows like a sword.

As the beams spill over the dusty floor and cracked plaster walls, a ray of sunlight lands on Delilah's eyes. She winces sharply, her eyelids fluttering as she hisses in pain. She sits up, burying her face in her knees, trying to shield herself from the harsh light, as an overwhelming repulsion from its shine grips her.

Suddenly, a sound erupts from her, a terrifying roar unlike anything she's ever produced before. It echoes with an unearthly, fiendish timbre, as if the devil himself has seized her voice, using her as his sinister mouthpiece. "Father Michael," she snarls, venom dripping from her words. He slowly turns toward her, his eyes wide with apprehension and fear over her knowing his name.

Her blonde tangled hair clings to her tear-streaked face, mixing with the fetid discharge from the open sores marring her pale skin. She lets out a low, guttural moan as her body convulses and vomits. The foul, acidic smell causes John to choke and gag.

Father Michael cautiously takes a step closer, his eyes fixed on her as he extends his hand. "You are a child of God," he says, his voice reassuring.

She sways rhythmically, her body rocking back and forth, lost in her own world.

"He is inside you," he continues, voice gentle but firm. "With his love, he will sustain you through this battle."

Her spine curves, contorting her body in reaction to his words.

Feeling helpless, John steps forward, attempting to offer some insight and break the tension with a quiet explanation. "I left her food, hoping to encourage her to eat," he says, his concern clear in his voice.

The once-white nightgown she wears is stained, its pristine fabric now tinged yellow, clinging to her frail frame.

John squinches his face, baring his teeth slightly as he inhales deeply through his nose. "Lord, watch over us, keep us safe," he murmurs, his nose wrinkling at the overpowering odors. His leg muscles tense and tremble as he carefully steps forward, each movement cautious and deliberate.

With its crumpled sheets and stained fabric, the mattress appears filthy and neglected. A sickly aroma of urine and vomit lingers heavily in the thick, stale air, making his eyes water and his skin crawl.

Suddenly, her rocking accelerates, her movements gaining frantic momentum. She begins to sing, her voice rising in a haunting lullaby: "With her long flowing hair and the devil so strong—oh, where, oh, where can she be?" Her voice echoes through the room, filled with misery.

Her haunting melody hits a nerve deep within Father Michael. His eyes soften with a strange mix of recognition and concern as he searches for what to say. "Delilah, please stop," he insists. He tightens his grip on the cross, knuckles blanching, as if anchoring himself amidst the chaos. "Who has done this to you?" His voice cracks under the weight of emotion, the ache of helplessness clear.

"They..." she whispers, her voice barely audible, shaking with a blend of pain and defiance. She lifts her chin, revealing eyes that glitter with a fierce, untamed light, peeking out from beneath matted hair that obscures her face.

His knuckles go from white to a sickly purple as he grips the cross's wooden edges tighter, veins bulging beneath tense skin.

A hiss escapes from her throat, reminiscent of a cornered feral cat, raspy and strained. Her breathing is ragged, shallow, as if invisible forces constrict her lungs.

He speaks, his voice rising slightly in urgency. Fear flashes in his eyes as he leans forward, searching her face with concern as he repeats the question again. "Who—who has done this to you?"

The crooked edges of her smile lift her face, forming deep pillars of wrinkles that cut through her cheeks and push the creased skin around her eyes into pronounced folds. Her skin resembles a poorly adhered latex mask, its uneven surface stretched tightly and unevenly.

The room's temperature steadily decreases, causing a thin layer of frost to form on the saliva pooling at the corners of their lips. Their skin takes on a pale blue tint, lips trembling slightly as the cold penetrates deep. The air feels crisp and biting, with an icy sheen that clings to every surface.

John moves cautiously, keeping close behind the priest, matching his footsteps. His gaze stays fixed upward, watchful and alert, as if sensing danger in the silence.

"Answer me." The priest's voice wavers, his body shaking as he maintains eye contact with her.

She lifts her chin defiantly, thrusting it forward, while her facial features sag slightly from weariness. Her lips purse, and with deliberate control, she spits.

The saliva arcs through the air, just inches from the priest's face, then splatters onto the floor near his feet. The liquid sizzles when it hits the ground, bubbling and smoking, turning the wood black, like charred wood. It emits a foul sulfurous odor as it burrows into the floor.

"I answer to no one!" she snarls, clenching her fists, her eyes blazing with unwavering resolve as her words echo through the icy room.

Father Michael winces, glancing toward the ground. His eyes flicker rapidly, blinking away a fleeting speck of liquid that swiftly turns to its frozen state, as if caught in a moment of doubt. His muscles tense as he steadies himself and recommences his mission to save her.

"Our Father, who art in heaven, hallowed be Thy Name—" he begins, his voice unwavering as he recites the Lord's Prayer.

Suddenly, Delilah jerks violently, her body convulsing as her back arcs. Her spine, resembling a twisted branch, emits a loud, disturbing crack. "He won't save you!" she screams, her voice jagged and raw.

The priest raises his voice, desperation creeping into his tone. "Thy kingdom come, thy will be done," he says louder, almost shouting over her chaos, trying to anchor himself amid the turmoil.

Delilah continues to writhe, her movements jarring, disjointed, disregarding the pain in her ribs concealed beneath the cotton fabric of her nightgown.

Chapter Thirteen

THE TOYS ARE ALIVE

With her back pressed against her bedroom door, Lillie strains her ears to listen, trying to catch every sound beyond the wooden barrier. She had lost all track of time, but with the sun setting and her room growing noticeably darker, she knew it had to be getting late.

Faint cries and groans seep through the narrow gaps around the door frame, curling into her ears like uncomfortable whispers. Her hands tighten around her trembling legs as she says, "Momma." Her voice trembles with fear and helplessness.

As the horrific sounds down the hall escalate, the noises transform from muffled cries into agonizing screams that make her heart race.

Desperation floods her mind as she tries to cling to the thought: *She is a princess—princesses are strong.*

An unsettling creak echoes from the old, worn floorboards across the room, its groan piercing the stillness.

She squints tightly, trying to steady her breath. "He—hello?" She says, fragile and hesitant.

The creaking persists for a moment longer, then gradually subsides into an eerie silence.

She presses her back tighter against the door. "Is someone there?" she whispers, her breath catching in her throat, each inhale shallow and quick, as her eyes dart around the dimly lit space.

A slight shift in her weight makes the floorboards squeak, the sound slowly rippling outward and hanging in the air for what feels like an eternity.

The walls seem to absorb the noise peacefully, while the windows rattle, their glass trembling as if disturbed by an unseen presence.

Lillie runs her fingertips along the wall, searching for the light switch. Her fingers brush against its edges. A moment of relief washes over her.

A faint hissing sound comes from the corner, where a shadow twists and turns. She squints, struggling to focus on the elusive figure cloaked in darkness, her vision blurred by tension.

The form slowly becomes clear: the hunched figure's limbs twitch oddly, like a spider's legs. An elbow appears from beneath a torn cloak, and its movements are unsettlingly slow, almost calculated, as if it savors even the smallest reaction from those it is sent to torment.

Lillie jolts, her hand flicking the switch with urgency. A sharp click reverberates in the stillness, yet the light remains off.

Frantically, she flips the switch repeatedly, the rhythm now harsh and irregular, resembling the uneven ticking of a dysfunctional clock. Despite her frantic efforts, the fixture refuses to turn on, only emitting a brief, flickering spark that stabs the darkness momentarily.

Each brief burst of illumination highlights the figure perched in the corner.

Her breathing quickens, chest rising and falling rapidly as her heart pounds in her chest. The room feels heavier, expectant, as she waits in silent frustration.

The figure's blackened eyes gleam as it shifts position, coiling its hand beneath its body. A sudden crack echoes from its joints as it moves into a spider-like stance, its limbs twisting into sharp, unnatural angles, leaving its frame fractured and held together by tendons.

Lillie gasps, her eyes widening as she hesitates, her finger hovering uncertainly above the switch. She draws in a hurried breath as she again says, "He—hello?"

A flick of light accentuates the elongated neck as the head spins fluidly and extends outward toward her.

Her finger trembles on the hard plastic switch, causing tiny vibrations that are nearly audible.

A sudden chill skulks into the air, sending a thin icy film creeping across her lips, making them feel numb.

A deep, foreboding voice calls out with an unmistakable sense of menace. "Lillie." Her name echoes through the air with a familiar tone, accompanied by a foreboding scent of death. Every time her name is spoken, a chilling wave spreads outward, mixing the putrid stench with the air and deepening her despair.

Her heart pounds fiercely in her chest, sending shocks through her entire body. Her stomach knots up as a visceral reaction to the rising tension and stress becomes overwhelming.

In the darkness, the creature's long, tangled hair flows down its back, swishing softly as it moves with deliberate, precise steps toward her, each move slight and premeditated.

"Are you—" Lillie stammers, her eyes filling with tears, her voice trembling as the icy breeze slips down her throat.

A terrible scream surges from her mother's room at the end of the hallway.

"Do you hear that, my child?" the creature asks with a sneer, its voice dripping with cruelty.

Lillie trembles, pulling her knees to her chest, trying to block out the distressing noise that consumes her mind. The sting of fear grips her stomach.

"It's a cruel twist of fate, isn't it? Someone summoned here by your father to save a soul becomes the catalyst that ends a life." The creature continues, its voice purring with malevolence. "While you sit all cozy in this room, someone else will soon breathe their last." It pauses, savoring the moment. "Their final gasp for air, their last wretched wheeze on this earth." It leans closer, saliva spattering onto the floor as a twisted thrill radiates from its tongue.

"No..." Lillie whispers, her voice cracking, desperate to hold on to hope. "Daddy said that man—he's a special doctor—" Her voice falters. "He's supposed to help make her better." As she clenches her fists tightly, knuckles whitening, the girl whispers urgently, "Daddy wouldn't do that. He would never do anything to hurt us."

She presses her ear cautiously against the door, closes her eyes to heighten her senses, and listens intently for any sound of her mother from behind the barrier.

The creature mocks her as it extends its fingers, curling them threateningly and scraping its claws along the floor. Its eyes sparkle as it watches her.

She strains her ears, catching another muffled cry. "You don't know Daddy," she says quietly to herself, a desperate attempt to cling to hope. "He loves us," she says louder, voice quivering. "More than anything."

An unsettling smile flickers across the ghostly, pallid skin of the creature's face. Its voice drops to a sharper, more accusatory tone. "He locked you in here, didn't he?" it snarls. "He confined you in this suffocating darkness and threw away the key." Its speech quickens, words spilling out with increasing enthusiasm, spindly teeth gleaming like a Cheshire cat. "He took you away from her—"

"No, that's a lie," Lillie replies, her voice shaking as she tries to control her emotions. Her eyes flash with anger and sadness as she says, "He is helping her—"

But the words are cut off by a sharp, seething retort. "He is killing her bit by bit." It sneers, eyes narrowing with contempt. "He doesn't accept her for who she truly is. He doesn't love her, or you," the voice snarls, voice rising with a vicious edge. It cackles wildly, a harsh, mirthless sound echoing around her. Frothing at the mouth with excitement, it taunts her. "He doesn't accept her special nature. Just like he won't accept yours."

She winces, jerking her head back as if recoiling from an unseen blow. Her fingers tighten around the edge of the doorframe, knuckles whitening under the strain. Sniffling, she presses a trembling hand to her nose, trying to hold back tears.

The creature gently bobs its head, feeding off her unstable emotions. Its dark, unseen eyes spark as it tilts from side to side, intently watching her every movement.

Her voice wavers as she breathes heavily, desperate to maintain control. "That's not true," she says. She balls her hands into tight fists, her eyes fierce yet unfocused.

Saliva gathers at the edges of its mouth. A thick, yellow foam forms at the edges, and it gradually disintegrates into a sticky flow. Like molasses, it drips slowly from its lips to the floor.

"My Daddy would never hurt us!" she yells, standing her ground.

The creature's face remains hidden beneath a glob of viscous fluid; its form is vaguely humanoid, but twisted with decay. Its movements are slow and deliberate, creating the impression of a serpent stalking a rat as it slinks across the floor.

A high-pitched, mocking voice escapes it. "Daddy wouldn't hurt us." The creature's head tilts, exposing the jagged, vertebral-like protrusions along its neck, the skin stretched tight and marked with areas of paleness and decay. Its eyes, if they can even be called that, glint briefly through the slimy curtain, flashing with a disturbingly cunning spark. Its tone echoing with unsettling inflection, it repeats, "Daddy wouldn't hurt us!" It raises its voice in a loud, frenetic cry and repeats. "Daddy wouldn't hurt us!"

Lillie lunges toward the doorknob, her fingers shaking as she reaches out and grabs hold. With each frantic turn of the knob and no click of the door latch releasing, she knows it is hopeless now, sealing her fate with the unforgiving lock.

She shifts her focus to pounding on the door, slapping her palms against it with a loud *thwack ... thwack...thwack*. She keeps going, desperation clear in her intensity. "Help!" she cries out, voice trembling. "Daddy, please help! The monster—it's going to eat me—it's going to—"

A harsh, sarcastic voice cuts through the air. "Daddy, help me! The big, bad monster's gonna get me! Boo Hoo. That's what they want you to believe—they want you weak and pathetic; they don't want you to be a princess like your mother." A sinister, almost manic voice interrupts, quick and cutting. "That's what they desire. They want you to be weak and beg for help; they want to change you." The creature's words whip around like a frantic storm, each syllable a blade. "They want you to scream—they want your crown."

Lillie freezes, her hand glued stiffly against the door. The creature leans closer, eyes glowing with malevolent light.

In an instant, her hand is yanked with brutal force toward the creature's gaping maw. The skin around her hand prickles painfully as it seems to melt and dissolve into the wood.

The creature's mouth curls into a seething snarl, foaming at the edges of its teeth. It whispers with venomous intent, "The crown upon your head is a gift that you shouldn't dread. It's a power that threatens the weak and misled." Its voice is a raspy growl as it spills its poisonous words.

Suddenly, an intense pain shoots through her forehead, radiating outward from the place where a crown would sit. The burning spreads, searing through the delicate skin. Her body collapses forward onto the unforgiving floor, hanging by the palm that seems fused to the door, her knees barely able to support her weight. Sharp, tiny thorns cut the flesh around her head, causing a burning sting as they erupt from deep within.

The creature's oppressive presence casts a dark shadow over her, its form barely visible in the darkness. Lillie screams, a deafening cry, as the cruel crown of thorns pierces her scalp, each serrated spike tearing into her flesh with brutal finality. Her body shudders uncontrollably under the weight of fear and pain, the oppressive force pressing down on her in relentless silence.

Desperation grips her as droplets of cool ichor, thick and shimmering like an aged merlot, drip slowly from the edges of the torturous circlet. They trickle down her face like shimmering waterfalls, mixing with her sweat and tears, staining her pale, smooth skin with vivid, crimson streaks.

As the blood pools thickly on the wooden planks beneath her, the creature's agile body shifts in the darkness, preparing to strike. "Let the darkness in, and soon it will win," it hisses.

Remaining concealed in the gloom, it slinks silently, crawling backward along the wall, the form melding with the night.

She listens intently, her breath quick and shallow at the sound of scurrying overhead. The creature stops, hanging from the ceiling, perched like a bat above the bed.

With each heavy, ragged breath, she listens intently to every sound and movement—while her mind is battling a surge of pain and dread. The darkness thickens around her like quicksand, pressing in from every corner.

"It is coming," the creature wails.

A cold, metallic-tasting droplet slides down her face, crossing over her eye and dripping into her gaping mouth. "Help," she gasps, her eyes narrowing in distress as she struggles to breathe. The bitter taste coats her tongue, prompting her to purse her lips tightly, her face contorting with unease. Every muscle in her body tenses as she fights to escape, desperation flickering in her eyes.

Razor-sharp claws extend from its shadowy form, reaching toward the crucifix hanging crookedly on the wall.

Her eyes sting as she follows the figure's movement.

"It is here!" it bellows. It snatches the rusty nail from the wall.

Lillie's body seizes, a disorienting wave of weakness washing over her. Her bones tremble from within, and her knees grow shaky, threatening to give way. She gasps, desperation filling her eyes as she struggles to maintain her composure.

Glancing at her hand, which once seemed melted to the door like wax, now clutches the doorframe tightly. Her knuckles are white, straining with the effort. Her nails dig into the grain of the wood as if clawing for a hold on reality.

Lillie's voice trembles as she calls. "Daddy!" Her plea is filled with vulnerability. Tears well up as she cries out, "I don't want to be a princess!"

It opens its mouth, revealing a serpentine tongue that flicks out lazily, glistening in the faint light. "Your Daddy is gone," it hisses. "Your mother is gone as well—"

"No," she whimpers, trying to hold it together.

It sneers. "And you will be next." The creature's eyes gleam with malicious intent as it moves the old wooden crucifix closer, pressing it into its mouth with a crunch.

Wood chips spew from the creature's grotesque mouth, scattering a trail of tiny splintered pieces across the rumpled bedspread.

She presses her ear into her shoulder, trying to make the sound stop, and tightly closes her eyes. "Make it stop!" she cries. "Go away!"

Its maw slowly widens as a gaping smile spreads across its face, revealing sharp edges along its upper and lower jaws. From its spidery, unsettling form, it gazes at her with its head tilted, its eyes glinting with a strange, unnatural glow.

Suddenly, a piercing scream erupts from its throat, and in response, the toys scattered around the room light up in a cascade of glowing colors.

The sudden burst of bright light floods Lillie's senses, jolting her backward with a startle. Her trembling hands grip the doorknob, knuckles bone-white as fear and desperation wash over her.

As she pulls and struggles with the handle, dark thorns sprout rapidly from her palms, curling around her fingers, while sharp, twisted tendrils grow through her feet.

She frantically kicks at the door. "Daddy!" she screams, voice cracking with terror. "*Help me!*" Her knees hit the two-inch barrier, but she can't kick quickly enough, so she leans into her last attempt, driving her knees into the door again.

The toys lie scattered around her in disarray, their bright, cheerful colors contrasting with the evil chaos. Soft melodies drift from the music-playing toys, initially innocent, but gradually, the tunes descend into a disturbing minor key; the notes curling through the air like specters.

The creature lifts its spindly finger, creeping toward the worn mattress in the dimly lit room's corner. Its obsidian eyes fixate on her with a sinister curiosity as it slinks closer, every movement barely disturbing the stale air. "I dwell in your mind, one dark thought at a time," it sings, its voice blending eerily with the haunting melody of the toy noises, a chaotic chorus of twisted tunes. "Oh, where, oh, where has my little girl gone—oh, where, oh, where can she be?" the creature croons.

With a flick of its knuckle, Lillie's head snaps upward, her face tilting toward the ceiling as her mouth hangs agape. Her eyes flutter open wide, shimmering with an intense, almost frantic energy, then half-close, as if struggling to focus.

"With her crown of thorns and her face half gone—oh, where, oh, where can she be?!" it squeals.

Her pupils dart wildly before rolling back into her skull, revealing only the strained whites.

Toys on rollers glide smoothly across the floor, their bright colors flashing. They whirl and shift effortlessly, transforming their shapes into whimsical figures and curious creatures.

A low growl escapes from the creature's snarling mouth. With glowing, piercing eyes, it beckons, voice dripping with venom. "Come to me, my child," it calls. The sound is rhythmically haunting, forming a melody that takes over the mind.

As the toys continue to move, their shapes seem to animate, eyes glowing with an eerie crimson light that cuts through the darkness, producing an unsettling yet mesmerizing spectacle.

In a sudden surge of momentum, Lillie's palms rip away from the door's surface, fingertips leaving unspoken traces of contact as her body stiffens, veins visibly pulsing beneath her skin. Fighting for her life, her vocal cords tighten, not letting out a single sound or breath. As she struggles to breathe, she is overwhelmed by the stench of decay that hangs heavy in the air.

The creature's slithering tongue flicks back into its mouth, disappearing behind razor-sharp teeth that shine with a sinister gleam. Its lips, elongated at the corners, stretch into a slimy, dripping grin, menace radiating from its wide, gaping smile. It edges forward, its evil expression promising only harm.

"Please," she whispers urgently, her voice barely audible and laced with fear. Her eyes are wide with terror, her trembling lips barely forming the words as her hands shake, praying for rescue from her knight in shining armor.

Chapter Fourteen

DON'T LET HER OUT

I nside Delilah's room, a sharp, cracking sound resonates as a piece of the place shatters under John's foot, scattering porcelain shards across the floor.

Her veins swell in her neck, protruding like twisted electric cords beneath her taut skin, as she strains to turn her head toward the source of the noise. Her eyes are wide, darting anxiously before fixing on the jagged shards scattered at his feet. "John," she says. "Baby," she adds, her tone accelerating with quiet desperation, "You know this will all be over soon—I—I don't need help." She inhales sharply, her chest rising and falling rapidly. "I just need you. I'm fine. I'm just tired and need a little rest, that's all."

John studies her, conflict evident across his face. He nervously removes his glasses, rubbing the rims with hurried fingers before placing them carefully on the bridge of his nose. "Delilah, we need help," he says, his voice tight with worry. "This isn't just about you or me. You need to get better for Lillie. We can't keep doing this; she needs her mother."

"Please," she sobs, taking a shaky breath. "John, don't do this to me." Her voice cracks, and she gasps, tears welling in her eyes. "He's going to hurt me." Desperation claws at her voice, breaking with her fear. "Look at me, baby—look at me. I'm still the woman you married, the woman you fell in love with."

The raw plea stirs something in John; her distress makes his pulse quicken, and his fingers twitch involuntarily, as if he is fighting an internal battle.

An eerie, guttural moan echoes from the shadows, its volume steadily rising until it hits Father Michael's ears with a disorienting surge.

John's knees quake, and a strange, inexplicable gravitational pull draws him closer to her, urging him to take another step forward.

The priest raises the rosary in front of him, gripping it tightly, his knuckles whitening as he steadies his approach. "Our Father in heaven, deliver us from evil and bring justice for all!" he recites, his voice cutting through the chilling noise that drowns out his speech.

With each rapturous word, a sharp, agonizing pain shoots through her limbs, causing her body to jerk violently in convulsions, as if the very words unleash a malevolent force within her.

"Who inhabits this body?" Father Michael demands as he thrusts the religious relic toward her.

Her eyes widen in terror, and a visceral scream rips from her throat, a sound of fractured hope and fear. The sounds tumble out, disjointed and broken, as if her voice struggles to claim coherence. "Ba—" Her entire body shudders, trembling with a mixture of fear and defiance.

"Reveal yourself!" he shouts, his grip tightening on the crucifix.

Her eyes suddenly roll back into her skull, veins visible beneath her translucent skin, and her mouth snaps open in a horrific, involuntary gape. Her tongue undulates like a serpent trying to squirm free, flickering wildly within her mouth, while cold sweat beads on her forehead. An animalistic sound escapes her, barely human, as she proclaims with strained intensity, "I am Baal."

The atmosphere thickens with supernatural energy, each moment stretching the limits of reality itself.

"Who—who is that?" John stammers as he listens to the deep, gravelly tone of her voice, rough like sandpaper.

The name hits Father Michael like a lightning bolt. His cheeks flush dark red, burning with embarrassment and anger. He recognizes the name—an echo from his painful past that reopens old scars and triggers wounds in his soul anew.

Suddenly, a surge of fervent conviction overtakes him. His voice rises in a fierce, desperate cry. "I condemn you, demon! Get out! You are not welcome in this vessel! Leave now, and return to the Hell from which you came!"

A loud thud strikes the window, creating a spiderweb of cracks that spreads across the glass.

John quickly pivots, eyes darting to the window as a dark, feathered shape tumbles off the surface, sliding slowly down the smooth glass until it vanishes. An icy shiver runs down his spine.

"You must fight what is inside, Delilah—you must not let it win," the priest urges. "That demon—he—he wants you weak, broken—" His words hang heavy, each syllable resonating fiercely, filling the room with an unrelenting force.

Delilah's screams tear through the air, her back arching violently, as if jolted by a powerful surge of electricity. Her chest heaves with ragged, panicked breaths. Her face flushes a deep, glistening purple, sweat dripping from her skin as she fights for each gasping breath. Tears well up in her eyes, shimmering with despair, threatening to spill over. Her body convulses and shakes with each agonizing inhale, muscles tightening unwillingly.

The air around her grows oppressive, thickened by a tension so palpable it is suffocating.

Every muscle in her body contracts, spasming in a painful, unsteady rhythm, her suffering clearly etched on her face.

John senses her life slipping away, and his instincts compel him to rush to her side.

"Get back!" Father Michael yells, intercepting him, grabbing his arms, and holding him back with an unyielding grip. John's muscles tense as he strains and grunts with effort, trying to break free while the priest attempts to restrain him.

"She needs me!" John shouts, flailing his arms and fighting to break free. His voice cracks with desperation as he insists, "My wife needs me." His words fade into strained gasps as he struggles against the priest's hold.

Father Michael's expression shifts to one of compassion. "She needs God," he says, voice trembling with fervor and exhaustion. As he tries to wrench John away, his grip slips, and the rosary in his hand tumbles to the floor with a soft clatter, momentarily forgotten amid the chaos.

A crazed gleam erupts in John's eyes, shining with wild intensity. "Let—" He gasps as he struggles to form words. "*Go of me!*" His plea hangs heavy in the air.

Delilah's back arches further, releasing a terrifying snap as her bones shift unnaturally. A bone-chilling scream rips from her throat, piercing the silence and making the hairs on their necks stand on end.

Shadows elongate and swirl in the room's dark corners, creeping forward like living things. They grow taller, twisting into grotesque skeleton-like figures that loom menacingly.

The priest's grip falters, his strength waning as panic overtakes his face. He cries out desperately, "This is what the demon wants—he wants us to turn against one another! He wants chaos!"

The room is oppressive, the air thick with dread, as the shadowy forms draw ever closer.

John feels an unseen force surge through the room, cold and cruel. It seizes his foot and wraps around his ankles like an icy vice. His eyes widen in panic as he stammers, "Wha—"

Before he can finish, his legs are yanked out from under him, and he crashes onto the hard floor with a thud. The force drags him backward, his body skidding across the surface as he strains against the invisible pull.

Father Michael reaches for his crucifix, his fingers trembling as he grips it tightly. An unyielding force pushes back against his hand, as if the darkness itself resists his attempt to invoke Holy protection. Summoning every ounce of resolve, his voice firm but strained, he shouts, "Release me!"

As he fights to hold his ground, his gaze darts toward Delilah. Hovering in midair, her body stiffens, then slowly lifts higher from the bed. Her torso is pointed upward, limbs suspended as if caught in an invisible grip, eerily still against the shifting, shadowy threats that pulse and writhe around her.

A voice drifts softly through the air, weaving through the darkness like an ethereal vine. "I own her soul," it intones insistently. "She is mine."

From the shadows, Father Michael's voice rings out urgently, filled with authority and desperation. "Release her soul! I demand you listen!"

A sinister chorus responds, its mockery echoing and swirling in the gloom. "When she dies, she will drift up into the sky, and only then will she be let go—a fallen angel cast into the depths where she belongs. Her soul sold long ago." The voices hum and snarl, their malicious tone resonating through the void, sealing her fate in a tapestry of darkness and despair.

John shouts as he is pulled inescapably toward the bed. Tears stream down his face as he cries out in fear, "Father!" As he nears the shackles that bind his wife, an unbearable heat surges through his skin, as if flames lick at his flesh from within, melting away his resistance and searing his bones.

From the shadows, a sinister voice hisses sharply, each syllable like a dagger piercing the silence, echoing with malevolence. "He belongs to me!"

The words claw at Father Michael's ears, wrapping around his mind with malicious intent.

Heavy blows slam against the sides of the house, each strike shaking the walls with force. A window shatters with a deafening crack, shards of glass scattering into the air.

Father Michael ducks as a barrage of crows hurtles through the open space, their wings flapping wildly, claws raking the air, aiming directly at him.

"The power of Christ compels you!" he shouts fiercely, brandishing his rosary high in the air.

A lone bird streaks across the ceiling, wings spread wide, claws extended like jagged knives, then suddenly swoops down, dragging sharp talons across his face.

Blood streams from the gashes, marring his skin. "You have no power over me!" he roars defiantly. "We have the love and protection of Jesus, our Savior—the Son of God, light from light, true God from true God, begotten, not made, one in being with the Father…"

John's flesh reddens from the relentless heat, sweat glistening on his brow as he stumbles to the foot of the bed. Pain sears through his body, sharp and unrelenting, making every breath laborious.

Delilah tilts her head, eyes blazing with fury, and hisses, "No one can save you now!" Her voice is venomous, each word saturated with spite.

The priest, gripping the worn leather of the Bible, desperately tries to open it amid the bedlam. A sudden gust of wind sweeps through the room, flipping the delicate pages rapidly. He frantically fights to hold them in place while trying to invoke the sacred words that might still save them.

The shadows in the room stretch and deepen, slowly creeping along the worn plaster walls. They swallow the faint moonlight that filters through the jagged edges of the broken windows, which rattle as the room trembles. Dust particles dance in the air, casting a hazy glow over the uneasy space.

The priest's hands quake as he takes a deep breath, feeling the weight of the moment. His voice wavers, yet he forces himself to speak, words coming out hesitantly, but with growing clarity. "In the Name of Jesus Christ." He shudders visibly, a flicker of vulnerability crossing his face. His voice cracks unexpectedly, a fragile edge betraying his confident demeanor.

Taking a shallow breath, he continues, words tumbling out faster, driven by an urgent need to speak. "Our God and Lord, strengthened by the intercession of the Immaculate Virgin Mary, Mother of God, of Blessed Michael the Archangel, of the Blessed Apostles Peter and Paul and all the Saints and powerful in the Holy authority of our ministry," he says, and, picking up his pace, he talks faster. "We confidently undertake to repulse the attacks and deceits of the devil. God arises; His enemies are scattered, and those who hate Him flee before Him."

The heavy chains rattling around Delilah's limbs clink loudly with each frantic movement as her body jerks into the tangled mass of hair. An unbearable pain shoots through her, causing her to emit a piercing, desperate wail. The oppressive metal cuffs bite into the tender, bruised skin of her wrists, the cold metal pressing deep into her flesh, intensifying her torment.

Above, a dense cascade of bright sparks erupts from the tiny, single bulb fixture, casting fleeting glimmers in the dreary surroundings. A cloud of smoke billows upward, tinged with the acrid scent of burned toast, its thick tendrils weaving around them.

"As smoke is driven away, so are they driven; as wax melts before the fire, so the wicked perish at the presence of God," the priest continues louder.

A relentless, oppressive weight presses down on her chest, forcing her into the unyielding mattress stained with vomit, excrement, and sweat. Her body trembles as the relentless pressure continues to constrict, each breath shallow and strained, her ribs audibly cracking beneath the force. She gasps, desperation flickering in her eyes, and cries out, "Tell him to stop!"

In a sudden surge of strength, she snaps her wrist and clutches her husband's arm, her grip surprisingly fierce and unyielding, almost inhuman in its intensity.

Frantic to escape, he scrambles to find his keys, his fingers quivering as he dives into his pocket. The warm, familiar weight of the metal bundle provides a fleeting comfort as he grips it tightly.

Outside, the sky changes rapidly; the once-clear horizon darkens into a threatening gray as thick, churning clouds fill the sky.

Cold sweat beads on his forehead, and his clammy hand slips against the metal object of his freedom, heightening his sense of urgency as the storm approaches.

She tightens her grip, her nails digging sharply into his skin, leaving indentations as her fingers tighten further. He wails loudly, the sharp sting of skin tearing echoing through him as fiery pain shoots through his nerves. His body tenses painfully with each breath, his face contorted in anguish, overwhelmed by the relentless sensation of suffering.

Delilah hisses sharply, nostrils flaring as a faint, deathly scent wafts from her nose. Her piercing eyes scan her surroundings with intense caution, pupils dilating with focus. Her fingers twitch involuntarily, trembling with alert anticipation as her muscles tense in readiness. Every movement she makes mimics that of a hunting feline—silent, lethal, and poised for action.

A sharp crackle of thunder rumbles deeply as lightning cuts through the clouds, casting a fleeting purple hue across the sky. Every flash of light highlights the red streams of ichor streaking down his skin as her nails penetrate deeper.

The priest presses his chin defiantly upward toward the ceiling, his eyes burning with unyielding resolve as he confronts the malevolent forces swirling around him. Clutching the rosary tightly, he raises it high above his head, feeling the rough, weathered wood scorch his palm as if infused with a sinister energy. His breath catches, and his voice wavers briefly before exploding in a mighty, defiant yell, resonating with urgent fervor, refusing to succumb to the encroaching darkness that seeps from every wall. "Behold the Cross of the Lord, flee, bands of enemies! He has conquered, the Lion of the tribe of Judah, the offspring of David! May Thy mercy, Lord, descend upon us, as mighty as our hope in Thee."

Delilah screams in agonized despair, her face contorted with pain as she grits her teeth. With a trembling hand, she clenches her fist around a jagged piece of flesh torn from John's arm, blood slick and warm on her palm. Her chest heaves wildly, eyes wide with terror and defiance as she gasps for air. "You fool! I don't want to be saved!" she shouts, her voice cracking with a raw edge of anger and grief. "I can't be saved!" Each ragged breath shudders through her, defiant amidst the chaos.

The agony etched across his wife's face grates on him, piercing his guilt with every flicker of her strained features. His mind races, and he frantically tries to stop the bleeding, holding pressure on the fresh wound on his arm as his desperation mounts.

As he fights to stop the bleeding, a sharp metallic clang echoes softly. He hears the key drop to the floor, skittering across the worn, uneven floorboards, creating an unsettling tinny sound.

Father Michael inhales sharply, feeling his chest tighten as he gathers his resolve. He pushes forward, each step tentative yet purposeful. His hand reaches out, and, with a steadying breath, he raises the cross and recites, "We drive you from us, whoever you may be, unclean spirits, all satanic powers, all infernal invaders, all wicked legions, assemblies and sects; in the name and by the power of Our Lord Jesus Christ, may you be snatched away and driven from the Church of God and from the souls made to the image and likeness of God and redeemed by the Precious Blood of the Divine Lamb."

Her spine arches, and her chest heaves rapidly, each breath shallow and desperate. Her eyes widen with panic as she screams. "John! He—he's killing me!"

Her scream escalates into a desperate, tearful wail, carrying with it a sudden gust of chilled, musty air that sweeps across the room. The acrid stench of rotting flesh and decay assaults the senses, causing the priest to flare his nostrils in disgust and recoil. With a commanding voice, he declares, "Most cunning serpent, you shall no more dare to deceive the human race, persecute the Church, torment God's elect and sift them as wheat."

A steady drip of fluid slips from her nostril, streaking her upper lip with a glistening trail of crimson. She opens her mouth wider, revealing a set of teeth that are mottled gray, each one catching the light as her lips peel back to release a demonic hiss. Flecks of bright blood splatter across her teeth, contrasting starkly with their discolored surfaces.

John's gaze locks onto his wife's twisting, shuddering body, his eyes widening in shock and despair. Every muscle seems to contort involuntarily, a haunting display of pain and vulnerability. His breath catches as tears well up, shimmering at the corners of his eyes. "I'm sorry," he chokes out, voice thick with emotion, as he quickly averts his eyes, darting them to the cold darkness sprawled across the floor, seeking refuge or perhaps trying to block out the scene.

Gaining strength with each breath, the priest steadies himself and advances another step forward, muscles taut and eyes fixed sharply ahead as he navigates the shadowed path. "The Most High God commands you. He with whom, in your great insolence, you still claim to be equal; He Who wants all men to be saved and to come to the knowledge of the truth—God the Father commands you."

John's face drains of color, the tension tightening his jaw. He trembles, his hand shaking as he clenches his fist. His other hand reaches out, fingertips exploring the floor beneath him. The texture of the floorboards presses against his fingertips as he searches, eyes darting around, seeking clues or stability in the chaos.

The priest's gaze lingers on her twisting form, his eyes unwavering as he observes every movement. With a steady voice, his words echoing through the charged silence, he proclaims, "God commands you."

She shouts at the top of her lungs.

"I'm hurrying, darling," John says.

"God the Holy Ghost commands you," the priest declares firmly, his hand steady as he thrusts the cross toward her rising chest. The wooden relic catches the crash of lightning, casting a faint glow on his determined face. His eyes, unwavering, lock onto hers, conveying a silent plea for obedience and faith. "Christ, God's Word made flesh, commands you; He Who to save our race outdone through your envy, humbled himself, becoming obedient even unto death—He Who had built His Church on the firm rock and declared that the gates of Hell shall not prevail against Her, because He will dwell with Her all days, even to the end of the world—the sacred sign of the cross commands you, as does the power of the mysteries of the Christian Faith."

Sweat and perspiration bead intensely on her brow, trickling down in cool streams that catch the light. Suddenly, her complexion rapidly pales to a ghostly white, her lips turn blue, and her nail beds take on a purple hue. The whites of her eyes redden as her gaze fills with distress, and tears well up, turning crimson as they roll down her cheeks.

"The glorious Mother of God, the Virgin Mary, commands you!"

She jolts suddenly, her head striking the unforgiving metal rail of the bedframe with a sickening thud. Her eyes widen in shock as adrenaline courses through her veins.

Meanwhile, John grips the key tightly in his hand, his muscles tense as he leaps to his feet in a rapid motion. "Stop it!" he yells fiercely, his voice cracking with emotion, and he lunges forward, quick and determined.

Father Michael steps into his path, raising an arm to block John's approach. His face is etched with concern. "Son—" he begins, then raises his palm to stop him. "Stay," he urges, pressing his hand against John's chest to create distance, his eyes begging for composure.

John pushes back with force, his chest heaving as he struggles to find his voice. Shadows flicker and sway, their dark shapes stretching across the dim room, inching the darkness nearer. A faint creak echoes as a floorboard shifts beneath their feet.

The priest, his face set and eyes sharp, grunts softly, then swiftly redirects his gaze to Delilah, speaking in a hurried tone. "She who, by her humility and from the first moment of her Immaculate Conception, crushed your proud head. The faith of the Holy Apostles Peter and Paul and of the other Apostles commands you. The Blood of the Martyrs and the pious intercession of all the Saints commands you."

Whispers swirl eerily around them, their soft voices weaving through the room as the temperature steadily drops. A chilling layer of ice forms on the surface of the words they speak, shimmering with a faint, icy glow. Every breath becomes visible in the frigid air, and the silence deepens, broken only by the delicate crackle of chill taking hold.

Each of the priest's words tumbles over one another in a frantic, aggressive rush, the voices rising and falling with urgent intensity. "Thus, cursed dragon, and you, diabolical legions," he declares, his voice echoing through the air with a commanding force, "we adjure you by the living God, by the true God, by the Holy God—the God who so loved the world that He gave His only Son, that every soul believing in Him might not perish, but have life everlasting." His eyes blaze with fervor as he gestures passionately toward the heavens. "Stop deceiving human creatures and pouring out to them the poison of eternal damnation! Stop harming the Church and hindering her liberty!" The words hang in the charged atmosphere, a potent declaration striving to pierce the darkness.

Delilah's back arches violently, her muscles clenching so tight that her ribs crack audibly with every breath. The pain is sharp, a brutal reminder of her fight.

"She—" John's voice breaks, and he presses harder with his hand, desperation flashing in his eyes. He inhales sharply as the truth slams into him. "She's going to die!" Panic claws at him, and his hands shake as he fights to control it. "Let me help her!"

Her eyes are wide with shock as the veins in her neck visibly swell, pulsating with each frantic heartbeat. Blood seeps silently from her ears, staining her hairline with dark, glistening drops. Her body trembles, every muscle taut with tension, as she struggles to breathe amidst the growing sensations of dizziness and pain. The metal cuffs of her restraints cut into her wrists, sawing away at the delicate skin.

Standing at the bedside, the priest holds his hands over the woman's chest, his fingers gently curved as though channeling some hidden power. His gaze is intense, focused, and reflects both authority and compassion. He loudly commands, "Be gone, Satan, inventor and master of all deceit, enemy of man's salvation." His voice rings out, resonant with spiritual power. "Give place to Christ, in whom you find no foothold; give way to the one, Holy, Catholic, and Apostolic Church, which Christ acquires through His bloodshed. Stoop beneath the all-powerful Hand of God; tremble and flee when we invoke the Holy and terrible Name of Jesus!"

She screams hysterically as the shadows in the room stretch and coil, thickening the darkness that creeps toward her. The frigid grip of the unseen forms lifts her from the mattress, her body taut with panic, her voice the only thing breaking the suffocating silence.

"Can't you see she's in pain?!" John yells, reaching out to grasp her arm gently as Father Michael pushes past him.

The air thickens with Holy authority as he pronounces the sacred name, sending a palpable ripple of reverence through the air. "This name makes Hell tremble; the Virtues, Powers, and Dominations of Heaven humbly submit to it, while the Cherubim and Seraphim continuously praise it, repeating the refrain: Holy, Holy, Holy is the Lord, the God of Armies," he proclaims with unwavering conviction.

With a ragged gasp, Delilah collapses limply onto the mattress, her body limp as if surrendering to an unseen force.

The priest, breathless, clutches his chest as if to hold his heart in place, eyes fixed on her motionless form.

John's face contorts in horror as he observes her lifeless body; her chest remains still, unresponsive, refusing to rise or fall with breath. He notices the slight, unsettling droop of her chin pulling her head to one side, her jaw slack.

Their gazes lock—her wide, open eyes stare back at him, marred by a clouded, bloodshot veil that hints at the traumatic event, the whites tinged with a resounding crimson ripple.

Silence hangs heavy in the room, thick with dismay and the suffocating weight of loss.

The whispering voices suddenly stop, and the storm subsides, leaving the peaceful moon's glow, erasing all sound in an eerie silence.

Shadows that once rippled and stretched now shrink back into the corners as if called to return to the place from which they came.

The once-burned-out bulb suddenly flickers, giving off a soft glow that casts their distorted selves dancing along the walls with each movement.

"Delilah," John whispers, voice trembling as he takes a cautious step forward. Her unresponsive gaze remains fixed, vacant and distant, holding him in a silent, unyielding stare. "Darling," he repeats, voice strained and desperate, his lips struggling to summon a reassuring smile.

Father Michaels's palm presses against his back, the weathered texture grounding him in the difficult moment. "John—" the priest begins, his voice low and steady, but suddenly, his words are cut off by a muffled scream, raw and desperate, echoing through the tense air and breaking the fragile silence.

"It's Lillie," the priest whispers urgently, his voice barely more than a breath. "Go to her now." His eyes dart nervously toward the door, scanning for any sign of danger.

John's face twists with horror as he glances toward the doorway, his heart pounding in his chest.

"Now!" the priest insists, placing a firm hand on John's shoulder and giving him a gentle but decisive shove toward the door.

John stumbles forward, gripping the wooden door frame as he moves through the dark hall, every footstep feeling heavy and uncertain as he makes his way toward her screams.

Chapter Fifteen

DARK MISTAKES

John's footsteps gradually fade as he walks down the hall to check on Lillie, leaving a heavy silence behind.

Father Michael walks to the door and quietly closes it. He returns to Delilah's bedside, his gaze fixed on her unmoving form as he strains to catch any sign of life.

Suddenly, a high-pitched sound, reminiscent of a spinning top, whirls across the floor before coming to a halt just at his feet. Its sharp, rhythmic vibration briefly contrasts the reverent quiet.

Father Michael, though momentarily confused by the sound, keeps his eyes fixed on the bed. He cautiously kneels, hoping to get a better look at what made the noise. Feeling around near his feet, he finds a small object, partially hidden by the bed frame.

He slowly lifts it to eye level, examining its unique pin-like shape. The moonlight streaming through the windows and the faint glow of the bulb illuminate it, creating shimmering patterns that dance on the walls and ceiling as he turns it side to side. After a moment of analysis, he recognizes what it is from his time as a priest at the state mental hospital: a key for the shackles. His gaze returns to Delilah's open eyes, which stare back at him, filled with a silent plea and desperate hope. His voice barely a whisper, he mutters, "John must have accidentally dropped this."

A crow's sharp cry echoes eerily through the night from outside the windows. The sound is piercing, shattering the room's quiet. Father Michael jumps, nearly dropping the key from his hand. He quickly pivots on his heel, his eyes narrowing as they dart toward the window.

He positions himself defensively, almost like prey, scanning for any signs of danger, his gaze lingering on the opening with heightened vigilance.

Outside, the bird persists in its call, a sequence of sharp, urgent notes that fracture the night's calm. Its voice crackles with a wild, unrestrained energy. The creature's expansive black wings shimmer with an iridescent sheen beneath the moonlight, the feathers reflecting a silvery green hue that flickers with every subtle movement as it thrashes.

As the priest glances toward the window, he ponders how late it must be. Seeing no immediate threat, he leans in closer to the bed, a mixture of curiosity and resolve in his expression. "I suppose I can free you from those restraints, my child," he whispers. He turns back to look at her, still cautious and alert, scanning her face one last time for any sign of life.

Her body remains unflinching, as if frozen in time. She lies limp on the cold, stained mattress, her features strained and pale. Her eyes are wide open, hollow with fatigue and distress. Even though they are lifeless, they are still begging for answers. Her mouth, a deep shade of purplish blue, slightly gapes as if she wants to speak, but remains helplessly silent.

He reaches out slowly, taking her limp wrist and feeling for a pulse. Her skin is cold under his fingertips. He pauses, holding his breath to concentrate, but there's nothing, not even a flutter. His gaze shifts, and he slowly traces the edge of the key still resting in his hand, the dim light flickering across his tense features, casting shadows that dance across his face. In a soft voice, he whispers, "Your suffering is over; you're with God now. You deserve some peace."

He inhales sharply. His gaze traces the soft lines of her body once more, searching for any sign of life, and seeing none, he settles on the restraints. "I don't think we need these anymore," he murmurs.

She remains perfectly still, eyes unblinking, as a fly lands on the white of her eyeball, its tiny legs gripping the moist surface.

The priest leans closer, his brow furrowing as a bead of sweat forms at his temple. He straightens the stiff white collar of his cassock; the fabric creases beneath his fingers as he adjusts it. Even though the situation seems settled, his actions are measured, and a hint of doubt occasionally flashes in his eyes.

Suddenly, the tiny pest flutters its fragile wings vigorously, attempting to burrow further into her tender cornea, its movements relentless, as if driven by an urgent need to penetrate deeper.

He bats the fly away, mumbling, "Have some respect for the dead." His lips curl into a subtle smirk, his eyes glinting.

The bug, recovering from the heavy swat, languidly flies toward the window, its wings shimmering as it soars. It suddenly collides with a large shard of glass sticking out from the frame, and a gentle tapping sound echoes in the room. The insect loses momentum, gently drifting downward until it lands on the floor, twitching as it restores its fluttering.

The priest chuckles nervously and slowly sets the Bible down on the nightstand beside the bed. He moves with quiet deliberation, almost hesitantly, as though trying to avoid any abrupt sound. "I'll just put my things down so I can give you my full attention," he says, his voice tense but steady.

As he looks away, her eyebrow twitches.

"You remind me of a young woman I helped many years ago," he says, his voice carrying a faint sense of nostalgia. As he speaks, he relaxes his grip, slowly slipping the rosary from his fingers and carefully placing it into his pocket, the beads rustling softly against the fabric.

His eyes grow distant for a moment before he continues. "She had a little girl, just like you—bright, curious, with wide eyes that seemed to hold the universe. There's a nursery rhyme she used to sing to her daughter, a melody similar to the one I overheard from your daughter's lips just before I entered your room." The words linger in the air, heavy with memories and unspoken stories, as if the past and present are woven together in this moment.

Her toe twitches, sending a faint ripple through her foot.

"I must confess, it rattles me more than I let on," he says, a shadow crossing his face as memories surface. "Her ending unfolded differently—far from the peaceful conclusion you have reached. It haunts me to this day, deeply etched into my mind. Something I will carry with me forever. I never learned the name of the Demon I spoke to that night, but I sensed it was the closest thing to the devil himself—its presence was dark and malevolent, shrouded in shadows that crept into every thought and dream."

As he is caught up in his trail of words, the bulb flickers and goes out. He feels his way through the room, which is now completely dark aside from a hint of moonlight. His fingertips brush against her icy skin as he works carefully to unlock her wrists from the heavy, oppressive shackles. The thick chains are cold and unforgiving, clanking loudly as they fall against the iron rails behind her head.

The surroundings are eerily silent; both John and the crows have vanished into the night, leaving him utterly alone.

An unsettling chill runs down his spine, yet amidst the darkness, a sense of protection washes over him; it's as though a divine entity is watching over them, its presence comforting.

As he prepares to release her ankles, his eyes are drawn to the moonlight illuminating her face with a silvery glow. The light touches her features differently this time, revealing a delicate beauty that sparks a strange familiarity inside him. His brow furrows as he gazes at her, muttering to himself, "It's strange ... You look so much like her."

Bewildered, he freezes, rooted to the spot. He carefully scans her features for a moment before returning to releasing her.

He shakes his head and chuckles. "It's been a long night."

As he returns to unfastening the restraints, a nearly silent breath escapes from Delilah's lips. Her chest rises and falls slowly, and her eyes blink, then open wide with panic. She struggles to find words, her voice airy and fractured: "H-help..." Her lips part desperately as she tries to speak again.

He turns slowly and faces her, unable to believe what he just heard.

She suddenly gasps for air and croaks, "Please, help me."

He stands frozen, staring in shock, certain she died in the battle for her soul. But hearing the words, there is no mistaking the speaker, nor the chilling reality that it was her corpse.

He carefully studies her, trying to interpret her intentions, then sharply demands answers, his voice firm and commanding. "Who am I speaking to?" he asks. "Is the Demon moving your lips, or is this..." His question hangs in the air, unfinished.

Before he can complete his sentence, she abruptly cuts him off, a gasp escaping her throat. Her eyes bulge with surprise and fear as she breathes out, "Delilah." The name trembles on her lips.

He moves closer, gazing at her with eyes full of disbelief. "It's a miracle," he says, visibly over-whelmed. Adrenaline courses through him. "Thank you, God, for this miracle of saving her and bringing this child back to us."

The darkness of the room deepens, unnoticed by Father Michael, pressing in around them as he rushes to the foot of the bed.

As he fumbles with the restraint around her ankle, a strange, pulsing movement radiates from her hands. Her fingers curl into a tight fist, and her eyes bulge suddenly, as if pushed from within by an unseen force. He moves faster, the key sliding into the lock.

"Father," she murmurs, watching him. She slowly taps her rigid finger against her chest.

"Yes? What is it, child?" he asks gently, turning the key in his hand. A soft click echoes as he unlatches the first heavy anklet. He steps back, eyes scanning his work with pride, then moves to the other side of the bed.

"Do you remember the story you mentioned earlier?" She asks, her voice trembling and faint, yet tinged with curiosity. Her eyes flicker with a hint of recognition, as if a memory is emerging.

He pauses as he reaches the last lock, his fingers fumbling trying to align the key as he works to unlatch it. The moonlight subtly illuminates his face, revealing a blend of anticipation and solemnity.

As the last lock falls open, he stands still, gazing at her silently for a moment.

"Well ... I remember you." She says.

Father Michael looks at her, thinking it must be a joke or a bit of delusion from her near-death experience. "Oh ... that's quite interesting. Where do you remember me from?"

Breathless, she continues, "That was me—I was the little girl from that night."

"But if I remember correctly ... the little girl's name was Avery," he says.

"Yes, you are correct, Father—Avery Delilah Monroe."

The room's temperature shifts with her words.

"Oh, but you wouldn't know that, would you? Because you didn't stick around long enough to find out."

He eyes the doorframe, calculating his exit as the shadows seem to throb with a menacing energy. A slow, unsettling creak emanates from the springs of the old mattress as Delilah shifts her position.

"I—I couldn't help your mother," he stammers. "I tried—I really tried ... but she was too far gone. The evil had taken root inside her. It devoured her soul and every aspect of her humanity from the inside out." His words catch in his throat, and he buries his face in his palms as a wave of emotion crashes over him.

Delilah's voice breaks through his sobs, soft and childlike, laced with accusation. "Is that why you abandoned us?" she asks. "You left me alone with her—"

He quickly interrupts, voice strained but steady. "I didn't abandon you. You had your father to care for you," he insists, desperation lining his words.

She stifles a bitter laugh, her voice trembling with emotion and pain. "My father," she repeats slowly. "My father ... He couldn't handle her darkness either. Eventually, he couldn't take it anymore. He left too—left me behind with her."

Father Michael's face flushes vivid red, jaw tightening as humiliation and anger surge through him.

"I am not responsible for what is out of my control!" he shouts sharply, cutting her off mid-sentence. His words are drowned out by the creaking of the mattress springs as she pulls her legs back, her tension evident in her posture. She snarls with bitter frustration, her eyes blazing. "What kind of man of God are you?" she demands, voice trembling with outrage. "You lied—you claimed you could help—our family relied on you, and you simply abandoned us."

He stammers, his face pale and sweaty. "It was right after I was ordained and began my priesthood; I tried my best to help, but it was too much for me and well beyond my scope of training," he admits, voice trembling. "There was nothing more I could do." His hands tremble as he states his defense, trying to justify his failings.

She swings her limbs slowly, her body perched on the bed's edge, eyes fixed intently on him. Her voice lowers to a venomous growl. "Coward," she says.

A scent, heavy with the smell of death lingers in the air around him.

From the shadowed corners of the room, murmurs drift like ghostly echoes, barely audible, but chilling in their whispering.

He pauses briefly, senses heightened, ears alert for the quietest sound. Carefully, he lifts his head, eyes narrowing suspiciously at Delilah. "What do you want?" he asks softly, his voice tinged with unease.

An inhuman shriek escapes her lips. "As you have stolen my essence—now I hunger for yours in return," she whispers. "For the souls you've forsaken, your soul is mine."

He hears the door lock and spins around quickly, eyes searching for any sign of salvation. Apart from the chaos of broken windows and some scattered furniture, all that remains are his Bible, rosary, and an empty, disheveled bed.

She has disappeared into the darkness, leaving behind a haunting emptiness.

He hyperventilates and glances at the nightstand, which holds an open Bible to Luke 11:2-4, the Lord's Prayer. The moment swiftly reconnects him with his faith as he starts reciting, "Our Father, who art in heaven, Hallowed be Thy Name—." His voice quivers as he speaks the familiar words, providing a fragile comfort amid his despair. Slowly, he reaches into his pocket, searching for the rosary. The cloth initially feels empty against his skin, returning his sense of susceptibility.

At that moment, he hears footsteps scampering up the walls, echoing strangely in the empty room.

A chilling cackle breaks the silence. "Looking for something?" Delilah says, laced with sarcasm and a mocking cheerfulness. Her laughter then reverberates, the sound bouncing off the walls.

He doesn't glance up, frantically patting down his pockets until his fingers brush against the smooth wood of the beads. A sigh of relief escapes him. His lips part slightly as he continues to say, "Thy Kingdom Come. Thy will be done, on earth as it is in heaven." His voice is barely audible. He lunges toward the Bible, its pages fluttering softly.

Suddenly, whispering voices resound, their tone transforming into a Latin chant that reverberates through the room, shaking the walls. His hand grips the Bible tightly, trembling as he frantically flips through the delicate pages, searching for something.

He hears footsteps outside the door, growing steadily louder as they approach. His stomach clenches, and he drops the Bible, and it skids across the floor. As he steps to retrieve it, he stumbles and falls. Using his unsteady limbs, he propels himself forward, pressing his palms and feet against the floor. "Come on," he mutters, his voice strained as he realizes his Bible is just out of reach.

A sharp, distinct creak pierces the silence from a floorboard nearby. He flinches, a sense of danger washing over him, and his pace quickens, crawling faster, desperation driving his every step.

A sudden gust of wind whips through the room, pushing the Bible further away and sending its pages into a frantic dance. As the pages turn wildly, ominous voices chime in, intensifying the disorder, their unsettling Latin chant echoing amidst the turmoil.

A spectral force presses one of its pages open, revealing a faded illustration. Father Michael holds his breath, his eyes fixed on the haunting image faintly illuminated by the silvery glow of the moonlight. "Baal…" he whispers as he stares at the demon's depiction—sharp, menacing, and grotesque—illuminated with an unnatural glow, its features twisted into an eternal snarl, ranking just below the devil himself in malevolence.

A jarring, disjointed chuckle booms from the corner of the room.

He hesitates, then slowly, reluctantly, lifts his gaze toward the sound. He glimpses a shadowy presence, its sinister energy rippling through the darkness. Its body moves, and the moonlight illuminates its face, showing that it is Delilah.

Delilah's body hunches forward, her torso curling toward her toes. Her spine twists agonizingly as her upper body pivots sharply to face him, every muscle taut with effort. Her drooping face shifts, a slow smile emerging as her palms press firmly against the floor. Her elbows bend, and a crimson flush spreads through her veins, bloodshot and pulsating beneath her skin.

He kicks his feet anxiously, pushing himself back further into the wall behind him. His voice softens, trembling with urgent emotion. "Delilah—" he says, lowering his tone as he attempts to reach her, "I know you're still there deep inside. I urge you to fight this darkness and resist the evil that has seized your soul. Please, Delilah, confront the demon lurking within you before it's too late."

A thick darkness spreads like a heavy, suffocating blanket, spilling forth from the shadows that enshroud her statuesque, fractured body. Her form is rigid, partly revealed beneath the fabric of shadows that cling to her, accentuating the stark contrast between light and dark.

Tears cascade down his cheeks as he struggles to contain his emotions, his voice trembling with regret and desperation. "I beg of you," he pleads. "I'm sorry for leaving you in harm's way, for not helping all those years ago, but I am here now. I'm standing before you, asking for your forgiveness and for you to overcome this agony, just as I should have asked your mother to do long ago," he says, voice thick with remorse.

Her head slowly turns, her lengthy hair cascading in dingy, tangled waves, falling like a shadowy curtain in front of her face.

"Instead of sinking into this demon's trap, we can conquer this together," he cries, his voice steady but urgent. His eyes lock onto hers, filled with fierce determination. "Delilah—what do you say? You and I—we can change this family's path for good."

He stands and steps closer, every movement charged with conviction, as if the very air around them crackles with the promise of change. "Please, Delilah, let me help you," he pleads.

"Delilah is gone," she bellows, her voice echoing with a fierce finality and resolve.

Chapter Sixteen

OPEN THE DOOR

John feels his way cautiously through the lightless hallway, each step tentative and deliberate. The familiar distance to his daughter's room now seems elongated, as if the darkness itself has stretched the space, making his heartbeat escalate into a frantic race. Though no one is behind him, an unsettling heaviness lingers in the air, as if an unseen presence shadows his every move.

A scream from Lillie's room pierces the oppressive void, making his stomach sink.

"Daddy!" Her desperate cry rings out with anguish, her voice trembling with fear and pain.

Chills ripple down his spine at her distress. "Lillie," he says as he struggles to maintain composure. Hearing her suffering, he raises his voice louder with purpose. "Lillie, don't worry! I—I'm coming!" His hand flails outward, fingers desperately searching the wall's features. Frantically, he presses his palm against the surface, patting for the familiar ridges and divots as he speeds up, driven by the sound of her pleas, desperately seeking her doorway in the darkness.

"Daddy," she cries again, her voice muffled by her trembling lips, a desperate plea woven with fear and urgency. "Please—hurry!" Though the door conceals her cries, they are painfully loud to him.

He pats the cracked lath and plaster wall repeatedly, each contact igniting a growing heat beneath his fingertips as he struggles to find his way. The texture under his hand becomes unbearably hot; sweat beads form on his brow. "Shi—" he starts, nearly cursing, fighting to control his fear and frustration. He quickly pulls his hand back, cradling his fingers to soothe the burn.

A pungent smell of smoke wafts through the air, growing increasingly thick and oppressive with each passing moment. The sharp, acrid scent clings to his nostrils and lungs. He coughs, trying to clear his throat.

Oblivious to what is causing his daughter's terror, he remains unaware that the creature's grotesque form looms behind the door, its jagged claws scraping the walls as it slowly approaches her. Terror rises in her as she shrieks, "The monster—it's going to eat me!" She screams louder, her eyes wide with terror, echoing the chaos unfolding just beyond John's reach.

His fingers fumble in his pocket, desperately searching for the keys as panic escalates within him. "I'm coming, sweetheart!" he shouts.

At last, he clutches the keys and fishes them out of his pocket. The frantic sound of metal scraping against the lock's edge as he fumbles in the dark, trying to find the right key, silences everything else.

After a tense moment of frustration, the correct key finally slides into the hole. The metal grapples inside briefly before settling, his grip tightening on the key as he turns it slowly, and with a satisfying click, the door unlocks.

A whisper, soft yet urgent, calls his name. "John..." It creeps through the air, along the hallway's ceiling, growing ominously close.

His gaze flicks upward, heart pounding.

"John, why did you want to hurt me?" The ethereal cry shatters the air, echoing sharply against the corridor's empty walls. The haunting voice of his wife resonates with chilling clarity, each word dripping with sorrow and accusation. Her voice, fragile yet piercing, seems to float in the stale silence, anchoring him to the tragic moment.

As her voice fades away, a wave of guilt hits him, causing him to stop. Her words replay repeatedly in his mind, a constant reminder of the choices he's made and the love they once shared, now only painful memories in the empty hallway.

"I would never try to hurt you. I'm not a—" he responds defensively as he tries to suppress his emotions. "I'm only trying to do what's best for our daughter and you. I'm trying to do what's best for our family." He slowly put the key back in his pocket, a soft jingle accompanying the movement. His fingers shake as he steels himself to open the door.

The woman's voice suddenly shatters the quiet again, raw with accusation. "You're a monster and a murderer."

He hesitates, his hand hovering over the door handle, expecting the warmth of the wall through the metal. Instead, he feels the icy touch of the knob.

Confused, he quickly retracts his hand. A shiver pulses down his spine as he freezes in place. The world around him sinks into a suffocating silence, thick with unspoken words that seem to press against him from all sides.

Finding momentary comfort in the quiet, he reaches out again, carefully gripping the cold handle with uncertain fingers. "I'm doing what's best for us," he mutters, reassuring himself.

The handle gives beneath his touch, and he slowly pushes the door open. A punishing screech pierces the air as the hinges groan loudly.

He startles, his heart pounding against his chest. He takes a deep breath, then forces his focus back on the pitch-black room. "Lillie?" he whispers.

A sharp, icy gust of wind swirls past him, causing him to shiver. "Sweety?" he says, his voice slightly louder, trying to sound reassuring.

From the darkness, a child's faint, distressed cries resonate.

He cautiously nudges the door open a little more, squinting into the gloom, searching for any sign of her. "Lillie, are you okay?" he asks gently, his tone careful to avoid startling her.

Mid-scan, he notices a tiny figure tucked away from the moonlight, in the back of the room. Lillie's small frame trembles visibly as her chest rises and falls rapidly, her breath shallow and quick as she hyperventilates.

She sobs softly, her voice trembling, "I—I didn't mean to—" Her hands clutch her knees in a desperate grip. "I—I don't know what happened—Daddy, I don't know what happened—" Her words come out in a frantic, stuttering rhythm, her speech muddled and uneven.

He steps cautiously closer, his gaze fixed on her tiny form, his voice gentle but steady. "Whatever it is, we will get through it," he assures her. He nudges the door open wider and takes a tentative step into the room, inching toward the switch by the wall.

Her body rocks back and forth with each ragged breath, hysteria threading through her trembling frame. He keeps his eyes on her, noticing the way her hands clutch her knees as if holding herself together.

He pats along the wall near the entrance until he touches the light switch, ready to give her some relief. "We will get through this," he says softly. "Let's just figure out what the problem is, so Daddy knows how to help." His hand hovers for a moment before flipping the switch.

As the bulb flickers to life, a warm yellow glow floods the room.

He scans the room, noting the furniture and the faint outlines of objects cast in shadow. He quickly shifts his attention toward the side of the room where a tiny figure once huddled, but is now absent. "Lillie?" he calls as his eyes search for any sign of her.

Feeling an icy chill, his attention drifts toward the open window and the cool night air sweeping inside. John reflects for a moment, flinching at the memory of having locked her in the room alone. He rushes to the window, calling out again in a soft, urgent voice, "Lillie?"

Through the quiet night, he hears a faint chuckle, its origin hidden in darkness.

He quickly moves closer to the window thinking the voice is outside, anxiety sharpening his senses. "It's okay, everything will be fine," he says. He takes a deep breath, then slowly peeks out the window.

Raindrops fall softly, each one delicate and calm, the wind blowing them inside, grazing his cheeks with gentle persistence as he gazes into the misty darkness. His voice is barely audible as he calls out, "Lillie?" Listening intently for a reply, he leans further out, cautious of the slick, wet surface beneath him.

A child's sniffles cut through the rhythmic pattern of rain on the rooftop, a fragile sound of distress.

He looks up toward the edge of the roofline, recalling the last time he saw his daughter when she was frightened—the small figure huddled near the precipice.

Then he sees her, her tiny frame wet and trembling, her shoulders hunched as she sustains herself near the dangerous ledge.

"Lillie," he says sternly, mindful of the slippery rooftop as he climbs out the window and edges closer to where she sits, careful to avoid slipping on the mossy surface. His eyes scan for dry patches, searching for any secure footholds.

Dispirited, she sniffles, her gaze fixed forlornly on the distant silhouette of the cornfield. He extends his hands toward her, voice strained but firm. "Are you listening? Come here before you hurt yourself—"

"I-I'm sorry," she cries, her voice quivering as tears stream down her face. Her chest heaves with every sob as she clings to her sense of shame.

He hesitates, studying her with a careful, measured gaze. He slowly inches closer, uncertain, aware he needs to close the space gradually so as not to frighten her into scooting too close to the edge.

She shifts nervously, scooting toward the roof's dangerous brim, her body tense and guarded. "I'm sorry," she repeats, her voice a fractured whisper, sounding like a broken record.

"Lillie, come here," he calls, his voice urgent yet gentle, as he extends his arms, eager to reach her. He gestures with open palms, inviting her to step closer, his eyes filled with worry. "Take my hand before you hurt yourself—it's dark out here, and I don't want you to fall and get injured."

She hesitates.

He shifts his tone, voice growing softer and more coaxing. A flicker of remorse for abandoning her crosses his face, fleeting but noticeable. He wrings his hand behind his neck, thinking back to the moment he threw her into the room. "I didn't mean to be rough on you earlier. I was trying to protect you, to keep you safe from danger."

Her muscles tense, and she takes short, shallow breaths as she fights back tears.

His words spill from his lips, jumbled in a frantic rush. John's voice is thick with panic and concern. "I just want us all to be okay again, to find our way back to the way things used to be," he says. His eyes search, trying desperately to connect with her, pleading for connection. "I only want to do what's best for you, my darling. You are what's important to me—no one else." He hesitates as he waits anxiously for a response.

Her breath slows and deepens with each inhalation. Her body sags, limbs slackening as weariness overtakes her. The thick misting cloud cover shifts, parting slowly to reveal the luminous golden surface of the moon glowing softly against the night sky.

"Please, Lillie, just take my hand," he says, extending his palm closer. Carefully, he inches closer across the slick shingles. The surface beneath him is fraught with patches of moss, slippery and treacherous, reflecting the moonlight in shimmering patches.

"You lied!" she shouts, her voice consumed with anger. Her body shudders uncontrollably as she clenches her fists, tears welling in her eyes. "I saw it—I saw it in my bedroom," she insists, voice cracking, horror etched into her features. "Mommie's not a princess—she—she's a monster." Her words catch in her throat as she doubles over, trying to catch her breath.

He pauses, eyes wide with shock, the weight of her accusations settling over him like a nightmarish fog. "What did you see?" he asks almost hesitantly, as if afraid to hear the answer, his gaze searching hers for any sign of truth.

"I don't want to be a princess." She sobs uncontrollably, her shoulders shaking as she struggles to form the words. Her voice is raw with desperation, as if the very idea of that future terrifies her.

He takes a slow, cautious step closer, his face a mask of conflicted emotion. "I just wanted to keep our family together," he murmurs, voice shaky, thick with regret. "I didn't know if I could do it without her. A child needs both parents," he continues, but his words soften into a murmur, almost like a prayer under his breath. "A child needs their mother," he repeats, louder now, as if trying to convince himself as much as her.

"I'm just like her," she whispers. "I—see things."

Suddenly, his foot slips, causing him to teeter dangerously near the edge. His entire body strains as he fights to regain balance, muscles trembling with the effort, heart pounding in his chest as he barely holds himself upright, vulnerable on the edge of a fall.

She quietly inches closer, her foot stepping onto the gutter with cautious hesitation. Her shoulders tremble as she whispers again, voice barely audible over the distant thunder. "I'm—I'm sorry," she murmurs, eyes glistening with tears. "I—I didn't mean to hurt anyone—"

The distress in her tone sparks a surge of panic within him. "Lillie," he says desperately, fighting the tremor in his voice. Summoning his courage, he shifts closer as he pleads, "Just come towards Daddy—please—come here—get away from the ledge—stay with me." He stammers each word with fear.

The storm flares up again; a sudden crackle from above releases a drizzle, sending small droplets scattering everywhere.

He looks up, fearful of losing his footing, but his gaze quickly returns as a faint flicker of movement catches his eye.

Like a whisper of the wind, his daughter's tiny figure is swept off the roof, dissolving into the darkness below.

"Lillie!" John screams. "*No!*" Ignoring his own safety, he lunges forward, rushing toward the edge of the roof.

Her body leaves behind a gentle warmth that lingers in the air, mingling with the faint scents of lavender and rain.

Hyperventilating, he presses his gaze into the darkness, eyes darting in search of any sign of her presence. His heart pounds fiercely against his ribcage, each beat loud and insistent, as he struggles to maintain a flicker of hope that she might still be safe. "Please, God—let her be okay," he says. He clenches his teeth while tears blur his eyes and sting his cheeks, intense emotion flooding through him, overwhelming his senses.

Something shifts beneath him, a tiny rustle in the dense hedge below. The faint flicker of moonlight outlines the figure, causing it to ripple like a wavering ghost.

"Lillie?" he calls sharply. "Lillie!" he yells, voice strained. "Stay where you are!" His eyes dart around, frantic to find her. He notices the warm, inviting glow spilling from the open bedroom window. Without hesitation, he pivots, fighting against the rain, and begins to crawl forward.

The light pouring through the window is bright, intense, and glaring, casting shadows across the room.

He steadies himself, his trembling fingers gripping the windowsill as he tries to anchor his shaky body. Squinting against the brightness, he shields his eyes from the misting rain streaking down his glasses, blurring his vision.

A sudden gust of wind rattles the window, causing it to tremble. Startled, he flinches, eyes snapping open wider as he observes the heavy glass pane vibrating ominously.

The windowsill abruptly shifts, slamming down and crushing his fingers. "Sh—" he chokes out, wincing as he hears the sickening crunch of fractured bones. A spike of agony shoots through his hand, amplifying his panic. He screams, struggling to process the sight of his broken fingers.

The room's light flickers erratically. Heart pounding, he uses his free hand to force the window open further. Clenching his jaw, he fights through the throbbing pain in his bones as he slowly eases the pressure. His hand feels unnaturally hot to the touch, with sweat beads forming on his forehead.

Once again, the flickering light dances across the room, heightening his sense of chaos and fear.

Someone has just opened the door to Lillie's bedroom, the creak sharp in the silent air. Heavy footsteps echo from the dark hallway, each step deliberate and measured.

With pursed lips, he fights the urge to react and freezes in place, his hand still in midair, not making a sound. He peers through the small window, watching the shadowy corridor outside her room. He listens intently for any sound, every movement holding his attention, alert and tense.

The thunderous sound of footsteps grows louder, each step echoing ominously as they close the distance. With every advancing thud, a surge of electric tension charges the air, making the hairs on his neck stand on end.

He hears Delilah's voice humming a lullaby softly. "Oh, where, oh, where, has my little lamb gone, oh, where, oh, where, can he be?" The soothing melody contrasts sharply with the growing menace approaching him.

He wants to gasp as a sharp, searing pain shoots up his arm, but he holds his breath to stay unnoticed. John carefully slinks down, trying not to be seen, peering in just enough to watch the scene unravel inside.

A crack of thunder echoes through the thick, swirling clouds overhead.

With each deliberate, dragging step against the wooden floor, a growing sense of dread tightens in his chest.

Standing alone in the dim light, Delilah appears suddenly, stark nude, her skin covered in what appears to be a slick sheen of blood—cloaking her like an ichor-stained armor. She continues to sing, the haunting melody filling the tense air, then stops abruptly as she stands in front of the bedroom door. Peering inside, she scans the room with an unsettling calm.

Her body is distorted, grotesque, her enormous belly stretched taut and misshapen, with the skin unevenly pulling, hinting at unnatural growth or transformation. She resembles an anaconda mid-digestion, the aftermath of swallowing prey much too large for comfort.

John trembles visibly as he observes the outline of a grown man's face pressing from the inside against the wall of her abdomen. He recites the Lord's Prayer under his breath, but then, realizing something horrifying, he stops. His eyes widen with distress as he notes the subtle movements beneath her skin.

The man's mouth opens wide, revealing a deep indentation that seems to imply a silent scream from within.

In her hand, she clutches a Bible, its cover bloodied and its pages yellowed with age. Her knuckles blanch as she raises it high, a menacing glint in her eyes.

"Father Michael..." he murmurs, voice trembling, as if trying to summon the courage to acknowledge the possibility that it is him. Thunder roars overhead, jagged lightning illuminating the sky. In that moment, he realizes her grip has consumed his last hope, her ruthless expression erasing any trace of mercy.

Cruel, mocking laughter escapes her lips as she tears into the fragile pages, ripping them out with ferocious ease. She stuffs a handful of torn paper into her mouth, the crumpling sound echoing ominously as she chews and swallows, the binding of the book slipping down her throat as effortlessly as a drink of water.

He pictures the priest's last moments—fear etched into his features, screams lost in the chaos. Fighting back tears, he turns toward the pouring rain, the cold droplets soaking his skin, offering a fleeting sense of solace.

The sky weeps alongside him, mourning the loss of a noble soldier whose sacrifice now lingers only in the echo of the storm.

"I promise if you deliver us from this madness, oh, Lord, I will do better," he cries. "Not only for me, but for my daughter."

Abruptly, a snarl curls on Delilah's lips as her mouth extends into a jagged tooth-filled snout, nostrils flaring with a feral flicker. Her expression twists into a grimace as she eagerly laps her lips, then shifts her gaze toward the fogged window, eyes gleaming with predatory intent.

Hearing the subtle shift of movement, John turns his head sharply, his eyes snapping toward her. Mid-run, he catches sight of the flickering lights inside, shadows dancing erratically behind the glass. Despite the searing pain stabbing through his hand, he is still able to force the window shut, the glass vibrating from the impact.

Inside, darkness swallows the room as the lights extinguish, plunging everything into pitch-black

.

His heart races, nerves on edge, as he steels himself to move. He glances anxiously toward the rooftop's edge, confusion and fear battling within him.

Suddenly, a loud thud echoes as flat palms slam against the glass shards, followed by silence.

Startled, he spins around and notices the smeared handprints—deep burgundy streaks—left by her frantic movements.

Panicked, he scrambles away from the window, placing his injured hand on the rough surface of the roof for leverage. As pain jolts through his fingers, he quickly yanks his hand away, desperate to avoid further injury, and, losing balance, he starts to roll, trying to distance himself from the terrifying scene.

The creature pounds the glass relentlessly, its snarls growing increasingly ferocious and irritated.

John strains to hear beyond the cacophony, catching the sharp crack of glass breaking amidst her guttural sounds, muffled yet intense.

Above, dark clouds churn violently, rolling ominously as a fierce thunderclap splits the sky, casting flashes of harsh intermittent light that reveal the shadowed edge of the roof rapidly approaching. Rain pours down fiercely from above, droplets slamming on the ground below with relentless force.

He desperately attempts to press his shoes against the slippery, uneven shingles as the rain turns the mossy patches into treacherous slicks, accelerating his fall. The rough texture of the roof, coarse and splintering, scratches at his palms as he claws at the surface, fighting to slow his fall. His vision blurs, adrenaline surges through his veins, and suddenly, he feels himself tipping forward into an uncontrolled descent, plummeting through the air.

He reaches out desperately, pawing at the gutter in a frantic final attempt to grasp or steady himself, but the rain and his slipping grip doom him. In the final instant, he succumbs to the inevitable, panic rippling through him as he falls into the dark void below.

Chapter Seventeen

CONFESSION

Stunned, he lies flat on his back, staring up at the swirling, tumultuous sky above. A sudden spasm shoots up his spine, causing him to flinch involuntarily. With a trembling voice, he whispers, "Why—" He pauses, then mutters, "Why, God—what did I do to deserve this?" His tears well up as he cries out, "What did I do to deserve this? This life, her—"

A sharp crackle cuts through the heavy air, echoing across the open space and causing the porch steps to tremble.

The breath knocked out of him and stunned, he watches as a jagged bolt of electricity arcs through the air, striking a weathered metal shovel protruding from the earth near the garden bed. Sparks crackle and shimmer as the energy surges through the ground, sending ripples through the soil and stirring a faint tremor beneath his body.

Shaking, he turns his gaze back, feeling the dull ache of his recent fall radiate through his limbs, and senses the soft, damp leaves of the shrub that broke his fall brushing against his bare arms and back of his neck. He quickly scans the perimeter, eyes darting with cautious alertness. "Lillie..." he murmurs silently, voice barely more than a breath, as he struggles to grasp the sequence of strange, unsettling events unfolding around him.

The joyful laughter of a child resonates across the open field, blending with the gentle rustling of the tall corn stalks swaying in the breeze.

He quickly gets to his feet, each movement sharp and hurried, accidentally putting weight on his injured hand as he uses it to balance himself while a wave of dizziness hits him. A sting of pain shoots through him, reminding him of his wounds. "Lillie!" he yells, his voice trembling.

Consumed by the sound of her laughter, he scans the horizon frantically, eyes darting toward the source of the distant sound. Somewhere amidst the shimmering green sea of corn, a shadow stirs, breaking the stillness of the night.

Thunder rumbles loudly from the darkening sky above, carrying fierce gusts that cause the screen door of the weathered home to flap open and shut violently.

His nerves are rattled, making his heart pound anxiously as he twists his head to look. He observes the shadowy outline of the door slamming shut with a deafening bang. He grabs the sprigs of the nearby bush to help him steady himself.

A sharp ringing cuts through his eardrums and throbs loudly in his head as the sounds of the storm's chaos worsen.

"Daddy!" Lillie's cry pierces the crashing rain, a desperate, trembling call that cuts through the roaring weather.

He remains fixed on the looming cornfield ahead, convinced she is there, his eyes scanning desperately for any sign of her.

An animalistic scream erupts from behind him, raw and feral. It mirrors the cry of a beast caught in a trap, its frantic voice desperate to escape.

The house lights flicker wildly, throwing erratic, strobe-like flashes across the walls and ceiling. Shadows stretch and contort in the unstable light, creating jagged, shifting figures that seem to breathe and move within the surrounding darkness.

He glances behind him, his eyes narrowing as he witnesses a disturbing sight through the upstairs window.

There, the grotesque figure of his wife looms—her form twisted and terrifying, shadows dancing across her features. She lurks in the darkness, engaged in a desperate, silent struggle before shifting abruptly from Lillie's bedroom window, as if being summoned by an unseen force.

He squints his eyes tightly, furrowing his brow as he concentrates intently. His voice is strained but focused as he whispers, "Focus on Lillie. Keep your mind on your little girl."

A sudden sharp movement emerges from the corner of the crops, as if a small, furtive creature is quickening its pace, darting swiftly and silently.

Turning toward the noise, his pace quickens as he pushes through the relentless downpour, each step marked by a painful limp from his injured ankle. Water sluices down his face, blending with the tears he fights to hold back.

The more he moves forward, the more adrenaline surges through his veins, dulling the ache in his muscles and numbing the pain that grips his body. His voice breaks as he cries out a raw plea. "Lillie!"

Just ahead of him, her trembling voice responds, "Daddy!" Her cry is thin with fear. "I'm scared."

He freezes, eyes scanning the area, searching for her. His voice softens with urgency. "Just stay where you are—everything is going to be okay." He quickly pivots his head, scanning the surroundings with determined focus. Seeing nothing in the open space, he knows she must be hiding in the cornfield. "I'm going to find you!"

Suddenly, the door to the house creaks loudly as it swings open, its tired hinges protesting the force. The sound slices through the tense atmosphere, followed by a deafening slam that echoes like a gunshot, reverberating through the air.

He quickly hides in the cornrows, listening closely and searching for any sign of Lillie.

The childlike melody drifts across the distance from the house, carried by a brisk wind. The haunting sound of his wife's voice echoes faintly in the distance, lingering in the rain-soaked air. Her tone is tinged with a strange mix of longing and solemnity as her words curl into the chill. She sings, "Oh, where, oh, where has my little lamb gone—oh, where, oh, where can she be?"

Each minor note reverberates through him, stirring a complex swirl of emotion.

A childlike whisper drifts softly from his side, fragile. "She's coming," it murmurs, delicate yet insistent.

Startled, he gasps and spins around, eyes searching the shadows. "Lillie—" he begins.

Suddenly, another voice echoes from a different direction, colder and sharper, carrying a sense of urgency. "It's coming." Its tone cuts through the air.

He moves cautiously through the towering rows of corn, traveling deeper into the field, each step deliberate to avoid breaking stalks or rustling leaves.

The dense green stalks sway gently around him, their husks glistening.

Suddenly, a joyful sound traverses the air—it's his daughter's laughter calling to him from a distant point among the foliage. Heart pounding, he whispers urgently, "Shh—" He presses a hand to his mouth to still the rush of sound from his lips. His senses sharpen as he strains to locate her amidst the rustling greenery, eyes searching through the maze of crops.

"Daddy..." she whispers.

He hesitates for a moment, cautious in his movements, then takes a tentative step closer, narrowing his eyes as he scans the shadows.

From somewhere nearby, her voice drifts again, clear but strained, saying, "I'm over here." Her words feel disjointed, barely holding together, as if she's fighting to keep control.

He shifts his foot to take another step, but his toe unexpectedly catches on a fresh mound of dirt, causing him to stumble and fall onto the ground. As his palms hit the cool, damp earth, he is instantly overwhelmed by the smell of death. In his rush to escape the foul odor, his hand contacts a patch of matted fur. He recoils, his heart pounding, upon realizing that someone has dug up Kitty.

John can hear his daughter's shallow breaths, and, frantic, he crawls through the darkness, feeling his way as he searches desperately for her. The sky churns above, swirling with ominous shades of gray and deep purple streaks that shimmer against the turbulent clouds.

As he shuffles over the moist, uneven earth, a strange coldness bites into his skin, and he feels a small, clammy hand grasping his. His breath catches, and he whimpers softly, heart pounding.

"Daddy..." her voice whimpers, trembling with fear as tears streak her dirt-smudged face.

"Lillie," he stammers, his voice strained with concern. "It's okay, baby—Daddy's here now," he says swiftly, trying to reassure her. "It's okay, everything's going to be okay."

He takes her wrist gently feeling her pulse. It's faint and irregular, her skin clammy to the touch. She is covered in mud and has minor abrasions from her fall.

"I—" She coughs sharply, as her body shakes uncontrollably from the cold.

Behind her, a wild, piercing screech echoes through the space, sharp and unsettling.

Without hesitation, John carefully lifts her into his arms, supporting her delicate frame with gentle but firm certainty. His hold remains unwavering as he moves swiftly through the shadowy landscape, anticipation flickering in his eyes like a distant spark. "Daddy's going to tell you something very, very important," he whispers, his voice barely more than a breath. "Whatever you do, do not look into the darkness, and stay very, very quiet—"

She sniffles softly, pressing her tear-streaked face into the fabric of his shirt, seeking comfort.

He feels the subtle nod of her head against him, a silent agreement. "And if anything happens to me," he adds, his voice tense with urgency, "you must swear to me—you run as fast as you can, don't look back, no matter what, just run."

A faint rustling echoes subtly through the nearby row of crops, as if something is silently observing them from within the greenery. The stalks sway, trembling with unease, as the wind carries a faint, musky scent of damp earth and decaying leaves.

"We have to go," he whispers, his voice edged with mounting urgency, then sharpens into a demand. "*Now!*" His words, tinged with alarm, spill from his mouth as he listens intently, every muscle in his body tightening in alertness to any sign of threat. His eyes scan rapidly between the rows, searching for movement or shadows that might betray their stalker.

Leaves tremble softly as they come into contact with the unseen presence, their fragile forms whispering secrets to the wind, heightening the sense of lurking danger and tension in the air as anticipation mounts with every heartbeat.

He takes a deep, labored breath, muscles tense with adrenaline.

A sudden flicker of moonlight catches his eye, reflecting off a pair of dark, piercing pupils that peer through the leaves of the cornfield. The eyes seem to watch his every move with a predatory patience, lurking just out of sight.

Without hesitation, he leaps forward, sprinting in the opposite direction. He maneuvers skillfully, ducking beneath twisting cornstalks and weaving through the dense, rustling husks.

The piercing squawk of a crow echoes loudly through the air, masking the faint sounds of shifting footsteps and distant movement.

Fixating on reaching the last row of crops, he notices the glow of a window upstairs through a break in the foliage. He quickens his pace, each step steady and purposeful, driven by the anticipation of escaping the field and reaching the house.

With each stride, he feels the weight of Lillie in his arms lessen, almost dissolving into the night air, as if the act of running builds strands of their connection.

Approaching the edge of the corn, he tightens his grip around her small, fragile body, his fingers curving gently but firmly. Her limbs hang limply, swinging with each of his steps.

The rush of wind stings his face as he presses forward, his eyes fixed ahead. Every step is urgent, driven by the need to escape, to keep moving without looking back.

Behind him, the towering cornstalks bend and break, snapping loudly as their pursuer pushes through the sea of green. He presses on, fleeing into the darkness, the only certainty being the relentless pursuit behind him.

"Oh, where, oh, where…" the voice begins, gradually transforming as a female tone shifts into something monstrous. The words unravel, distorting into jagged shards of sound, as if torn from the throat of a creature in torment. It gradually morphs into a fractured cry, echoing with desperation and primal hunger. "Has my little lamb gone—oh, where, oh, where can she be?"

Wind gusts around them, carrying haunting whispers and mournful wails. The whispers ripple through the air like ghostly vines, blending with the moans that rise and fall in the night's cold hush, creating a chorus of sorrow and longing that seems to seep from the shadows themselves.

Out of breath, John halts abruptly just beyond the edge of the cornfield, his chest heaving as he frantically scans from left to right, eyes wide with terror. "Leave us alone!" he shouts. Then, without a moment's hesitation, he sprints through the darkness, his footsteps pounding across the uneven ground toward the front porch of the house.

A crackle of lightning crashes through the sky. He jumps, startled, his eardrums ringing.

A piercing scream cuts through the night air. "She belongs to me!" the woman bellows, with fury and anguish.

Almost at the gravel path leading to the house, John glances over his shoulder, heart pounding in his ears. His eyes catch a horrifying sight: the creature he glimpsed earlier in the hallway now stands motionless in the yard, illuminated by the moon's glow reflecting off the clouds.

Her form, cloaked in shades of black and blue, is gaunt and almost translucent, revealing veins and skeletal structures beneath her pallid skin. The moonlight stresses her distortions, revealing a face that faintly reflects his wife's features, yet twisted with an evil that ages her flesh prematurely—eyes hollow, lips cracked.

The creature tilts her head slowly back, her neck stretching unnaturally as she emits a wailing cry—a chilling call to dark, unseen forces lurking in the night's void.

In a split second, John's plan to hide shifts to an escape as his eyes catch sight of the station wagon parked nearby. "The keys," he whispers urgently, panic sharpening his voice, and, without hesitation, he launches into a frantic dash. His legs propel him with urgent purpose.

A sharp, grating noise escapes her joints as she steps forward. She moves slowly, dragging her decrepit feet across the uneven ground, each inch deliberate as she shadows their path, her eyes fixed on the retreating figures.

They reach the threshold of the house and dash inside, slamming the door shut with a loud bang behind them. His hands tremble as he fumbles with the metal lock, every movement infused with fear. His fingers scrabble, searching for the light switch, flipping it futilely—nothing happens.

Gently, he lowers Lillie onto the worn cushion of the sofa, her tiny frame trembling. He grabs the faded quilt from the nearby ottoman, the fabric soft against his grip. Heart pounding, he quickly wraps the blanket around Lillie's body, pulling her closer. "Stay here—Daddy will be right back," he murmurs reassuringly, spinning around with unwavering urgency.

Suddenly, a heavy thud reverberates through the doorframe, causing the walls to tremble. He quickly dismisses it, aware he can't lose focus on his plan, then rushes into the kitchen with urgent haste.

Again, the relentless knocking pounds louder, each strike resonating with increased weight and anger.

Inside the dark kitchen, he frantically runs his fingertips over the wall, searching for the small, unassuming metal hangers mounted near the switches. "Come on, John," he whispers under his breath. "Get it together." His fingers fumble in the darkness, unable to find the car keys, leaving him to come up with a different option. He approaches the window, hoping to spot their tormentor, assuring himself it has not somehow gotten inside.

He pulls back the curtain cautiously and peers out. It is too dark to see any details, with only the faint glow of moonlight reflecting off the storm clouds. John watches for a moment, hoping to catch even the slightest movement.

A sudden flash of lightning splits the sky, illuminating the yard with stark, jagged brilliance. In that fleeting moment, he sees her—the decaying, contorted figure of Delilah outside the glass, her body eerily still and silent, eyes fixed on the window with a terrifying intensity. Her face is a grimacing mask etched with pain and darkness, blood staining her skin from head to toe. Her beauty, once striking, now warped into something monstrous, a chilling reflection of the demon she harbored within.

The silence that follows the sight of what she has become is grotesquely hypnotic, broken only by the distant rumble of thunder as he stands frozen, staring with a mix of fear and disbelief.

Suddenly, her eyes look up and lock onto Lillie's room, the window dark and partially open.

In a quick, fluid motion, she grasps the home's wooden siding, her claws finding grip as she shimmies upward, tearing off boards as she climbs, scattering their fragments onto the ground below.

Without hesitation, she pulls herself onto the roof, each of her heavy footsteps making a thud that reverberates through the entire house.

Seeing what she is doing, he sprints toward the wall, his hand rummaging through the clutter on the kitchen counter, desperate to find the keys.

He notices the faint gleam of the station wagon key resting in a pile of mail beneath the key hook, just as a sudden loud creak from the upstairs window opening echoes through the hall and reaches the lower level.

His palms sweat as he grips the ring, its comforting in his trembling hand. He casts a quick look at where Lillie was left just moments ago and rushes toward her.

The wooden steps of the staircase groan loudly under the weight of footfalls, their aging joints protesting with every movement.

Reaching the living room, he scans the space where Lillie once lay, now empty. All that remains is a crumpled, faded blanket, its fabric fraying at the edges.

Confused and worried, he swiftly surveys the living room, his eyes darting from shadow to shadow. "Lillie," he murmurs, trying to keep his voice calm as he strains to hear any response. A faint, mirthless laugh erupts from behind an oversized chair, and he freezes. "This isn't funny," he says urgently. "We have to get out of here—your mother—"

His words are swallowed by a flurry of frantic, whispering voices that ring from every corner.

A dark shadow stretches upward, gradually revealing itself from behind the oversized armchair chairs, its form shifting and writhing with an intangible menace. The flickering light casts eerie patterns across the room, emphasizing the shadow's ominous emergence.

His gaze fixes on the source of the laughter, eyes narrowing as he follows the sound with intense focus.

As he turns, the shadow's silhouette stretches farther across the wall. He comes to an abrupt halt, a tremor coursing through his body as a cold, wicked darkness consumes the surrounding air. His eyes dart desperately, voice trembling as he demands, "Wha—what have you done with her?" Every word is edged with fear.

"Two went to the river—never to return; even if drenched in water, their souls the fire will burn." The woman's haunting voice sings, ethereal and echoing, weaving through the stifling air like a penetrating wind. "They'll sink, sink, sink, like a submarine deep in the dark abyss, but alas, they will drown and be quite dead—oh, their company you will miss." Her words linger, thick with mystery, but he recognizes the voice; it's Delilah.

John watches intently as she inches forward, creeping. The moonlight casts a silvery glow across her features, which have deteriorated further since just a moment ago.

"What did you do with her?!" His voice booms, with desperation and anger.

The ominous shadows deepen, creeping along the floor, swallowing the corners, exerting an oppressive presence that presses against his chest. The air feels charged with evil, and he's reluctant to breathe.

"Tell me—" John's voice cracks as he desperately pleads. "Just please tell me, Delilah." He shifts his gaze toward the coming figure, studying every detail of her grotesque form as it slowly stirs from the darkness.

She moves closer with deliberate slowness. Her face is more hag-like than before, with deep-set eyes gleaming with mischief and age; her cracked lips curl into a sinister grin, her tongue licking the dry, cracked skin.

He flinches, muscles tensing, trying to mask his unease and maintain a facade of composure. His voice softens into a strained whisper. "I promise—wherever she is, I—I won't be mad."

"She's gone," she hisses, her body coiling as she shifts her weight onto her hands. Her torso arches backward into a backbend, muscles taut and defined under her skin. Gravity pulls her breasts outward, causing them to spill over the sides of her chest, while her head tilts slightly to the left with her neck in a delicate yet tense curve.

Uncertain of what her answers mean, he leans in, his posture tentative. "What do you mean?" he asks, his voice shaking nervously.

Delilah slowly licks her lips, her tongue tracing a lazy arc around the edges, revealing serrated, burgundy-red teeth that shimmer in the dim light. For a moment, neither makes a sound except for the creaking sound created beneath her coiling fingers as they shift positions on the floor. The faint drip of the kitchen's leaky faucet punctuates the quiet, adding an almost rhythmic backdrop to the tense atmosphere.

John flinches at the sudden creak beneath her grasp, instinctively shrinking back. He squints into the shadows, struggling to focus on every sound that may or may not be a threat, uncertain if his mind is playing tricks or if danger lurks nearby.

"I thought you loved me," Delilah snarls, her voice edged with bitterness, yet her eyes flicker with unresolved pain. Her gaze wells up as tears threaten to spill over, blurring her fierce exterior. She mocks him passively, voice dripping with disdain, "In sickness and in health. Till death do us part. Wasn't that the promise, John?" She slowly inches forward, her movement deliberate and menacing, her presence filling the space with silent threat.

"You told me who to call," he says, his voice strained with a blend of frustration and resolve. He gestures emphatically, making sharp sweeping motions in the air. Carefully, he takes a step back, his eyes fixed on her. "You told me you wanted help."

Suddenly, her face twists with fury. She jumps to her feet and screams, *"Liar!"* Her voice echoes with primal rage, and her hands gesture wildly as she emphasizes her words.

He recoils, startled, and quickly leaps aside, dodging her frantic movements, his muscles tensing in response to her explosive outburst.

"You want me dead, don't you?" she says, her voice rising in pitch and speed, words tumbling over each other in a frantic, desperate rush. Her eyes burn with a wild, menacing intensity, and her lips twitch into a sinister smirk. "I think you would love nothing more than to see me suffer and die?" she taunts, her tone sharply laced with deadly sarcasm.

"Where is Lillie?" he asks. She swiftly advances, faking a lunge as he warily backs away, her body coiled like a predator ready to pounce.

"Who?" she asks, tilting her head with a playful, almost innocent expression that contrasts with the sharp glint in her eyes.

"Our daughter," he says through heavy, panic-stricken breaths, his chest heaving as he tries to steady himself.

A crack of lightning ruptures the sky, illuminating the tension within the room with a sudden, stark glow, followed by the distant rumble of thunder.

"Oh, her," she says, a slight grimace crossing her face. She sighs, then murmurs, "She's such a sweet girl."

He fixates on her callous behavior, his eyes narrowing in disbelief as he struggles to comprehend what's happening.

The faint trickle of water grows louder and closer, each drip echoing in the tense silence. It merges into the soundscape and amplifies the growing tension.

His confusion deepens as he looks down at his feet, watching the water creep past them with almost hypnotic persistence. A strange unease rises inside him, tightening his chest. His eyes follow the shimmering stream as it winds from the living room floor, ascends the aged wooden staircase, and overflows the top step on the second floor like a waterfall.

The cool mist hangs thick in the air, swirling gently above the water. It catches the faint, flickering light, shimmering like fractured glass, floating weightlessly before vanishing into the shadows.

He keeps his gaze fixed on the unyielding rhythmic march of the mist, feeling its icy chill seep deeper into his skin with each passing moment. The air hangs heavy and damp, and he can't help but shiver. "Did you leave the water running upstairs?" he asks, his voice tight with concern. He flinches, his gaze sweeping over the couch, then quickly back to the stairs as a horrifying realization grips him.

She watches him intently, with a smirk, her eyes narrowing as her head spins slowly around, savoring every subtle change in his expression.

John takes off in a dead sprint as water sloshes inside his shoes, each step splashing against the slippery floor on his way to the stairway.

Delilah twists her monstrous body suddenly, her muscles tensing and coiling as her wide mouth opens in a deafening, rage-filled scream. The flickering single bulb explodes, plunging the room into darkness as shadows dance across the walls.

As John ascends the staircase, he notices, at the top, the first delicate glow of dawn filtering through the windows. Soft amber rays of sunlight stretch lazily across the worn wooden floorboards, illuminating the tense scene unfolding below.

Delilah's snarls grow more ferocious, fueled by her wrath. Hunting him, she heads for the stairs. As she passes the sofa, she bumps a small table with a lamp on it. In a frenzy, she throws it against the wall, sending shards of glass and wooden splinters flying. Then, she climbs the staircase.

The muffled sound of rushing water grows louder and more insistent while the hurried footsteps echo against the walls, creating a chaotic symphony of urgency.

He quickens his pace, his heart pounding, determined to put as much distance as possible between him and Delilah as he desperately calls for his daughter. "Lillie," he shouts.

Delilah releases another deafening scream that cuts through the morning air, shattering the fragile calm with its raw intensity.

John's instincts sharpen as he senses the threat trailing closely behind him. "Lillie," he calls out urgently.

The daylight streaming in from the outside grows brighter, flooding through the windows with a vivid, almost blinding force as more rays push past the glass, illuminating the chaos inside.

He sloshes over the water-soaked floor runner, the cold wetness seeping into his shoes. Shielding his eyes from the harsh glare of the window, he gazes past Lillie's open bedroom door toward the source of the rushing water—it's coming from the bathroom, where the volume seems to be intensifying.

An ear-piercing shriek reverberates from behind him, resembling the agonized cry of a wounded animal. He covers his ears, spins around sharply, and his eyes land on Delilah, who is perched precariously above him on the ceiling.

Clawing at the plaster with gangly hands, she recoils, suddenly exposed to blinding sunlight, her skin sensitive to its rays. With a labored heave, her body drops helplessly to the floor, contorting into a fragile, unsteady pose as she paws at her eyes desperately.

He watches intently as she forcefully yanks her head upward, trying to regain composure. Her mouth twitches, and her tongue darts out like a striking serpent, releasing a stream of crimson liquid. As she shifts her head left and right, a deafening crack echoes through the room.

He flinches, catching a fleeting glimpse of her eye; despite her darkened, monstrous appearance and feral actions that make her unrecognizable, something within her gaze pulls at the strings of his heart. A wave of guilt washes over him, heavy and relentless.

An inexplicable force seems to take hold of his legs; he moves a cautious step closer to her. Her head snaps backward, her neck arches, veins and tendons taut beneath her skin as her jugular visibly pulses. "Please, God, she doesn't realize what she's doing," he whispers, a tear forming in the corner of his eye, trembling as it wells up. "She is simply weak."

His words seem to trigger her; she staggers upright with unsteady legs, then is suddenly soaring, light and wind filling her lungs, the sun's penetrating rays igniting her skin and digging deeper into her consciousness. A deep, gravelly voice emerges from within her, resonant and menacing. "Don't say his name."

He raises his hands defensively, feeling the threat emanating from her posture. Cornered, he shifts his weight backward, careful to avoid sudden movements, retreating slowly.

She observes him intently, then lowers herself onto all fours. "You think your God will save you?" she hisses. "You're the reason our daughter is missing. You're the reason I am this way. It's always been you." Her voice rises with each deliberate, sinuous step forward.

He flinches, the sharp sting of her words like daggers piercing through his chest, each syllable slicing deeper as they enter his ears. "That's not true," he says, emotion flooding over him until his body feels ready to collapse. "I'm the one who holds us together—I'm the one who stays strong for us," he stammers, voice trembling.

She slowly creeps closer, like a predatory spider coiling for the leap, her nostrils flaring as she revels in his growing fear. "Are you afraid?" Her voice transforms into a piercing shriek, screeching like a needle scraping a vinyl record, sharply through the tense, suffocating air.

John slowly shakes his head, trying to convince himself as much as her, while backing away until he can go no further. He trembles, his back now against her bedroom door, desperately searching for the doorknob. He twists the knob, feeling it turn under his sweaty grip, then freezes as he realizes it's unlocked.

Delilah's joints crack softly as she inches forward, movements sly and deliberate. "I'm going to eat your flesh and devour your soul," she growls, her lips curling sinisterly at the corners, revealing a hint of decay as they break the skin.

"You would never do anything to hurt me," he whispers, fingers tightening on the handle. His palms grow slick with sweat as the metal doorknob slips in his hand.

With a blood-curdling howl, she scrambles forward on all fours, with primal malevolence.

John throws open the heavy door with a violent jolt just as she leaps at him. He ducks low.

She barely misses him, but then slams headfirst into the sharp corner of the bed. The impact splits her head open, momentarily knocking her cold and sending a tremor through the bed frame.

Dazed, she lies crumpled on the floor, gasping for air. He slowly turns around, eyes wide with shock as he fixates on her.

A sudden gleam of sunlight catches the metal key resting in a dark pool of burgundy, its surface shining ominously in the gore. Avoiding her bloodied face and the source of her injuries, he swiftly reaches out, snatching the key and wiping it on his sleeve to remove any debris.

Then, without hesitation, he drags her limp, blood-streaked body toward the chains mounted on the bedframe, securing her with trembling hands to prevent her from slipping free.

Coming out of her stupor, she gnashes at his hands as her consciousness sharpens. Her eyes flutter open, revealing a flicker of fear and confusion.

He slips the shackle key into his pocket and slowly approaches the door, dreading his next task of confronting the truth of what happened to Lillie. As he steps through the doorway, he glances back at the wall stained with ichor, a remnant of the priest's presence. He closes his eyes, shakes his head, and takes a deep breath. John gently shuts the bedroom door. His hand trembles as he reaches into his pocket for the keys and locks the door, ears strained for any sound.

A faint voice, small and fragile, echoes down the hallway. "Daddy…"

Hearing that the sound of water has ceased, he pauses, slowly turns around, and scans his surroundings with cautious eyes.

The dim corridor, now brighter than before, seems to hold its breath in anticipation.

He whispers Lillie's name softly, his voice barely more than a breath. Gaining his bearings, he glances toward the bathroom, and a wave of emotions sweeps over him.

Although the flood of water appears to have subsided, an overwhelming sensation grips him when he looks at the closed bathroom door; tears start to flow uncontrollably down his cheeks.

He moves toward it hesitantly, his legs feeling suddenly burdensome, muscles weakening with each step.

Silence envelops everything around him, thick and oppressive.

Near the bathroom door, he gently places his palm on the cool wood, eyes fixed on the ground. "Lillie," he whispers, voice trembling, his chin lowering as he stares downward.

A soft, hesitant voice whispers again, fragile and uncertain, saying, "Daddy."

Startled, he quickly straightens, heart pounding fiercely in his chest. He doubts his sanity, wondering if the sound he heard was really her or just a ghostly whisper. He turns abruptly, eyes darting across the dimly lit space beyond, searching for any movement. "Lillie?" he calls, desperation slipping into his voice.

Her voice rises sharply, louder now, echoing through the quiet house from her bedroom in an urgent, frantic tone.

He rushes forward, his chest heaving with shallow breaths, fists clenched as he quickly scans the space, desperately trying to pinpoint her location. "Lillie, where are you?" he shouts, voice strained, trying to steady his nerves while listening intently for a response.

From inside her bedroom closet, realizing it's him, her panicked voice responds, trembling with fear. "I'm in here!" she calls out, voice cracking.

He races to her room, frantically searching as he follows the sound of her voice, and then he swiftly throws open the closet door.

"Daddy!" she exclaims, her small face bright with relief as she leaps into his outstretched arms.

He feels her quaking body pressed against him, warmth spreading despite her fear. Overcome with emotion, he sinks to the floor, gently wrapping his arms around her fragile frame. His voice thick with feeling, he whispers, "You scared me." He pulls her closer as tears well up in his eyes. "When I didn't see you on the couch, I thought I'd lost you forever."

She stammers, trying to find words, "I ... I."

He gently silences her with a calming touch, hushed voice soothing. "Shh, it's okay—everything is okay—you don't need to explain—Daddy's got you." He pulls her in even tighter, feeling her tiny body against his.

He leans back slightly to get a clear look at her face. As he takes a moment to absorb her presence, his gaze drops to her dirt-streaked skin, noticing the grime caked on her cheeks and hands. Her small nail beds and lips have a faint blue tint, hinting at cold or exhaustion.

"Wha—what about Mommy?" she asks softly, voice trembling with a mixture of curiosity and worry. Her wide eyes search his face for reassurance, her small hands clutching her blanket tightly.

"What about her, sweetheart?" he responds gently, trying to keep his voice steady despite the knots tightening in his stomach. He rubs the back of his neck and breathes in slowly, searching for the right words.

"Is she going to be okay?" she whispers, voice barely audible, eyes glossy with unshed tears. Her gaze fixes on his, seeking comfort amidst her confusion.

He purses his lips, hesitating. "Mommy—" He pauses, taking a deep breath to gather his thoughts. "She—um—" His voice falters briefly, and then he forces a warm, reassuring smile. "Princess Mommy—"

The mention of her mother's royal title ignites a spark in the little girl's eyes, a flicker of hope and admiration.

"Princess Mommy—she makes a courageous decision—" he explains, his tone carefully serious as he gently tightens his grip on her shoulder to ensure she listens. His eyes soften with a mixture of respect and concern, emphasizing the weight of the moment.

"He helps her," she stammers, her voice trembling slightly, searching his face for reassurance.

His expression relaxes into a kind determination as he prepares to offer comfort amid the lingering uncertainty. "Well," he begins thoughtfully, searching for the right words, "the knight does everything he can. But in the end, it's ultimately her choice—what she wants her life to

be ..." His voice trails into a soft pause, emphasizing her autonomy.

Radiating a mature calmness beyond her years, she interjects with quiet confidence. "She wants to stay a princess?"

He pauses, his gaze lingering softly on her face as a gentle warmth blossoms in his eyes. A slight, almost imperceptible smile curves his lips, revealing tenderness. "Yes, my darling," he begins, his voice gentle and steady. As he observes the innocence shining in her eyes, a weight seems to lift from his shoulders. "It's not that she doesn't love you; she—" he starts to say, but is interrupted.

With a tender, guiding touch, she gently rests her hand on her dad's shoulder, delicate yet firm, signaling him to stop. "I know—it's okay, Daddy," she says gently, offering comfort and understanding. Her calm demeanor radiates serenity amid the emotional turmoil.

He gazes intently into her eyes, wanting to say more, but deep unspoken emotions keep him silent.

As they share a quiet moment, she suddenly breaks the silence with a firm voice. "Don't worry, I don't want to be a princess." Her words hang in the air, fragile yet resolute.

His eyes shimmer with unshed tears, and he quickly averts his gaze, trying to mask his vulnerability and maintain his composure.

She clears her throat, her voice gentle but direct. "Do you want me to get the duct tape?" she asks, her nose faintly sniffing, her tone matter-of-fact yet tender.

He nods slowly, striving to steady himself. "I'll get the trash bag," he replies, pausing briefly as he turns his head toward the window, where sunlight streams in sympathetically, casting warm patterns across the room.

It feels like a new day, a fresh start for both of them.

"Lillie—" he says, his voice heavy with emotion. She looks at him attentively. "I'm really sorry about your cat," he murmurs.

She averts her gaze to the ground, her voice tinged with sadness. "He's in a better place now."

After a moment, John rises to his feet and turns away from her, and his eyes fall on the crucifix lying on the bed.

Gently, he reaches out and delicately lifts it, his fingertips brushing the surface gently. He carefully puts it back on the wall, pausing briefly with a look of reverence before letting out a soft breath. "I see Kitty watching, imagining him playing among the puffy clouds, batting a ball of yarn with innocent delight," he whispers, his eyes fixed as sunlight streams through the window, illuminating the crucifix and creating a shimmering golden glow that bathes the room in a warm, spiritual light.

Her expression relaxes further as she slowly approaches him. "Maybe this time, things will be different," she says, reaching into a nearby drawer, her fingers sliding over the smooth surface to retrieve a roll of tape.

He turns to her, his expression stiffening to hide the turmoil inside, and drops to one knee, his pose both humble and hopeful.

A scream pierces the quiet, coming from the next room. It's followed by the jarring sound of metal chains slamming against a bed, instantly creating an atmosphere of unease.

"I'll go fetch the bags from the kitchen. I'll be right back," he says, then pauses briefly, his brow furrowing as he mentally prepares for the task ahead.

Lillie calls out to him as he steps toward the doorway, her voice tinged with urgency. "Daddy..." she begins, rising slightly on her tiptoes.

John turns his head over his shoulder, his eyes meeting hers with a glance full of unspoken understanding.

"Don't forget the scissors," she adds, lifting the roll of tape in her small hands.

He sighs, a mixture of resignation and anticipation, then nods in acknowledgment. His muscles tense slightly as he commits to what's coming next.

Brigitte, "Gitte," Tamar was born in a small rural Oregon town. From a young age, she was enthralled by scary tales featuring poetic tones and gravitated towards writing her own dark narratives. Upon graduating from Jesuit High School in Portland, she pursued her studies in Film, Television, and Media at Texas Christian University in Fort Worth, Texas.

However, her path took a different turn when she was crowned Miss Oregon USA in 2015. Following her Miss USA experience, she pursued further education and earned a business degree from Southern New Hampshire University, an MA in Law Studies from the University of Southern California, and graduate certificates in business law and entertainment law and industries.

As an author, she fearlessly delves into the gritty truths of modern society, unearthing the depths of peer pressure, addiction, homelessness, mental illness, childhood trauma, discrimination, loneliness, the allure of fame, and the horrors of abuse. She strongly believes in the importance of sharing narratives that don't sugarcoat the difficult topics society tends to shy away from and she does so in a brilliantly haunting fashion.

Aside from being an Amazon New Release Best Seller, her work has garnered recognition from Mystery Tribune, POPSUGAR, Online Book Club, and Broadway World. She has also received the prestigious Mom's Choice Awards® Gold and many of

her works have been awarded a five-star rating by
Reader's Favorite.